Fellow Traveler

Fellow Traveler

James D McCallister

Muddy Ford Press

Chapin, South Carolina

 For information, address Muddy Ford Press, 1009 Muddy Ford Road, Chapin, South Carolina 29036.

"Treat you Right" lyrics courtesy Jenn McCallister and Michael Mahoney. "Calm Before the Storm," Shadows Fall," and "Day Without a Daydream" lyrics courtesy Greg Bates. Hear Stillhouse at www.reverbnation.com/stillhousesc and www.facebook.com/pages/Stillhouse/77204880678.

FIRST EDITION.

Cover design by Emily Kay Songer.

Library of Congress Number: 2012943795

ISBN:978-0-9838544-2-5

A good traveler has no fixed plans
and is not intent upon arriving.

—Lao Tzu
Tao Te Ching

FIRST SET

'Treat You Right'
(Partland/Sobel
©1968 JOR EL Publishing)

My mind's an awful mess, just don't know what to do
He's been runnin' 'round this town, and I thought he was true
Yesterday he was mine, today he holds you tight
But he ain't the man you think, and soon he'll do you wrong

So you better listen to me sing song
Cause I'm telling you, he ain't gonna treat you right
He ain't gonna treat you right
He ain't gonna treat you right

He's full of fancy talk and struts his handsome walk
You think you'll be with him right until the end
But then one day you'll wake in an empty bed
And you'll remember all these things I said . . .

–1–

I'm tone deaf, neither capable of singing nor playing any instruments, and yet I dream music—the most wondrous melodies and unique syncopated rhythms, passages that in my waking moments remain undefined, yet no less insightful. In the dreamtime, these tunes seem to weave a profound story, a story more ancient than the world we know, a narrative in song that's somehow older than life itself.

Upon awakening I'm unable to remember this music, but I don't need to—I had, and have, Rose Partland to serve as teller of the tale. Anytime I need her and her band, Jack O'Roses—the pied pipers of rock, the last of the 60s bands who kept the vibe alive, so to speak—I conjure her euphonious, fragile alto of a voice out of the sleeves of silver discs that lay nestled in a thick binder in the passenger seat, recordings of the shows she and her bandmates played. A representative sample of their work, anyway—until she died on us in that grim summer of 1997, Jack played thousands of concerts. Playing to live, living to play. For themselves, and for those of us who so loved them for their efforts.

The CDs, my only traveling companions.

Kipling's maxim—he who travels the fastest travels alone—offers no comfort, however, only reminds me of all that I've lost: my wife Halsey, to our freshly minted divorce decree, and my best friend Brian, to the big divorce that is death. Once, they'd have both been with me on an I-95 drive like this, either heading to or returning from an east coast Jack gig—RFK or JFK Stadium, a basketball arena like the Spectrum or MSG, or the last leg of a jaunt that'd taken us into the midwest. No longer. Childhood ends, never more so than in the instance of death.

Brian Godbold and Rose Partland, together again. I'm surprised he lasted the seven years since she left us. I'm not sure Brian had any other reason to get out of bed in the morning than going to Jack O'Roses shows.

Hell—he told me as much, almost from the first moments that I met him, on the Southeastern University campus a week after Jack played our football stadium on their 1987 summer tour:

"I was born to get high and go to these concerts," he said over bong rips in his dorm room. We sat smoking and listening to tapes of the Redtails Stadium show, which I couldn't believe he had in his possession—I didn't understand that the band allowed their fans to record the shows. "I know how that must sound," he added, self-conscious.

"I hear you," I said, not truly understanding in the least. Concerts were entertainment, not a lifestyle. I'd find out there was much I didn't understand. "That show was one of the coolest times I ever had."

Other than the last Jack show we saw together, which turned out to be the final concert Jack O'Roses would ever play, by the time of his death I hadn't gone on tour with Brian for a few years. I'd outgrown it, or so he accused me. I tried to tell him that it wasn't that way, that I'd taken what I needed and left the rest—for him, for anyone who needed what Jack had to offer.

But to him, my recalcitrance was a betrayal of Rose herself, and all she represented. Hah. As though there weren't other kids to take my place. We were legion, the followers—would we deign to be led. As a famous bumper sticker noted with sardonic wit, *Who the Hell is Jack, and Why is He Following Me?*

Alone, no more! Not long after I cross from Virginia into North Carolina, the pulsing pinpoints of a cop's electric blue rollers begin firing in the rearview, a psychedelic light show that does its sole job with alacrity and efficiency—my attention, wandering, has been gotten.

Pulled. Not good.

I dig out my bona fides. If you got yanked on Jack tour, you sat there waiting for a miracle. Hoping he wouldn't have a dog. But I haven't been on tour in a long time, and don't look the part of the hippie vagabond, the stereotype most associated with followers of Jack O'Roses, known colloquially as F-Kids. Looking the way I do, my goatee hiding a weak chin and with a genteel Charleston cadence coloring my voice, he'll probably think I'm gay, not a pothead.

The state trooper hitches up his belt, approaches my vehicle. I'm not doing anything wrong. Nothing actionable beyond a speeding citation. Nothing to see here. For the most part.

Truth: Yes, I do have some weed in the car, but it's well hidden. The headstash, an O-Z of named-strain, stinky indoor hydro bud, modest in quantity, is still enough to get me detained, hassled and charged.

This isn't my first rodeo—the herb's vacuum-sealed and secreted inside a box full of candy and roasted coffee beans. Sounds elaborate, almost professional, but hey, I'm no Yankee drug dealer like William Hurt driving down south for his old buddy's funeral—my best friend's already buried. And besides, never dealt anything in my life, except maybe some bullshit.

"License and registration, sir."

As I fork over my papers, my hand betrays a slight tremor. "How's it going, officer?"

"Mr. Zemp," the trooper says, "according to my little speed-o-meter back there, I'd say it's going right at eighty-five miles an hour."

"Gee," I say, holding onto the wheel like I'd been taught from movies and cop shows, keeping my hands visible, "that's pretty egregious, I guess."

"Do what, now?"

Traffic howls by, vehicles sliding into the passing lane, giving a respectable berth to the captor and his miserable, penitent prey. A bead of sweat slips down my right temple. Courtesy. Contrition. Don't argue with them—all advice from my father to whom I'm trying to return, this pushing-forty man with nowhere else to go and who now suffers a State Trooper sniffing around his dope stash. "Sorry—you know how it is out here."

Mirror shades hide his probing cop eyes, which I imagine have narrowed. "Out here?"

"Here on the road."

"Out here on the road," he says, thoughtful. He taps my license on the doorframe and allows his gaze to drift across the six sizzling lanes of I-95, vehicles screaming by at ridiculous velocities, their drivers unmindful of a cop with some other asshole already pulled. "That's where we are, all right."

"Truth is, sir, I wasn't watching my speed as

closely as I should've. Won't happen again."

He grumbles *uh-huh* and excuses himself to go run my info through Big Brother's tangled web. I'm straight, though. No worries. A clean slate, in more ways than he and his cop computer realize.

After five brutally long minutes, I watch as the trooper strides back toward my vehicle. He hesitates at the back bumper—something's caught his eye.

"Mr. Zemp?"

I feel like I'm going to vomit. "Yes, sir?"

"I don't know what the speed limit signs look like in Maryland," the cop says it like *Murrahlynn*, "but the ones here in the great state of North Carolina—those black and white things you see every so often, about ten foot tall? You know the ones?"

"Yes, sir." I realize I'm white-knuckling the steering wheel, force myself to release the tension in my hands. "I understand."

"Glad to hear it." He scribbles on his pad of tissue-thin citations. "Look here, I'm going to take you at your word—that you're going to slow it down out 'here,' as you put it—and only issue you this warning." He snaps off the ticket, hands it over. "This time."

I hesitate—considering the last few months of my life, I can't believe this instance of good fortune. I nod, accept the citation, and begin rolling up the window.

"Oh, Mr. Zemp, hold on—let me ask you something right quick."

My heart's trip-hammering. I know this tactic—I'm fucked. "By all means."

"Walking up here earlier . . . I noticed something winking out at me from your license plate." He tilts his head. "That little decal you put on there."

This is bad. I've been made.

He's referring to a small Jack O'Roses sticker I put on there ages ago, the image the most familiar band icon—a red and blue rose in full bloom with a kind of glimmering, white starburst at its center, a symbol that's not only recognized all over the world, but one that's associated with individuals known to partake of the sweet leaf. The fact that the cop brought the sticker up *at all* means I have every reason to believe he's about to tear this car apart.

Playing dumb is all I have left to try. "A decal—which one?"

"The one on your plate."

"I'm—not sure what you mean."

He describes the sticker. I shrug.

"Back up yonder in Maryland, they allow y'all to put little flowers on your vehicle license plate?" His expression is blank enough to play world class Texas Hold'em. "What is that little old thing, anyway?"

"Don't really know, to be honest."

He's counting my lies: "You don't know what?"

A beat of silence. Thinking fast, the survival instinct kicking in, I hold up my hands and feign nonchalant acknowledgement. "Oh—this is my wife's car. *Was*. Was my wife's car. Now mine. Part of the divorce settlement." Irrelevant to the discussion at hand, this blatant play for masculine sympathy represents my last shot at weaseling out of this. "Didn't even know it was on there."

Hooking his thumbs into his utility belt, he nods. "Whether it's your car, or your wife's car, I can tell you this much—in this state? It ain't legal to deface your plate."

The moment hangs there. The big rigs blow past, shaking the chassis of the aging Explorer. I worry that he can see the pulse pounding in the side of my neck. I feel as though I'm going to pass out. "I'll get rid of it."

"I would." He holds my gaze. "If I was you."

And he's gone, back to his cruiser, gesturing and waiting for me to pull out first. Which I do, with him riding behind me for a few tenths of a mile. Only once he whips into the median to head in the opposite direction do I relax.

I drive only as far as the next rest stop, where I take his advice—with a lump in my throat, I squat behind the Explorer and use a flathead screwdriver to scrape the goddamn Jack O'Roses sticker off my license plate.

-2-

Back on the freeway and fortified by a soda and half a pack of Nip-Chee, I crank the music and continue where I left off, back to the tunes in which I'd been lost, daydreaming, and that almost got me into serious trouble. I drop back into a long and languid jam from '74, one of the stadium gigs Jack O'Roses played with the Allman Brothers that long ago summer, an excellent statement of the period of the band. The recording, a bootleg, is nonetheless pristine, the music issuing crisp and wonderful and transporting—not to 1974, but a happier time in my own adult life, more like '94.

I chose this show from the binder of maybe thirty or forty live concerts I culled from the collection I—we—have back in Maryland, discs made for us by Brian in the first flowering of recordable digital media, a collection of blue CDRs that, for the most part, anyway, I offered to leave with Halsey.

"You might want to listen to some old school tunes sometime. You never know."

But she refused, said she didn't want any. "Oh, honey . . ." Her face, so sad and weary, a pitiful attempt at a smile. "I'd rather you took them."

I felt hot inside, a flash not so much of anger, more like emptiness, a chasm. Brian's funeral a month ago, it struck me, now constituted the last trip she and I would ever take together as a married couple. What a season of loss, I thought, then as now.

Trying not to cry, I said, "I'll leave some anyway, if that's all right."

"Whatever you want, Z."

Halsey is the last, now, to call me by my road name, which is reductive to the point that it neither illuminates my personality nor my actual moniker, Ashton Tobias Zemp—'Z' is well nigh-on useless but for placing me at the end of every list. As imaginative, one supposes, as I got, even on acid.

Hers, however, had been supercool: Sally Simpson, like in the Who song. She'd never been as devoted to Jack O'Roses as her namesake had been to Tommy, however. And Brian, he'd been 'Nibbs Niffy,' a road name he never fully explained, but that seemed to sum him up anyway.

"I'll give you a shout when I get . . ." I didn't know what to call my father's house, all the way upstate in Edgewater County, where he'd retired to be near my stepmother's family. "When I get there."

"If you want."

"If you put it that way . . . I won't bother."

"It's up to you."

Halsey, I knew, was preparing for her own trip, a buying jaunt to NYC for her stores, a regional chain of a half-dozen high end boutiques I'd helped her grow from her modest beginning owning a sandal and T-shirt shop on the beach back in South Carolina. As a one-time accounting major at Southeastern University, where we'd all met and become Jack devotees, I'd been her original bookkeeper, financial advisor, confidant, roller of paint and assembler of store fixtures, all roles that would in the end be more important than the one of being her husband. When she asked for the divorce, I tried to convince myself that I was in shock, though any tears I loosed upon the atmosphere I kept to myself.

Who am I to complain? A clean break, no guilt or recriminations—we'll stay friends, sure—and I get a decent chunk of cash to boot, a fair settlement for the sweat equity I put into her successful business, stores that year in, year out all gross in the high six figures. Enough to live on for a while, buy a house somewhere, buy time to sort things out. Lucky me! God almighty, it's like I'm shitting gold here, nothing but net, out of the park, rolling sevens and elevens. And only a warning ticket from a North Carolina State Trooper. Don't forget that part.

With thoughts of having scraped off the metallic rose from my license plate, I say to myself, enough Jack O'Roses for today. I pop out the CD and rummage in the glove box. I find therein a studio disc by a young sensation named P. S. Jones, a singer-songwriter Halsey and I both liked enough to have gone to see once or twice, including a très cool acoustic show at the Beacon Theatre in New York we hit during one of the buying trips. Terrific, authentic songwriting, a voice and style like a growling, bluesier version of Rose Partland. Check. P. S. is a good choice, her breezy, optimistic lyrics and clean guitar lines all gentle on my mind as I haul this collection of junk home to South Carolina.

Besides my stash and personal effects, the rest of my smuggled cargo belongs to none other than Nibbs Niffy himself—I'd made a stop along the beltway, in an aging Silver Spring suburb of 1970s era McMansions, to check on his mother, who I found still in a state of bereavement.

She'd asked an interesting but uncomfortable favor of me, to which I agreed without hesitation: to read through his journals, his writing, of which there exists several boxes-worth of notebooks, a laptop, and an external hard drive or two holding god knows how much material—he'd been writing since his teens.

To what end, I'd asked of her; to seek a better answer, she said.

How could I tell her no? "Give me his things," I said. "I don't mind. I need an answer, too. But—you could read them yourself, couldn't you?"

"From the little bit I've seen, it will all mean something to you that it wouldn't to me. Or so I hope."

I knew what she meant—as a fellow fan of the band he so loved, I supposed that reading his thoughts, filled with subtleties and esoterica likely to be lost upon her, would indeed be a better task for me.

The real drama of my visit came not with the gift of my friend's papers, or saying a final-final feeling fare thee well one last time at the gravesite I'd visited before going to his mother's house, but rather in his old boyhood room—this, a space to which Brian retreated after leaving his job in the library at Southeastern, once he'd turned inward to the point that he couldn't work anymore, could only feed a jones. Another dead doper was all Nibbs became—what the reactionary punditry on the radio talk shows had said about Rose. Brian. My friend, my foolish friend.

Mrs. Godbold gestured, bidding me to follow her up the stairs. "Before you go, I'd like you to see something."

Uncomfortable, I asked what, exactly—I'd already loaded several cartons worth of notebooks and assorted ephemera into the Explorer. "If it's more papers, I might have to get you to ship them."

"No—it's something else."

When she opened the door, my breath, taken away—Brian had built three walls-worth of shelves to house his beloved music collection, which by the time of his death had grown beyond impressive, thousands of shows spread across numerous types of media: cassettes, DATs, CDRs, videotapes, DVDs, lining the walls floor to ceiling. Boxes of old, outdated cassettes piled in the corners. Unopened manila mailers, peeking out of stuffed drawers left hanging open. A small desk and a blue typewriter, the one he'd written on, he claimed, since the age of thirteen.

His obsession with owning the music had always been pathological, but grew to the point that, instead of trading for them after the fact, he'd begun recording the Jack shows we attended—the waiting, untenable, for the bubble wrap mailer to come with the pair of Maxell XL-IIS high-bias cassettes, in their heavy black shells that felt like weight in the hand, like you had something great, as Nibbs said. The taping, which despite being antithetical to any music industry and copyright protection norm the band had nonetheless allowed fans to do, had made them into the popular attraction they were more than record sales, an iconoclastic aspect of the group that no feature article ever failed to elide.

The feeling of triumph I'd see on his face as we rushed back to the hotel or campsite and put on the show we'd just seen, having captured the moment like a hunter bagging rare game. Cranked those tunes, and burned one down—another one, that is, to bring on the night and eventual sleep. To get ready for the next night's show. To do Jack all over again.

But the taper I saw at Drake Park, the horrible last show—the concert where the fences had come down, the F-Kids began to riot, and as a bleak, dark final encore, Rosie collapsed before our eyes—had by then become an enthusiast pushing past the point of obsessive, punctilious collecting to what a layperson might reasonably consider madness, perhaps no less so to the band themselves: every note captured and analyzed, even their soundchecks, by tapers using directional microphones from outside the venue, or in the later years, by cats wearing studio-monitor cans on their ears, hunched over fiddling with receivers picking up radio frequencies from the in-ear monitor system the band had started using onstage—Jack, always on the cutting technological edge. Straining to hear what the band might be working up. Conversations between Rose and Jake or Linus. A ghost of a chance at intimacy with the legends.

Maybe every note *was* worth hearing. But by Drake Park, Nibbs, in his own way, had become as selfish a taper as the gatecrashers, and by the time Rose pitched forward onto her piano, hearing and collecting every note had become a tainted, fool's errand.

And here, the shrine—his life's work—now debased and desecrated, by his own hand: He'd taken a can of day-glow spray paint and scrawled a message across the spines of all his tapes, the paint dripping down the shelves like fat, multicolored fluorescent tears:

RIDERS OF THE RAINBOW - LET IT GROW!

At the sight, my stomach dropped into my shoes. To Nibbs Niffy, the tapes meant more than life. But here, and quite apart from the inscrutable but somehow positive nature of the message, his life's work stood undeniably profaned—he'd never put a tape covered in spray paint into one of his sleek silver Nakamichi decks. Never in a thousand centuries would those tapes get near his gear. He'd stomp somebody into dust before it happened.

"What does it mean," his mother asked in a flat voice. "Please tell me you know."

I searched my brain—these were lyrics, but not of a Jack song. I shrugged, impotent and helpless and sickened. "I—haven't a clue. His way of telling us goodbye?"

"Us? Or *them.*" An accusation.

Before I could answer, this seventy year-old woman in a lime green wind suit and sneakers shrieked and flung herself against the wall of media, scattering plastic and chipping away at Nibbs's farewell message—a bereaved mother gone feral, jabbering, sobbing, a frenzy. Her fingernails, long and coral in color, began snapping off, her fingertips bloodied. Digital tapes the size of thick matchboxes fell off the wall in a clunky, clattering shower.

I grabbed at Mrs. Godbold, wrestling her into a bear hug and cooing nonsensical reassurances like, “Hush, hush now. It’s okay. It’ll be okay.”

She pushed against the wall of tapes with her fists and shoved away in a last lunge of roaring, aggrieved ire, forcing us both backward onto his bed, whereupon we bounced to rest on creaky old box-springs. Mrs. Godbold had run out of steam, clinging to me and whimpering in soft sibilance through her dentures. Tapes and blue CDRs had been flung all over—on the bed with us, on the floor, their covers colorful squares of paper with setlists and timings and artwork. Vessels of joy, these recordings, yet existing now to her only as evidence of a crime.

The two of us lay still and breathless, like lovers basking in grim, grief-stricken afterglow. Self consciousness flooded onto her aged features; she struggled to a sitting position. I pulled myself up, staring at the mess on the floor and the knobby, rough bedspread.

“That group, and these damn tapes,” she said, “killed my baby boy. And I want to know why.”

“It wasn’t the tapes.” Trying harder, making my voice quiet and soothing. “His overdose, it was an accident. He didn’t mean to. Nib—Brian, I should say, wouldn’t have done that to himself on purpose. He was just—he played a little too hard. That’s all.”

Her own heartbreak assuaged through her demonstrative release, in a sudden, sodden rush it then became my turn to weep. My stomach convulsed almost to the point of dry heaving. She put her hand on my shoulder. I held it with my own until I could stop crying. The tears were for Brian, for Rose, for my fading youth, the wasted time. I promised her I would read. I would look for an answer, an answer she could buy.

Driving away from the house and heading for the beltway that'd loop me onto to 95, I couldn't stop thinking about Brian's graffiti—as sick as it made me feel to see the music collection defaced, the content of the message resonated as optimistic, a last wish of a vastly different polarity than that of the scrawled, nihilistic memorandum Colonel Kurtz left for Captain Willard, in one of Brian's favorite movies that we'd watch late at night, waiting for an acid trip to ebb its way into a state allowing for sleep: *Let it grow*, I have to admit, is certainly no *Drop the bomb, exterminate them all!*

Let it grow.

And yet Brian hadn't wanted to stick around to see the continuation of all that he'd loved, of everything that'd made sense to him about life. A cowardly approach, to say the least, to give up on oneself like this. To give up on friends and family and greeting the morning dew by drawing breath. The band had quit, but the rest of the guys were alive. With or without Rose, they might play one day, and again bring the family together. The rumors came every year that, in one form or another, Jack would soon be back. Somehow. One would think that that'd have been enough to keep an F-Kid like Nibbs going.

Not that I'll be there at any Jack reunions—Drake Park forged a rift between me and my friend, but also between me and the band I'd once loved so much that I paid to see them play almost fifty times.

As for the estrangement with Brian, which had been one of never-returned calls and emails from him, that could have been fixed, had never felt irreparable. For the minimal effort I made to stay in touch with him, however, the alienation from one another might as well have been a chasm uncrossable.

I knew what the problem was: I blamed him for Drake Park. For Rose. And that was unfair.

Alienation, estrangement . . . concepts that lead me to think of my father and stepmother, to whom I now return. I pass a giant sombrero, an hour to go before I'll bypass Columbia and dogleg onto yet another highway to take me north past the lake country, to a little hamlet in which the remains of my family have settled, in the armpit midlands of a state to which I never thought I'd return. What my father calls a 'nice, quiet place in which to dwell,' Tillman Falls, will now be home for me, too, I suppose. A roof over my head. But a safe harbor, a refuge? From myself, perhaps, and the rest of the world. But not, as I'll find out, from Nibbs Niffy.

-3-

Putting off the last leg of the trip, I pull off the freeway in Columbia—the glorious shimmering jewel that is the state capital, and the city where I first met Brian and Halsey—and head into town for dinner and a beer in the Old Market, the commercial district and college ghetto near the Southeastern campus. I don't want to see my father tonight. I don't want to answer his questions.

At a pub I don't remember from my time as a student here, I order and consume a heavy Southern meal of chicken-fried steak and gravied mashed potatoes. With greasy fingertips I flip through a Nibbs journal I've chosen from one of the cartons of his papers, a Moleskine notebook labeled *Summer 2004*—the last of his diaries. I drink a heavy craft beer, one like he and I might have quaffed in the parking lot of a Jack show, and try to peer into his words for insight. But I find no edification, only page after page of navel gazing and illegible, drug-addled foolishness.

This nonsense is Mrs. Godbold's answer—he'd lost his mind, both to substances, as well as a dead rock star who, in her lengthening silence, could offer no comfort. If I didn't feel bad enough, I do now. Instead of reading any further, I kill time by flipping through the local alt weekly. From the ads, it seems none of the rock clubs we used to hit are still around. Columbia, despite its enormous state university, has never been much of a live music town.

After an uneventful trek on one last interstate leg, and afterwards a few turns on country two-lanes, I find myself in the woods of Edgewater County, a place to which I've come only once or twice since my folks moved here from Charleston. A newish house, in a settled and established subdivision. The dream, made real.

I sneak in the house to find the rooms dim and quiet. On the kitchen table a note from my stepmother, Phyllis:

SEE YOU IN THE MORNING, SWEETHEART.
WE ARE SO GLAD TO HAVE YOU HERE.

As I'd hoped, they're asleep.

So, I dig around in the Explorer and bust into my quote-unquote snack pack full of goodies. I sit down on the porch and mash a nug of herbal essence into a glass spoon I cleaned of residue right before the drive. I relax and smoke—discretely, carefully—in a rocking chair on the wraparound porch, gazing out at the yard full of oak trees, immense and steadfast in their long watch over this landscaped patch of Carolina ground.

The world is quiet, all stillness and dark—real country dark, oh my brothers—but inside I feel no peace. I try to shove the faces out of my mind, try to forget about Brian and Halsey. I consider digging out a portable CD player and ear buds to listen to some Jack, but that's all I did for the whole drive down here. No—the silence is what I seek.

I smoke and smoke, but don't feel high, which doesn't make sense—the pot is good, blueberry crossed with something or other, a very heady strain. Ah—there we go. Now my scalp feels as though it's being massaged by a supple, sympathetic hand—and if, pray tell, this is the hand of fate I feel caressing my bumpy noggin, do please allow this gentle touch to portend some measure of good fortune in my future. As with Brian's mom, I'd say that I'm on the hunt for answers, but I fear I cannot even muster the right questions, much less make sense of my friend's life and death to her. Or anyone, for that matter.

I tamp the bowl on the porch railing much too soon, and meteors of flaming blueberry streak downward in glowing arcs. Nibbs used to ride me mercilessly over my impatience about dumping bowls—"There's still good stuff in there!" he'd shout. I'd give anything for him to be here now to castigate me.

Reality descends: Brian, Halsey, the cop pulling me over, and now being back in South Carolina, ensconced in some podunk backwater instead of the beloved low country of my youth in Charleston, a city of charm and history and character, and probably where I belong—home, true home, as much as I've known one. Nothing to which I may look forward, not even a Jack show, but I'd gotten used to that.

There—at last, a question comes to me: What have I done?

–4–

At the breakfast table, my back aching from sleeping on an unfamiliar sofa, my father and I rattle newspaper sections and sip good coffee. Phyllis, on the other side of the huge kitchen, is humming and happy and busy cleaning a skillet of egg leavings, then moving on to the production of an enormous batch of chocolate chip cookies for a church function, she says, to be held later in the day. All-American, this household. Wholesome.

"So," my father says after a period of small talk and classic Southern family avoidance of the unpleasant issues at hand, "we're both just about eat up with curiosity about what you plan to do with yourself now, Tobey."

My father and Phyllis, both using my childhood name—once old enough to have control over the situation, from Ashton Tobias Zemp I became not the childish sounding family nickname, but Ash—much more dignified, more so than Z, which would come later, only after we'd begun following Jack.

I welcome my relatives to call me what they will—other than these family members, upon whom may I count to address me by any name at all? One supposes I'll have to find me some new peeps, folks who may call me yet another name.

In any case: this, no time for road names. Not once you're back home. "No offense, Dad, but I'm not sure I've ever felt like 'Tobey,' even when that's who I was."

Alston Lancaster Zemp looks at me over his paper and purses his full lips in displeasure, as though I'm yanking his chain. "Son, that may be the most obtuse and ridiculous notion I think I ever did hear."

"You'll always be Tobey to us," Phyllis calls over. She's dumping a sack of bittersweet 60% cacao chips into a giant stainless steel bowl of batter, followed by a few handfuls of crushed walnuts. "How else can we possibly think of you?"

"Identity issues are somewhat endemic to we Gen-X wastrels," I offer both as excuse and rejoinder. "We stand here in the long shadows of you baby boomers, still trying to figure out our place in the world."

"'Us' wastrels," my stepmother corrects, but I take no offense—I always scored better on math than verbal. It's why Halsey let me keep her books.

I last spoke to my father a few weeks ago, only days after Brian's body was found, cold and alone and surrounded by his disfigured tapes, tagged like the subways upon which we'd ridden on trips to see the band play at Madison Square Garden. When I broke the news, Dad sputtered and stammered his way through a grudging condolence that evolved, as I knew it would, into disparaging remarks about Jack O'Roses, the rootless and ill-behaved F-Kids, drugs, liberals, permissiveness, and the seemingly pervasive depravity of the human spirit that's part and parcel, in his world view, of the entire rock and roll milieu.

I took no umbrage: All that bluster was subterfuge. I knew my father's bitter oration was only his way of avoiding the truth of the matter, which was that I'd lost someone I loved. Al Zemp doesn't do tragedy all that well, not after what happened with my mom—a car accident left the mother of two small children dead, an event that as a teen I learned had been her fault: a mom harboring a secret pills-and-alcohol problem, a predilection that'd take her away from me before I'd ever get to know her as a person. She's like an iconic fictional character to me, one depicted in a famous book I've heard about, but never gotten around to reading.

My father, whom I know all too well, sits across from me at this small, round table in the breakfast nook, decorated, as is the rest of the kitchen, in floral accents and pale yellows. Thanks to the house's frontage and oversized windows, sunlight streams in—this was by design, of course, that the nook would receive the warmth of the morning sun—and the soft babble of a Christian talk show, so low in volume that it barely registers, plays in the background from the tabletop Bose radio. Dad's trying to enjoy the simple, sacred ritual that is his morning paper and coffee, and probably more annoyed than overjoyed at the presence of his only son.

Now retired, my father spent his working life as a successful businessman, retiring only a couple of years ago. Roundabout the time of my birth roughly four decades in the slipstreaming, receding past, he'd been hired by, and later bought himself an ownership slice of, an office supply company, one that grew into a strong, stable and well-regarded regional business, and that'd financed this handsome, comfortable, early retirement—his stake in the company, when sold, yielded strong and duly-taxed capital gains. He had accomplished that by which his generation had been charged: to be men, as men were once defined. To provide.

He married Phyllis when Lil, my sister older by a couple of years, and who remembers Mom in a way I do not, and I were approaching teenagerhood and pubescence. Despite Phyllis's kind treatment of us, I never accepted her, have never considered her my mother, nor did my sibling Lilliana Montgomery Zemp, living in New York, now, for many years. Like me, she wanted our real mother, a feeling hard to describe to someone who's enjoyed the natural progression of this most crucial of human relationships. Hadn't been Phyllis's fault, bless her soul.

But now, another reason for Phyllis to annoy me: Dragging Dad up-country to these ordinary and humid midlands of the state, which has resulted in me being stuck here, too. From his retirement largesse, I suspect my folks could afford to live on one of the Carolina resort islands, in a lovely marshfront mansion amidst the egrets and ospreys and sawgrass. It's what I did—Halsey and I, flush with her own successes that'd marched us up the Eastern seaboard, from Charlotte to Raleigh to Richmond to the last store she opened in Bethesda, bought an old farm house on the shore across the bridge from Annapolis, a beautiful piece of property so peaceful and secluded that it lay only a mile from a government electronic listening outpost, one sensitive enough, perhaps, to pick up the faint echo of a Rose Partland guitar solo drifting down from heaven.

Already I find myself missing that tranquil corner of the universe in which I dwelled in my dotage as a feckless and bored house husband, cooking and cleaning and wondering, occasionally, what I ought to be doing with myself. I got through the long days with endless reading—despite never again needing to take such a test, I worked on that verbal SAT score, and considered writing, a childhood dream that'd never come to fruition in any meaningful form. When I tried putting pen to paper, I found, unfortunately, that I had nothing to say.

Awash in these recent memories, I produce myself another cup of joe from a whirring automated grinding and brewing system by Bosch, a device that looks less like a coffee pot than set decoration from some cheesy old sci-fi TV show. The machine is one of a veritable family of glimmering stainless steel contraptions arrayed across granite counter tops: bread maker, food processor, juicer, and an indoor counter top grill, a nifty device that reminds me of a similar one Halsey gave me a couple of Christmases ago. I close my eyes and see it on the counter back home, can remember the last couple of hamburgers I made to eat by myself whilst she dashed this way and that in the running of her businesses, racing like mad from one town to the other, not unlike how we'd once followed Jack O'Roses from concert to concert.

I add some half and half to the strong coffee, clear my throat, and try to keep the conversation modest in scale. "I see you still take the old hometown rag."

My father scoffs in rank indignation. "I would not stoop to line a cat's litter box with that Columbia paper—animals deserve more respect than that."

I simply have to ask: "Don't you miss the holy city?"

"Not a bit." He pages through his crisp *Post and Courier*, hiding behind it, I think. "Wouldn't trade this home we've made here for anything—Edgewater County's got a kind of peaceful atmosphere I had no clue I was missing."

Despite a surfeit of scrubby, sandy pine barrens, sure, it's lovely here—in this part of the county are rolling hills and expanses of hardwoods, and down the ridge, the red clay banks of the Sugeree River that feeds the huge lake to the south of us—but I'm doubtful that father believes this to be heaven on earth.

"I'd have figured you for a place on the peninsula, or out on John's Island. Kiawah, Edisto . . . anyplace but here," cutting my eyes at Phyllis, who seems to ignore us as she plops quarter-sized dollops of cookie dough onto a baking sheet warped and blackened by use.

"Well, *Tobias,*" he says, haughty, "you were wrong."

"Had to happen eventually."

A harrumph for the ages—to him, I've always been more wrong than right.

"Perhaps," he says, "what we should discuss is not the decisions I've made regarding my life, but the ones you've made about yours."

I allow the suggestion to hang unanswered.

"What he's trying to say, Tobey," Phyllis interjects, cheerful and bright as the shaft of light in which my coffee cup sits steaming, "is that we were wondering—and if you were us, you'd realize that we can't help but ask—how long we can expect you to . . . be visiting here with us."

"'If you were we,'" I say in a mincing prattle, unsure whether that's correct or not. I laugh, alone, then give a proper answer in a normal voice. "Couple weeks, maybe? Until I get on my feet."

Dad, eyeing me with rank suspicion. "May I assume you have some money? Money to start over, since this divorce, as I understand it, was your wife's idea?"

"Yes, there's money. I meant 'on my feet' . . . emotionally."

They exchange an uncomfortable look. My father goes back to his paper, refusing to meet my eyes. "Well—you're always welcome, son. As long as you need to be here."

"I appreciate that. I won't be a burden."

Phyllis comes over and puts her arms around my neck, a motherly hug. "You stay with us as long as you need to."

I pat the hands of the woman I've never allowed myself to consider as my mother, push her gently away. "Thank you."

My father, never one to give himself over to rank sentimentality, folds his paper and places it next to the woven straw place mat on which sits the remains of his breakfast, a plate containing a half-eaten piece of wheat toast smeared with raspberry preserves and a butter substitute called Smart Balance. He puts the tips of his fingers together in front of his lips as though in prayer, then musters the words eating at him: "I'm very sorry about you and Halsey—truly, I am. But what is it you plan to *do* with yourself now?"

"Get used to bachelorhood. Probably move back to Charleston. I miss it."

"As I do myself, son." A moment of honesty between us. "I meant for a living."

I tell him I do not know, but that, in time, a new path will come to me.

"May I ask you something else?"

"Certainly."

"You're not still attending those silly concerts, I hope?"

I sigh. "No—Rose died. Remember? Rose Partland? The rest of the band gave up the ghost after that."

Sarcasm, oozing out of every word. "Isn't that a dreadfully terrific shame."

"I'd seen enough shows to last me, even before she croaked on us. Not Brian, though. He'd be there right now, if he could."

"I never understood why you people insisted on making those vagabonds wealthier than they already were."

"If I have to explain," I say with a smile, offering a slogan I once saw on a T-shirt some kid was selling in the Jack parking lot, "you wouldn't understand."

He shakes his head. "That's neither here nor there now, is it? My understanding?"

"No—making sense of all that doesn't much matter," which reminds me of Brian's various journals and manuscripts. "So listen, I've got some paperwork I need to print, and I'd like to work on a résumé—may I assume that a man who's late of the office supply trade has a PC and its related accoutrements at hand?"

"Phyllis has herself a workstation set up just off the master suite—if you ask her, I'm sure she'll be happy to let you use it."

Phyllis finishes filling the dishwasher and takes me to a guest bedroom. After arranging to use her computer, I feel a wave of raw emotion ripple through me, one she can see on my face.

"Oh, Tobey," her voice breaking, "I'm so so sorry—come here to me, angel."

I let her hold my stiff, bony frame to her plump body. "It's all right," I say as though it is she who needs comforting. "We weren't supposed to be, I guess."

"The Lord's will can't be fully understood. Life makes so much more sense when you finally accept that, and accept Him, son."

“I’ll keep that in mind,” I answer with a forced smile. “And thank you again for letting me crash here for a while.”

“Son,” she says, sounding offended. “We’re your family.”

She sniffles and departs, leaving me alone but for the words of a dead man, calling out to me, begging me to listen. And so, I do.

–5–

After Phyllis leaves for her church bake sale, I get comfy in her office-nook and connect a USB cable from Brian's laptop to the all-in-one ink jet printer, after which I watch his battered old computer decide if it knows this particular model from around the technological neighborhood. After a few clickings and other such machinations, saints be praised but it does.

I print up the first chapter of Nibbs Niffy's magnum opus, a manuscript he'd often described to me, but never shared—his 'making sense of who they were and what happened,' as he put it, and begun in earnest after Rose's death. After Drake Park. I take the sheaf of pages, along with a few of his most recent handwritten journals, back downstairs.

Feeling stir crazy after only half a day, I ask Dad if there's a coffee shop in Tillman Falls, but he says that there's not, so I decide to drive into Columbia, where I'll feel a little more like I'm still in the civilized world—back to the Old Market again already, a place I can lose myself among the hipsters, panhandlers, and other eccentrics. Assuming, of course, that there's a me to lose.

The drive, through hill country that descends toward the fall line, is pleasant—despite the lingering

Carolina heat of summer, the windows are rolled down and a Jack CD's cranked up, a lengthy and introspective 'Nebula Rising' jam sequence from '69 that's intense and rockin' and spacey, and then intense redux as it folds back on itself and the band wends its way from pulsatingly pure improvisational exploration back to the main theme, which reemerges one instrument at a time until resolving, fully, in an exultant and exciting buildup of a conclusion that melts, exquisite, into the next tune. Phew. But glorious—however many words and pages Nibbs Niffy expended trying to understand Jack O'Roses, to my mind what I hear now does a more than adequate job of explaining that which cannot so easily be explained.

A double-shot latte later courtesy of Maxine's Koffee Klatch, I'm sitting at a table halfway down the block from the pub at which I drank last night—I should have kept my parking space and slept in the Explorer. I know why I've come back, of course—it's where we spent our youth: Brian. Halsey. Me. For all the nice folks and the inviting vibe in the coffee shop—people clattering away on laptops, reading the newspaper, playing chess—this uneasy proximity to problematic memories offers me scant comfort.

I contemplate the pages I've printed, which from emails and infrequent conversations with Brian I know represented, he hoped, a literary exegesis expressing in concrete terms his deep and grand summation not only of his personal Jack O'Roses experience, but of the overall history of the band, and the era out of which they sprang and flourished; a kind of hippy dissertation, an acid test. I'm amazed at how much material there is, and how cogent and lucid passages read in passing seem—a couple of hundred pages in total, which owing to severe concentration issues, I'll have to read a bit at a time.

He worked so hard, put so much effort in, only to throw it all away on a fistful of Oxycontin and a fifth of bourbon. 'Tis a shame, a crying, pathetic shame, this. Nibbs Niffy, for all his effort, seems to me but a waste of flesh, and before I begin reading I find I must tamp down a ruinous, hot wave of futility and anger, reminding myself that to best honor his life I must let the words be his, now, for a while. And so, I quiet my inner skeptic, and begin to read.

The Ballad of Jack O'Roses
by Brian K. Godbold

Verse One

On the plane ride back home after the Rose Partland memorial in Golden Gate Park, which had been a throng of grief-stricken, spun out humanity, a sea of bodies, I felt like I was still tripping—could there be a better way to honor her life, this feeling, than a lingering dose? No, I thought. Surely not. But it hadn't been last night, it'd been a month since I'd done acid—since Drake Park. Still, there it was. A shimmering. A tingling. A lingering.

As Sunday melted into Monday morning, the redeye to Atlanta whistled along, still and cloaked in semidarkness. Fingers of light danced around the periphery of my vision; seated in the back of the cabin, the front bulkhead seemed a thousand miles away. The backs of heads stuck up from the seats in front of me, strange growths like those gray mottled monster eggs in the Alien *movies. Sounds, muffled and distorted by the constant thrum of the jet's powerful churning turbines. My consciousness, trapped in a slender hurtling metal tube. My soul, closer to Rose's, dancing cloud-high and exuberant in its freedom from her heavy, burdened body.*

The last trip, man. Acid or no acid, that's what I had been on. Hadn't sunk in yet. Not at that moment, anyway.

I had a small satchel with me containing dozens of print media accounts of Rose Partland's death, and I kept reading them repeatedly, as though the news simply couldn't sink all the way in. Some of the more insightful accounts went beyond the facts surrounding her life—and the mythologies—to delve into how We the Collective were going to handle the situation now that our muse was gone, an admirable but futile effort at such a moment, so close as it was to the tragedy.

And let me be clear, I say We with a capital W because we are more than just a bunch of fanatical rock music or celebrity worshipers. We are a societal subset. We are a movement. We are One of a Mind, like our favorite band.

One of a mind. The personification of gestalt. An unwritten social contract. Thus is described the relationship between Jack O'Roses and the F-Kids.

Her *kids.*

Of course such heavy ideas are in themselves simplifications—exaggerations, even, and rank generalizations dangerous and misleading to those not in on the joke. The idea of gestalt applies much more to the actual musicians than to us, the fans, although we indeed are a part of the mix in ways that other music lovers and arena-rock junkies are not. We as a group outside the show, however . . .? Well, we aren't always of a similar mindset. At times I wonder if there is much of a connection at all, other than the fact that everybody goes to these concerts, these rituals called Jack O'Roses shows. We are as diverse in thought and attitude as most big groups tend to be, even a herd of white, middle-class college fucks like us, but who shared certainly commonalities that transcended personality type: Latchkey kids—we all started smoking dope young.

But naturally, there are matters F-Kids can all agree on—like the bumper sticker says, a bad day on tour is better than a good day at work. Everybody in our scene wants to be one particular place, and that is at a show. THE show, which is the show that is, like, happening right then and there.

Be Here Now, and all that.

Now? That's yesterday's papers. The Now is gone. Look! You can see it, there, on the horizon, growing smaller. A line, now a dot, now a wavering mirage.

Rose.

Rose was the one who kept us in line, until the day a month ago when she couldn't any longer, when the devil appeared at Drake Park and showed his ass, as my southern grandmother would have put it.

Already, speculation about whether the band will go on without our Earthmother seems a profane, absurd idea going beyond any reasoned person's comprehension—those who are saying it's possible are those who haven't come to terms with the loss, haven't fully understood that whether she liked it not, no matter how often she denied that it was 'her' band, and for all the talents of the other virtuosi on stage, Rose was our leading light. Jack is gone, right along with her. Let's not kid ourselves.

What some are saying—in hindsight, mind you—is that tour is what killed Rose. That Drake Park, what is now the final-final show in a way that no tour's ever ended before, finished her off.

Maybe.

Tour sometimes does that to people. Not like going to war, unless you count the war on us that the government conducts. But you still get eaten up by the road. Ask any rock musician worth his salt, who's played the big rooms on a long bus tour, town to town, all the same, play, get on the bus, go to sleep, wake up someplace different, yet the same. You lose a sense of yourself on tour, especially when it's lots of single nights, like the summer stadium run all the way across the whole damn patch of American dirt. On the road you're a cog in a machine, the rock star, a shiny golden one that people notice, that fans—people you don't and can never know, thousands, millions of them, a global hive-mind—adore without reservation.

I'll admit it. I've seen people's lives get ruined by following this Jack O'Roses act around the country, getting mixed up with the wrong drugs, the wrong people, the wrong lovers, vending crap in the lot and living this outside-the-lines kind of life to the point that you know they just eventually crash and burn. Lives get ruined all the time in the 'real' world too, don't they? Of course they do. Of course they do. Think of tour burnout like being a workaholic—all for the good of the Family.

Rose. In her case, no question—tour, voracious to the point that it must eat that from which it'd sprung.

Her bones, picked clean, collapsed in a crumbling cairn on stage like the body of the vagabond poet Cassady, staggering along as long as it could on those cold Mexican railroad tracks, until he could take no further steps. Rose, in death as in life our silver headed, ethereal angel, will stand on stage forever, figuring out the set list of the show that they'll never play, the canceled show.

Now, the real work begins: the telling of the tale, wherein we begin Rose's story, and mine, working backward from the dreadful end, with this clipping, the first in my stack:

'FARE THEE WELL, FAT ANGEL': PARTLAND MEMORIAL DRAWS RECORD-SETTING THRONG TO GOLDEN GATE PARK

By Jasmine Ikiru
Examiner Arts & Entertainment Desk
August 14, 1997

San Francisco: A crowd estimated by the SFPD at nearly 300,000 gathered in Golden Gate Park yesterday for a massive, impromptu concert celebrating the life of rock musician Rose Partland, who died Tuesday of an apparent heart attack.

A diverse lineup including Bob Dylan, Pete Townsend, Willie Nelson, Elvis Costello, Crosby, Stills & Nash, and Pearl Jam eulogized Partland and performed, sometimes their own music, oftentimes hers.

The Sunday afternoon concert was almost uniformly somber and peaceful. The SFPD reported only nine custodial arrests during the hours-long event, all for public intoxication.

SFPD Captain Nguyen Huang described a subdued crowd. “All ages, mostly respectful and very sad, many of them. I don’t think I’ve ever seen this many sad people in one place before.”

A giant portrait of a smiling Partland standing against a vibrant tie-dyed background served as the backdrop. In front of the stage, a makeshift shrine took shape as fans laid a mountain of flowers, pictures, poetry, candles, marijuana joints and other symbols of their affection for Partland.

Early in the program an announcement was made that filmmaker Oliver Stone would be shooting a documentary about the memorial, but the crowd reacted negatively, booing and chanting “Let her rest!” until the next musical act came on. A camera crane and other film crew equipment stored next to the stage was never used.

Many had speculated that the surviving members of Jack O’Roses would perform in some fashion. Instead, the remaining band members, sans instruments, appeared on stage only during a segment of brief official eulogies that took place late in the program, just before a mass jam session of many of the music industry’s most important artists that concluded the afternoon.

The group’s rhythm guitarist Jake Sobel spoke for the band.

“There’s good news and bad news, but I don’t know which part is which. What I do know is this: Rose is through becoming, now she is being. She’s here, there and everywhere. So when I say this, I know she’ll hear it: Fare thee well, sweetheart. We’ll be along presently, all of us here today.”

Adelaide Partland-Sobel, the fiercely private

daughter of the songwriting duo from their early 70s marriage, her face obscured by a silk scarf and dark glasses, stood sequestered behind a partition, and did not address the crowd.

In the last decade Partland, whose band filled concert halls and stadiums for 30 years, had suffered numerous health crises, including obesity, drug addiction, and what is now suspected to have been heart disease.

Following an attempt on her life after a 1986 Dallas, Texas concert, she nearly died of an overdose of medication prescribed to help her recovery emotionally from the assassination attempt. A subsequent tour was cancelled so that Partland could address her health issues.

At a press conference before the New Year's series of concerts that heralded her return to the stage, Partland joked about the Dallas incident.

"Mark David Chapman. Ronnie Wayne Bundrick. What's the beef these three-name cats have with rock legends? Sheesh."

Through out the late 80s and early 90s she appeared to be in good health, and the band hit a new peak of creativity and popularity that continued until this summer's tour, on which every show had been a sellout, including stadium gigs seating 60,000 fans, known as F-Kids.

Her health began to decline again in the mid-90s, however, amid fears that longtime fans agree seemed to indicate she'd suffered substance abuse relapse, which was confirmed by no fewer than three rehab stays, in 1993, 1995, and early this year following a West Coast holiday tour during which Partland appeared disoriented and unsteady onstage.

On July 4 of this year, a concert at the Drake

Park Amphitheater in Indiana turned dangerous for Partland as well as her fans: following a gate-crashing incident, the rock legend fans called 'The Earthmother' and 'Fat Angel' collapsed onstage, while in the audience a full-scale riot already underway turned deadly. Three concert attendees perished in the melee, with scores more injured, including police and first responders, and arrests numbering over a hundred. The subsequent night's concert, what would have been the last show of the tour, was canceled.

On Tuesday in her Marin County home, after she'd eaten breakfast and gone down to her studio to work on songs for a new album the band planned to record over the winter touring break, that concert became Rose Partland's final onstage appearance for all time. She was found on the floor, only steps from her studio piano on which she'd written many of the group's most memorable songs.

The diverse group of fellow classic rock titans memorialized Partland throughout the afternoon concert, ending with an uncharacteristically emotional Bob Dylan, who led the crowd in the singing of the traditional hymn 'Will the Circle Be Unbroken' [. . .]

Already, this material, both manuscript and press clipping, feels as tiresome as it prompts other strong and sentimental emotion—I know the Jack story inside and out, and as much as I loved them, I was there for the party more than the spiritual and cultural aspects that Brian feels the band exemplified. Feeling bored and enervated by these few pages, it seems to me that Brian, in death as in life, is engaged in making me feel guilty for my tenuous and shallow so-called faith in all things Rose.

Wait. None of that is true. That's only the way Brian—Nibbs Niffy—made me feel. He was the one who'd been wrong in the end, though. Nibbs who'd been the philistine.

In any case, a mention of Drake Park, a show I didn't want to attend in the first place, and did so only under the duress of an obstinate, determined and drug-addled Nibbs's angry insistence, so skewed my vision about what it meant to be an F-Kid that I've long lost all perspective and interest in analyzing the Jack experience, as Brian would term it. It was good music played well, for the most part, and I enjoy listening to it whenever I can.

What do you want me to say? I don't want to read about Drake Park. I don't want to re-live Rose's death. Reliving the horror was what killed my friend—why should I subject myself to this torture? To what end?

A promise. And maybe for my own selfish reasons, too—an answer to my own emptiness and loss.

I watch the college kids, bustling and settling back in for the fall semester, coming and going from the shops and the cafe like the busy beavers they are. I feel like a cipher, a blank slate, waiting to be filled. Not with Brian's words. Not today. Mrs. Godbold's answers will have to wait. I linger in the afternoon sunlight, sip the dregs of my tepid latte, watch the world drift by languid and untroubled, finally put his papers away and go home.

–6–

On the drive home, loneliness forces my hand, and I make an ill-considered call.

Halsey answers, polite but wondering what it is I need from her.

"Just wanted to let you know that I made it here all right."

"That's super, hon. Folks doing okay? Tell them I said—well. Maybe not."

"They don't change. You've never in your life seen two people more happy and fulfilled and satisfied. It's sick, I tell you. Depraved."

Music thumps in the background, obscuring Halsey's strained but polite responses. She's at a huge fashion trade show in Vegas, and we'd said our goodbye-goodbye in the departures lane at BWI, the ride a last favor on my way out of town. Misty-eyed, we hugged each other. I wasn't supposed to feel hurt or spurned—we'd both agreed we didn't really love one another anymore, if we ever had at all.

Her words, not mine. I agreed only because I wanted her to be happy. No point in parsing that now.

"Did you stop to check on Brian's mother like you said you were?"

"I did. She gave me—" I grope for words. "She presented me with a kind of assignment."

Halsey tells me to hold on while she barks replies to a stream of questions: color assortments and piece counts and ship dates. “An assignment,” she at last repeats, distracted and impatient. “Oh—did he make you executor?”

“God, no, nothing that official—Mrs. Godbold gave me his diaries, his writing, and wants me to go through it all. She needs to know why—if there is a why, I guess, since there wasn’t a note, per se—he did this to himself.”

“You’re breaking up. She wants you to write her a note? About what?”

“Forget it—this is nothing of interest to you.”

“Hon—can we do this another time? What do you say. I’m busy.”

Her term of endearment rankles—‘hon’ is what she calls the girls who are her buyers and managers. Well—I had been an employee, I suppose. I release her, ring off.

“Take care,” she says, very small and sad.

I put Brian’s papers back in the car and spend some time strolling up the hill to the Southeastern campus, remembering this or that moment, alternately reveling in nostalgia but deploring the passage of time, seeking solace, I think, in memories of more innocent days.

In reminiscing, I find myself needing a Jack show more than ever, a sensation I haven’t felt in years. Jittery and full of coffee, I consider going to the pub to drink alcohol, now, to excess, but think better of doing so. With nothing to do and nowhere else to go, and no burning desire to look up what few old friends might still be around Columbia—avoidance, of course, of all the inevitable questions from those people about what I’ve done with my life, and what’s to come—I putter back to Tillman Falls, where my empty room awaits, and along with that hollow space another bleak, pointless night.

Lying in the dark, prone and alone, I don't pray—it's not something I would do—but in a sudden rush I do feel compelled to ask Brian-slash-Nibbs, wherever he is, to grant me an iota of forgiveness and understanding for my dreadful apostasy, but for what specific transgression I seek absolution, I know not.

The next day, the folks pack up their own SUV and decamp for Hilton Head along with another couple from their church, what seems to me a rather sudden getaway. Phyllis claims to be mortified that they're leaving so soon after my own arrival, and my father looks blue around the gills, like he's holding his breath until the moment he longer has to contend with the presence of his overgrown child. Or so I perceive.

Orphaned, I call my only other life connection, Lil, who's in New York where she works for one of the big publishing houses—not in creative, as she puts it, but marketing. She's done well. An exec. Decent coin. Townhouse in Brooklyn that I've never visited, even when Sally Simpson and I be-bopped our way to the city, whether to see Jack, or later, to buy to stuff at the boutique show. Oh, I'd give Lil a call when we there in the area, but with both of us so busy, we'd never get hooked up.

Her girl puts me through, and we get caught up. Lil tells me how sorry she is about Halsey, and about Brian, who my father told her about, and that she barely knew. Two or three minutes more or less exhausts what we had to say to one another, and I ring off with her half-interested questions about my future plans echoing in my head like an unpleasant earbug.

After a few days knocking around in the cavernous house—getting high and watching the tube; nothing better to do—I feel as empty as the spaces I inhabit, spectral, and as guiltily indolent as can be imagined. I have to get. Out.

The obvious solution? Charleston, beckoning. My true homeland. With all due haste I assemble certain combustible libations, go online and secure a hotel room using Halsey's Marriott Rewards number —gold status, an automatic upgrade—and within the hour, after first gassing up the old tub and procuring a tub of grape ICEE with a bendy straw for the ride downcountry, this free man in Paris hits the slab once again for a two-hour cruise to my old home, my old haunts.

-7-

After stowing the ride in a downtown garage, with a satchel of Brian's notebooks and papers I stroll happily on a side street over to the shopping district along King Street, looking for a place to light until I can check into the hotel, which I found to be busy and booked and not ready for my early arrival.

Tourists and students wander along amidst the elegant, increasingly ancient Old World architecture, but not many—for such a beautiful, bright and clear fall day, this fine September 11, 2004, my picturesque hometown seems terribly still and motionless.

A curly-headed college kid bolts by me on the narrow, uneven sidewalk, a rude, hard elbow catching me on the forearm and knocking the satchel out of my hand.

"Hey," I call out, incensed and in pain. "You little—"

"Somebody crashed a jet into the White House!" he shouts back over his shoulder, feral eyes bugging out. "The president's dead! *We're under attack.*"

"Excuse me?"

No reply—he's already hauled ass down the street and turned the corner. I hear him call out, strained voice echoing between the rows of three-story buildings, "We're at war, *we're at war*"—a mad Paul

Revere racing through the streets in a Red Hot Chili Peppers shirt and board shorts.

An elderly couple standing on the opposite corner have observed this incident, and after watching the boy run west toward the campus of the College of Charleston, they hurry across to me.

"Did he just say a plane hit the White House?" the coiffured, well-heeled woman asks. Her husband—quite a bit older, and squinting with that helpless gape-mouthed look of one who cannot hear what's being said—looks more skeptical and impatient than afraid.

"I believe that he did."

"That's—that can't be so."

"I agree—I feel like I'm in one of those apocalyptic Stephen King novels," I said. I point down the block to a set of double doors. "Look—there'll be a television set in that bar."

We rush inside the tavern, a place I'd eaten and frequented many times, where I'd passed off a fake ID and bought my first beer, in fact. Inside, we find a group of people staring up at the flatscreens mounted on the walls, at staggering visions of destruction like out of a movie: One of the World Trade towers is burning, and indeed, as the crier had foretold, the White House lies in ruins, a smoking crater of horror shot from circling helicopters, while on the soundtrack runs a cacophonous jabber of frantic news anchors.

But our newsbearer was wrong about one detail: President Gore and the First Lady, both safe, but many other high-ranking casualties are reported killed—Vice President Lieberman and several other Cabinet-level officers including Secretary of State Colin Powell, assorted journalists and other support staff and the brave Secret Service detail, all caught unawares by the screaming, dive-bombing 757 that Peter Jennings says clipped and also damaged the Washington Monument on its dreadful approach. "A further insult," the Canadian-born broadcast journalist notes, "but one in which, thankfully, no lives were lost. That we know of, of course."

A few minutes later, it seems, a similar aircraft barreled into the side of the North tower of the WTC, and that building now stands partially aflame, with oily plumes of ink-black smoke drifting across the occluded sky over Lower Manhattan. A split-screen nightmare across a dozen televisions of various sizes, all still unfolding—I keep waiting for there to be commercial breaks, to give us all a breather and a chance to get caught up to our feelings, but there are none.

I shake my head, grind the heels of my hands into my eyes: I feel as though I'm tripping. And not in a kind way, either.

But wait, there's more—reports are still coming in that more jetliners may yet be involved, and every plane in the country, we hear in breaking news, has now been ordered to land forthwith and immediately at the nearest airport or airfield, including the news helicopters piping in the video of the two instances of ground zero.

Dan Rather crumbles on the air, weeping at the images of people jumping from the high floors in stricken building, above the raging fire of hell that's gripped the city of New York, and the whole world. We all weep, or else look away.

No footage has emerged yet of the plane actually crashing into the smoking ruin in DC that'd been not only a national symbol, but our president's home; once those images do, I suspect we'll suffer another moment of visceral shock and awestruck horror. Between the live reports from DC about what the on-camera retired general who's now a news advisor to CNN has been calling the White House Rescue Op, the shaky, lone video clip to emerge depicting the American Airlines jet hitting the South tower of the WTC plays over and over and over, so many times that the longer I sit in the bar watching the image, the more numbed through recognition I feel.

A young server, blonde and creamy of complexion, looking innocent and troubled and barely old enough to be out of high school, comes over to the table at which I've plopped down and asks, shakily, if I need a beverage.

"Beer," I order generically, like in the movies. "Cold."

"Bud . . . Light?"

"I don't care."

"Yes, sir."

"Hold on—wartime or not, certain standards bear upholding. Sierra Nevada?"

"Bottle or draught?"

"Which is colder?"

That gets a smile out of her. "Ah-ha—good question. Our manager thinks it's the bottles, but my boyfriend says—"

She's cut off by the screams and gasps of the collective watching the coverage: WTC2, as the anchors are calling the south tower, half of a mighty pair of obelisks that'd once been the unimpeachable colossus of the wealth and power of the western world, collapses before our eyes—sudden, straight down, clouds of ashy gray material billowing, as when they demo buildings on purpose.

My sweet server, shrieking, drops the round tray she'd been holding against her bosom like a shield and races into the kitchen, crying. My arm jerks forward, involuntary, and the satchel drops off the table, pages of Nibbs Niffy manuscript scattering. On another set, marble-mouthed Tom Brokaw says, " . . . and . . . and . . . the tower appears to have collapsed. The south tower of the World Trade Center—that's WTC2—appears, um, to have collapsed."

Appears? No shit. This development, a fresh shock, casts a further pall over the roomful of upset Americans.

In a booth across from me, the old man from the street weeps and pleads loudly for his wife to explain to him what's going on. She's strong for him—I can see in her eyes that she wants to give in to the fear, but for his sake, cannot.

I go over, ask if I can get them anything from the bar—water or iced tea or a Coke.

"Gin and tonic!" the old guy shouts. "Top shelf! Same for my wife!"

She smiles at me, shaking her head with weary bemusement. "Have the girl bring us two iced teas, young man. And thank you—he doesn't even know where we are. I keep telling him it's a movie. Only a movie."

"I keep thinking that, too," my throat clenching.

"The ironic part is that this had been one of his good days, which aren't many. Ah, well."

After a brief interval, President Gore, along with a hollow-eyed Secretary of Defense Hillary Clinton, appears from an undisclosed, secure location to address the nation. You can see a hint of shock in his eyes and the shiny pallor of Gore's normally ruddy, healthy face, and yet his demeanor is one of resolve, calm, and control. Stalwart and brave, the President informs the citizenry that we are under attack by what are believed to be rogue Islamic terrorists rather than another sovereign nation, that in addition to the obviously successful attacks, several highjackings—all commercial aircraft of various types, intended for other, yet undetermined targets—have been foiled and forestalled and prevented.

"Despite all appearances," he says in his friendly, soft Tennessee regular-fella accent, "the attacks, for now, seem to be over. And so, we must turn to rescue, recovery, and research—to find out who did this, and to prevent them, or anyone, from ever attacking our beloved American homeland again."

Homeland? That word makes my insect antennae wiggle, but I don't know why—a vague, unpleasant connotation.

Gore promises to have a further statement later in the evening, and a full-scale press conference either tomorrow or the next day to address in detail, he promises, what the next steps are to be, how we're going to be able to capture what terrorists may still be alive, how we will resume air traffic, and how, by getting the bad guys who have done this terrible thing to us, we will right our listing ship of state.

Of the White House, now a smoldering ruin, he explains to us in a steadfast, soothing cadence that symbols are powerful things, yes, but also that destroyed houses are but man-made objects, forged of metal and wood and stone, and with a simple decision to do so, may be rebuilt—can even be reconstructed better and stronger, he points out, than before. The opportunity given to us now, he says, smiling, is that rather than cower in fear—rather than let terrorism do its job, in other words—we now possess the impetus and motivation to strengthen the foundation that is our country. To set our noses to the grindstone. To assert our moral superiority.

Unfortunately, he notes with grim disappointment, the presidential campaign would be suspended, a sort-of rematch of 2000, with incumbent Gore running for his second full term against another Bush, this time Jeb, who, if he couldn't deliver Florida for his brother four years ago, this time aims to do it for himself.

"They may think we have been hurt today, and on one level we have," he concludes. "But make no mistake—these terrorists haven't won anything, and our lives and elections and commerce will go on. No—despite all appearances, they've failed." He presses his already thin lips together. "And we are going to make them sorry that they ever woke up today and decided to attack the U-nited States of America. So take a moment to pray, to collect yourselves, and to get back best you can to your everyday lives. We'll tell you all more when we know it ourselves," he says. "God bless and keep us, and for now, a good afternoon to you all."

As Gore's face fades into the presidential seal and the networks resume their coverage, a stout middle-aged man, screaming and red-faced, leaps to his feet, knocking over his high-backed stool onto the tiled floor with a crash.

"Bullshit—that goddamn socialist just made a campaign speech if I ever heard one! They did this—it's got Bill Clinton wrote all over it. Look at his damn wife, still sitting there at Gore's right hand with that smug look of hers . . . don't y'all see? Don't none of y'all read no more? Bubba's been mixed up with the CIA since Arkansas—they say you can still go into that airstrip hanger down in Mena and find Contra-cocaine dust in every damn nook and cranny, the corrupt lying Democrat sons of bitches! He's had almost six years to turn this country around, and look at us. *Look at us*!"

Indeed, even after the weight of Monica Lewinsky became too great to sustain—an unkind and lowbrow joke that'd gone around during the week of Clinton's resignation in early 1999—it's inarguable that Secretary Clinton's been more involved in government than ever. The speech Bill made the day he left Washington and Gore had been sworn in had been such a stem winder that the pundits all said it felt more like the kickoff of his next campaign than the farewell and mea culpa most had expected. Maybe they were still calling the shots. No one really knows who's in charge. Nibbs used to say that all the time, but I never quite knew what he meant, not until today.

My well-tended Charleston lady, her husband occupied by manipulating the straw of an iced tea a different server's brought to them, stands on her high heels and castigates the unhinged man, who appears on the verge of tears.

"Sir, if you know what's good for you, you'll hush your smart-aleck, seditious mouth—the White House is in flames, that's our leader," jabbing a manicured nail at the flatscreen, which now showed WTC2 collapsing again and again, in slow-mo and from every conceivable angle, "and *we are at war*!"

"But that's what I'm on about—they want a war to make sure Gore'll be reelected. *Can't you people see that this whole thing stinks to high heaven*?" he wheezes in frustration. "They did this to us!"

The patrons in the bar, rancorous and overwrought, shout down the partisan naysayer, who dismisses his accusers with an angry slashing gesture of his arms like an umpire calling an out. Cursing, the aggrieved man rushes out onto King Street, where a police car screams past with its rollers popping ice-blue and its siren blaring.

In the quiet wake left by the dissenter's exit, another man, teary-eyed, begins singing 'God Bless America,' and we all join in like it's the end of *The Deer Hunter*. I begin to think, now, I've had enough.

As if on cue, the manager of the bar, a chubby, gone-to-seed frat boy type, claps his hands and gets the attention of the twenty or so of us staring at the TVs.

"Folks, I called the owner and he's decided that since this is a national emergency, we're going to close. That the employees should be allowed to go and be with their loved ones. In case—in case this isn't over."

Murmuring and throat-clearing. Not only is what we've watched on TV not a movie, despite the President's assurances this action sequence might only represent the first plot-point. The murmuring becomes a stirring, a rustling of garments, and then a sliding of stools and chairs across the floor.

"And the drinks you have in front of you, those are on the house. Please—please finish up at your leisure, and consider tipping your servers."

I think better of noting that I never got my icy-cold Sierra Nevada. I leave a tip for my distressed and now absent server anyway, a fiver I hope she will appreciate.

National emergency or not, I'm too shaken and freaked and lost inside to get right back in the car and head home—my parents aren't there right now anyway. So, I wend my way through the tourist district, the slave market, and out toward the water, into the park there past the Corinthian limestone columns of the U.S. Customs House, where one can sit for hours watching the freighters and tankers chug languid and massive through the green harbor toward the docks of the Cooper River. As a boy I loved sitting in this park and reading, an era of innocence to which I'll never return, though I couldn't have known so then.

As I stroll, I'm shocked by the number of people I encounter who seem to have no idea what has occurred. No wonder the young man had felt like running and yelling.

And while what I've brought along to read isn't light or fun or relaxing or remotely innocent—despite my reluctance to do so, I've brought an essay Brian had published about Drake effing Park, for pity's sake, a nightmare I've spent the last seven years trying to erase from my memory—I decide to take this moment to get the day's horrors off my mind by reliving old ones: I've been taught that there's no healing in avoidance.

I settle on a bench and begin to read Brian's account of the moment that signaled the end of all normalcy and order in the Jack O'Roses universe. The document is, by his standards, but a modest sheaf, a clipping from *Scattered Petals,* an F-Kid fanzine in which this piece had run the autumn after Rose's death. I gird myself, and begin to read.

-8-

The Drake Park Debacle: An Eyewitness Essay by Brian K. Godbold

No single concert Jack O'Roses ever played exemplified all that had gone wrong with the scene more than the tragedy of the performance at Drake Park Amphitheater, a beloved annual stop on every summer tour since 1989. The band would not only play its final show there, but Rose herself would collapse under the weight of the selfishness and egotism on display that day by people who purported to be her biggest fans.

Located amidst corn fields and wide open American skies twenty miles northeast of Indianapolis, Drake Park had long held the cachet of a tucked-away, favorite venue wherein the band would lay down some of its fattest grooves and most delightful setlist surprises, an amphitheater that exemplified the spirit of 'if you build it, they will come.'

And come they did.

The assemblage outside the gates of Drake Park on July 3, 1997 represented an unholy convergence of all the worst aspects that surrounded Jack O'Roses in the later stage of their career, which had long been encumbered by hangers-on with no interest in the music, only the availability of contraband in the parking lots outside the shows.

The long holiday weekend, coupled with the near-legendary status of the band's appearances at the secluded, rural amphitheater, resulted in a throng of concert-goers nearly triple the capacity of the sold-out, open air 'shed,' as such venues are known by music industry insiders. Authorities estimated that more than 50,000 people crammed themselves into the gravel and grass parking lots of a facility that, at capacity, was designed to hold around twenty. The presence of more 'tourists[1]*' than a venue could logically hold was not in itself unusual at a Jack O'Roses show, but at Drake Park the numbers were out of balance, the throngs seemed more frenzied, and the search for extra tickets—for entrance through the gates of heaven—felt more desperate than usual.*

Portents of darkness had been evident from the very first stop on that summer's east coast tour, manifesting in problems apparent both on and off stage: At Gatewood Downs, Vermont, where in 1996 the band had played to a peaceful crowd of nearly one hundred thousand fans, gatecrashers swarmed through a torn-down security fence. Along with numerous reports of excessive drinking and aggressive behavior—hardly the hallmarks associated with the usual audience of blissfully stoned, multi-generational, twirling tie-dyed followers—Gatewood Downs would be a signpost pointing toward the tragedy three weeks later that would be Drake Park.

---

1 'Tourist' being a derogatory term for a casual Jack O'Roses concertgoer rather than an F-Kid on tour with the band

Three days after Gatewood Downs, the second of two shows at Giants Stadium in East Rutherford, New Jersey saw Partland become confused during one of her signature tunes, 'Came a Day,' resulting in one of the most pitiful, unprofessional moments in the band's long, storied history of nearly 2500 concerts—again, not terribly unusual, but an egregious and troublesome example that had F-Kids very very concerned about her condition and state of mind.

The next week, lightning struck fans in the parking lot at Pittsburgh's Three Rivers Stadium, killing one and sending three others to the hospital, where they thankfully survived their injuries.

By the time of Drake Park, a new and terrible wrinkle had been added: on July 2, a depraved, unstable soul phoned in a death threat on Partland, one that the FBI deemed credible.

And while the result was not an assassination—not as such—the huge police presence before and during the show kept fans on edge, and most certainly contributed to the mayhem and chaos that was to come. This individual who made the threat has never been identified, nor charged with any crimes. This person remains at large.

Reacting to the death threat, on the creeping, interminable trip from the freeway to the parking lots, every third vehicle was pulled aside and searched, and the authorities greeted fans at the gates with hastily installed metal detectors. Tension remained high throughout the afternoon and evening, especially considering that many didn't know about the circumstances—instead, most assumed that the authorities had gone mad with lust for control, perceiving the increased police presence as yet another escalation in the simmering, ineffective war on so-called illicit drug use that, by 1997, had plagued F-Kids, and the band itself, for decades. And this despite of the presence of a baby-boomer, musician, and admitted marijuana inhaler in the White House.

Within the band itself, however, the death threat was very much known, but Partland, far from being deterred—it wasn't the first time in her life someone had been out to get her[2]*—made no bones about her willingness to play. A bootleg recording of the technical rehearsal (the 'sound check,' as it is also called) has begun to circulate, and the musicians can be heard joking about the grim situation, entertainers who seem in their nonchalant professionalism to shrug off the unusual and potentially dangerous circumstances under which they were expected to appear.*

Inside the show, as Partland sang 'Treat You Right,' an apropos Jack O'Roses blues original penned by Partland and her songwriting partner Jake Sobel, a disturbance began in the far corner of the sloping lawn of the open air amphitheater: a slow-starting, incongruous cheer, one that grew in intensity—like a prison riot that somehow began on the outside of the institution, would-be fans were not just pouring over the wooden fence at the top of the lawn, but actually pulling apart the boards and gaining entry through the gaping holes that appeared.

---

2 In 1986, Ronald Wayne Bundrick, the angry parent of a young woman who had died of a drug overdose during the April 20 Jack O'Roses concert in Atlanta that spring, attempted to assassinate Partland in the lobby of her hotel following the June 12 show in Dallas, Texas. Bundrick, thwarted by hotel security, was arrested, tried, and convicted, and the Jack tour went on as though nothing had happened.

Rose seemed to respond: she charged into 'Calm Before the Storm,' perhaps the band's most famous song outside of the core fan base, and as overt a political anthem as any tune they band had ever played.

But halfway through the performance, and what was turning into an out-of-control riot, Rose collapsed onstage, the music stopped, and a follow-spot normally kept on her at all times fell dark.

A crowd already gone wild boiled over into a true formless convulsion of violence and anarchy—scores stormed past the overwhelmed security onto the stage area, but the longtime, protective road crew had spirited Rose out, and the rest of the band were already locked away on their tour buses. The police and security forces beat back the crowd, which began to disperse.

As frightened fans surged out of the venue over the hill and through the broken fences, an even uglier scene awaited outside: Burning police cars, a pitched battle between the authorities and rock- and bottle-wielding rioters, and black helicopters belching pepper spray into the hot July nighttime sky. To this peaceful, longtime F-Kid, such a terrible terrible scene, so antithetical to the wondrous and open spirit of the Jack O'Roses experience, still defies adequate description.

The fallout, immediate: Three concert-goers were dead including a 14 year-old girl, with the cable news networks featuring the Drake Park riot in their cycle of top news stories for over a week.

Rose herself, having been taken to a metro Indianapolis medical center, was still very much alive, and pronounced in a press release to be 'exhausted and dehydrated'; commentators on TV speculated that she may also have suffered a mild heart attack, a stroke, a drug overdose, or other such malady, though none were ever diagnosed.

Around eleven in the morning on July 4, a press release was issued by the band: The second of the two Drake Park concerts—the last show of the 1997 summer tour—had been canceled. Rose's condition was listed as stable but serious, and more information would be forthcoming when there was anything new to report.

I think that I've picked the wrong time to relive Drake Park—considering the events of the day, the tears streaming down my face are noticed by other folks in the park, and I'm asked by a passing bicyclist if I have family or friends at the World Trade Center, or who work in Washington. I tell her, no, no—I'm just sad for all of us right now.

Brian goes on to describe Rose's purported recovery, the speculation about the fall tour, which had already been announced and ticketed, and then her death and the memorial in San Francisco, but this essay does not tell the whole story. It does, yet it doesn't. There is missing detail that I can feel, but not articulate. I should know. I was there. And yet, I do not. Drake Park, like Brian's death, should be no mystery, so why, then, does it still feel that way?

My phone buzzes, and it's my father calling from Hilton Head, understandably upset about the terrorist attacks. The sound of Alston Zemp's voice—shaky, uncertain, a frightened old man's quaver—foments a momentary stab of panic. He's always been a strong and righteous man, seemingly unafraid of much of anything.

When I tell him I've driven down to Charleston for the day, he's apoplectic: "Tobey—I can't believe you're not at the house. Oh, my lord—someone's attacking the country and there's no one to watch over the house!"

"Settle down . . . nobody's attacking Edgewater County. Not yet," I mutter, regretting the weak attempt at a dark bòn mót. "I'm sure the house is fine."

"I'm not worried about the house, son—I'm worried about you." In the background I can hear Phyllis's murmuring voice, either parroting or feeding him the lines. "We're heading back probably later today, but your mother's so upset that I don't think we should drive . . . for all anyone knows it might not be safe on the roads either. They're saying it's Arabs, and that they might also have targeted shopping malls and nuclear plants and general infrastructure targets," which doesn't sound like my father's words at all—something he's repeating off TV.

"Well, then—you might as well stay put. All of us. Until this blows over."

I hear Phyllis praying and calling out to the Lord. My father erupts in fresh panic. "We all need to get home. *Now*!"

"All right, all right, for heaven's sake," I say, getting worked up, leaping off the park bench and pacing back and forth on the pebbled jogging path. "What's happening is a long way from us."

"But *Tobey*, we don't know who's doing it or what's going to happen next —"

"Dad—stop this. Just—stop."

For the next few seconds my father's heavy

breathing is all that I hear - it reminds me of Brian, a wheezing tobacco smoker and committed pothead if there'd ever been one.

"So: you're not going home, then."

"No, I've checked into a hotel down here, as I'd already planned. The world may be ending," regretting the choice of cliched rhetoric, "but I came to clear my head and figure out my life, so that's what I'm going to do." We ring off with terse, perfunctory farewells, both of us sounding snippy and annoyed with one another.

Smelling the salt of the Charleston harbor, the horror in NYC and DC indeed seems a long way away. I can't help remembering me and Brian, blithe and stoned, standing atop those very WTC towers, back when we were in the city for the Fall 1992 run at the Garden. How we didn't even give a thought to the possibility that one of those structures could be struck by terrorists, although that'd happen only two weeks after Clinton got sworn in that next January.

How we laughed and joked there at the top of the world; how I stood, awed, perceiving the earth curving away from me in every direction. How terrible Rose looked and sounded later that night. How Brian had bitched and moaned and stomped his feet about seeing 'The Ballad of El Goodo' yet again as an encore, how he decried so many of the cover tunes the band did.

"They sing this song as a song of hope," I yelled over the roar of the crowd, defending the Alex Chilton power pop anthem, so little known that many people thought it was one of Rose's songs. "It's melancholic yet optimistic. '*There ain't no one going to turn me around*,'" singing along with the band in my frightfully off-key warble. How my arms had broken out in gooseflesh; how I'd swayed and danced, lost in the moment, lost in the message. A mere dozen years ago, but feeling more like a storybook epoch that only ever existed in my dreams.

I feel pitiful and small and sorry for myself, and before long I'm back at the Renaissance, getting my single overnight bag into the room and going back down to hit the bar.

Like everyone, I spend the rest of the day and evening glued to the TV, hypnotized by the thought of missing any fresh, hellish horrors to come. As the news gets out about all the firefighters who died in the tower, the other government officials still missing, President Gore's unknown but secure whereabouts, and speculation about who'd perpetrated this new Pearl Harbor-style attack on the homeland, my head begins to spin, and not in the way an F-Kid would want. Beers turn to vodka tonics and an ill advised glass of acidic red wine, then mini-bottles in the hotel room, all churning and turning until later that night I'm kneeling upon cool porcelain. My profligacy makes me feel no better, only more numb, until intoxication swirls me downward into a deathless quiet sleep, in which I dream not of airplanes flying into buildings but instead of Drake Park, and running with Nibbs Niffy and a horde of hellhounds amidst choking clouds of tear gas, shrieking through the hoarse ravages of my striated dream-throat, bidding the red and white Medivac airlifting Rose, our fat earth angel, to carry her away to safety—from all of us.

–9–

I awaken the next morning in the unfamiliar but comfortable hotel bed with the cable television blaring—all the same images, planes crashing, plumes of ash billowing—and a mouth that tastes of slow, hungover death. I orient myself, chug water, wonder if I did or said anything untoward.

The piles on Pennsylvania Avenue and at the WTC site are still choked with gray smoke and smoldering brimstone, the coverage ongoing and uninterrupted by commercials. I look from the searing images onscreen to the mini-bottles scattered around and the remnants of an unremembered late night room service extravaganza, all lovingly charged to my erstwhile spouse Halsey's credit card. At least there's no dead hooker next to me.

Halsey: I need to check on her.

I call my ex, but she doesn't pick up—I guess until the planes start flying again, she'll be stuck in Vegas.

I miss her more than ever. I wonder: if we hadn't called it quits, would the savagery of the days in which we're now living have brought us closer together? I decide this is the stuff of wistful fantasy. I need food, coffee, a newspaper—no. No news. I have to look away from the destruction playing over and over. As though I'm not anxiety ridden enough.

I take one of Brian's Moleskines, with their black covers and snap-bands still holding secure despite all the handling and time that's passed, downstairs to the hotel restaurant. But it's not for entertainment, and in a way it isn't more literary skullduggery—I'm convinced that I already have Mrs. Godbold's answer, at least in part: I've a primary role to play in her son's depression and death, in that my ex-wife chose me over him back when we were the terrible trio on tour. Yeah—Brian told me how much he wanted her, how she was his dream girl, and yet I still went for it with Halsey. Some friend I was. After a dozen years, surely he'd gotten over her. Over my selfish, hormonal perfidy. Right?

But, if I find such grim confirmation, do I look his mother in the face and report that melodramatic love-triangle nonsense contributed to her son's isolation? That his heart had been broken once, and again at Drake Park? That's the whole story, far as I'm concerned. But I'll read anyway. Before I say for certain, I'll have to hear it from Brian's lips—Nibbs Niffy, possessor of secrets that only dead men may know.

When I break open the first of the two 1997 volumes I've chosen, however, I'm shaken to my core anew, this time by a new form of dark obscenity I find concealed in these most intimate of texts. Over my Denver omelet and coffee, my face gets hot and a light sheen of alcohol-sweat springs dewy across my forehead.

Oh, Brian—how could you.

Like semi-declassified documents retaining security clearance issues, huge chunks of the 1997 Vol. 2 journal have been redacted—wide rivers of black, soaked in, I guess, from the chiseled tip of an oversized magic-marker, one that's all but obliterated enormous swaths of text, sometimes entire pages. I can almost smell the El Marko uncapped and bleeding its black oil onto the paper—that's how fresh the redactions seem. Perhaps this was one of his final creative acts. He may have written and published an essay about Drake Park, but his personal thoughts on what happened—what was in his heart—have been erased.

All is not lost: One example of text that's left intact is a cryptic, recurring pair of phrases I've found in the midst of ruinous, obscuring fields of ink—*I made the call, but I didn't call the tune.*

Calling the tune, an integral part of the Jack magic—they played a different show every time they took the stage, so the ability, or luck, to call a song with prescience was an idea Nibbs held as the mark of a true fan, an F-Kid of the first rank. As the years and tours went on, Brian became particularly obsessed with setlist prediction, like a statistical alchemist chasing a mystical formula. By the end he could call a show with the best of them—what could my old buddy's words mean?

I made the call. But I did not call the tune.

The server, a svelte and poised dark-skinned woman with whom I'd already discussed the national emergency, the weather, and her homeland in the Caribbean, appears and asks in her West Indian dialect if there's anything that I need, if everything is all right.

"I don't think it is," I reply, closing Brian's defaced journal with a snap and cursing under my foul morning-after breath.

She's taken aback, seems frightened.

I right myself, apologize, and explain that I've been given an impossible task, that I'm at my wit's end, and like everyone, sit here before her this morning more than a little freaked about DC and New York.

She sympathizes with a nod and an understanding smile, tells me that difficult times always make us stronger. I grunt and tip well for this advice.

"Did you hear?" she asks. "President Gore is appointing Hilary Clinton as Vice President."

I recall the ranting man from yesterday. "That has a certain symmetry to it, I suppose."

Outside in the humid Charleston morning, bright and clear but sticky, anger floods into my gut—not about the new veep, but Brian's redactions. *What did he not want me, or anyone else, to know?*

Brian kept journals that appear to go back to 1989, maybe earlier; for answers about my own role in his sad life, I hope it'll be as simple as plowing through his record of the early 90s. But as for Drake Park, I suppose the record with have to stand as it does—obscured by clouds of El-Marko.

Oh, what is there to know? He loved Halsey—Sally, actually; the real Halsey that emerged after college he couldn't stand—but I took her from him, didn't I? And not any old place—on Jack tour, when we were all together. His sacred time and place. Right under his nose, I'm boinking the girl of his dreams in a dome tent at the KOA. Nice.

He lost Halsey, and then he lost Rose. So finally, he lost himself. I played a role; guilt, and a cross to bear. This case is closed.

-10-

After the rest of the morning spent recovering from the prior drunk, I drank myself an overpriced but cold beer in the hotel bar, finally, as a hair of the dog, and felt well enough to drive back to Tillman Falls. I did so without accomplishing any of what I'd planned during my brief sojourn to the holy peninsula—no job seeking or house hunting, only the acquisition of guilt over squandering Halsey's money, along with a few other burdens on my conscience.

I arrive at stately Zemp Manor only moments after my folks, who've becalmed themselves enough to make the journey back home—the terror threat has subsided, no further attacks, and scads of information pointing to groups of Arab men who hijacked the planes means we have a handle on what occurred. No one has taken credit, though a former CIA asset turned revolutionary called Usama Bin Laden, a spiritual leader to millions of disaffected Muslim youth, has been named as the likely source of this terror. All much more complicated than old-timey warfare—where to send the tanks and brave young Americans in uniform?

After I help them unpack their giant, American-made old person's sedan, Phyllis and I sit in the kitchen discussing God's hand in the ongoing crisis, while my father stays glued to the round-the-clock coverage, which has abated with the arrests of several failed hijackers on what would have been the fourth and fifth jetliners, one of which never took off, and the other that crashed in Pennsylvania under unknowable circumstances, its rogue crew reportedly intent to strike at the Capitol Building.

Precious little rhetoric is heard on the TV about why Muslims from half a world away would want to attack us, however, only that It Has Occurred, And It Must Be Avenged. With the incessant, fiery talk of making retaliatory war now unleashed across all major networks of whatever political leaning, these attacks are going to result in military action. War, at last! People are terribly stirred up by this season of death, as they should be, but let us act out of reason and not purely revenge. I should fire off a letter to the editor.

Instead, I put all this uncontrollable nonsense out of my mind, try to concentrate on the cool buzz I have from hitting the bowl out back behind the gardening shed. I flip idly through the *Columbia Record* and coo stoney reassurances to my terrified stepmom, who keeps looking out the window as though an airliner might be hurtling our way.

Phyllis busies herself frying pork chops in a heavy iron skillet, holding a flat mesh cover over the top to catch the popping grease. I riff along with her about whatever she's babbling: prophetic verses in Revelations, the need for repentance, both in this house—glancing slit-eyed over her shoulder at me—and in the broader America at large, about how we're going to *have* to go to war now to beat back what looks like the very devil himself, and how letting men lie down with men and how people using drugs has caused all this angst and terror and unrest.

That's all boilerplate material with Phyllis, so I barely hear any of her prattle. Then, however, she throws a curveball that snaps me out of my half-engaged haze. "There's something I'd like to say. That I need to talk to you about."

Now, with a woman of persistent and ostentatious faith like my stepmother, that's a flashing beacon of danger if I ever did hear one.

"Phyllis, I'm going to be blunt," I say to her in my precise and dry manner, which Halsey used to complain made me sound like a Mr. Spock who has managed to utterly banish his weak human half, with its nettlesome emotions. "Withstanding the force of your constant proselytizing is one of the least attractive traits of my being here—and one that you ought to know by now is destined to keep us at arm's length. I assure you that I have the spirit in me—I call it by a different name than you do, is all."

She ignores me as though I haven't spoken. "I wanted to talk about your friend—I want you to know that, when I heard, I prayed for him," Phyllis says. "And for you. What on earth was wrong with him to die so young?"

"I'm trying to figure that out."

But she already has her answer. She pivots from the stove to look at me. Her voice drops to a whisper. "He had turned away from God. It's one of the awfullest sins there *is*," brandishing a spatula dripping with grease.

"He had issues, yes. However you want to put it. But don't we all."

Talk of Brian sends her trundling down the bumpy ruts of an unpleasant stretch of memory lane: "Lord help me—it used to worry us to death when y'all were traipsing around after that longhaired bunch of hoodlums. I never could understand wanting to keep making those, those rock music *people* even richer than they already were."

Doesn't she realize there's more to that world than commerce? That in rock and roll, there's more, as Neil Young said, than meets the eye? It doesn't matter—she's only repeating what Father said. I could ask the same of their weekly tithing, but I don't—it's none of my business what they do with their money.

I sip my iced tea, gather my thoughts. "Those concerts, they were special times. It wasn't all about the dope. The music, it was transformative, transporting. Transcendent. Magic." Most of the time. "In any case, you had to be there."

"When that fat awful woman died, what they showed on the news was just about the worst mess I've even seen. People with dirty feet spinning around and wearing rags, Tobey, *rags*—and their *hair* . . .! Oh, but we were glad you never let yourself go like that. We set there looking at the news and I says, I says to your daddy, I looked over at your father and says, I can't believe our Tobey would associate himself with such riffraff. And I think that I knew in my heart that, whatever you were doing there, you weren't one of them. You just *couldn't* be."

So to them, I never became an F-Kid—not really, not as long as I kept my hair relatively neat. Nibbs used to call me a tourist, which I took for ribbing, until he got serious about the insult, after Halsey and I dropped out of the Jack scene and she started running hard and fast with her boutiques.

If not an F-Kid, though, what was I?

I start to make a grandiloquent statement about how there may have been no uniform, but there was an unwritten, codified way of living that the faithful—a word that would most surely set her off—adhered to, including myself. I never took more than I needed. I always left behind only footprints. I bought dry goods and stores in the parking lot from the traveling vendors—T-shirts, art, food, psychedelics. I danced and gave myself over to the moment and served my brothers on the road, yes, and was in turn served and honored by them—for the most part.

So why do I feel that she's right? Is it because, when we quit going to shows and started chasing dollar bills, as he put it, Nibbs accused Halsey and me of having lost our so-called faith in the road, in Rose, in the band?

You had no faith to lose—and you know it. You hush up, now, Bob Dylan. That isn't true.

I sense that regardless of my prior admonishment, Phyllis' monologue will soon take a decidedly spiritual turn—her brand, at least—and so without another word I get up and stroll into the living room. I plop down on the couch smelling the pork-grease on my skin and in my hair—I can't keep on eating like this, or I'll get as big as the side of a house, as they say 'round these parts.

Got to pull myself together, get a move on—as I feared, my continued perusal of Brian's journals and other writing is leading me down a path of great pain, one that consumed my friend. His grief in the years following Rose's death is palpable on nearly every page of his private spiritual and emotional ledger—the pages I can still read, that is.

I'll say this—he put on a good show of being over things and ready to move on, at least in person. I could sense a darkness there inside him, and that he was, for lack of a more elegant term, fucked up most of the time—but then I just dismissed it all as bitterness over

Drake Park, bitterness over Rose's inability to remain healthy (and alive), disappointment about having hitched his wagon to a star that would burn out in such a relatively brief time. Heartache, I now believe, over Halsey. As I've seen, his journals prior to Drake Park are plenty legible, and contain multitude regarding Halsey—Sally, as he always refers to her—and my life together, rank disapproval the prevailing emotion and assessment.

But like Brian's mother had suggested, there are subtleties to be gleaned: I've discovered two thick binders of show and tape reviews that I never knew he'd written. He'd said that along with some other hardcore tape collectors he'd worked the last few years to publish a comprehensive compendium of documentation regarding the unofficial Jack recordings that circulated—thousands in total—but the project had had a tough time getting off the ground, another frustration about which Brian expressed dissatisfaction during our infrequent, recent conversations:

"These other guys," he said of his erstwhile literary partners, "are in this fucking thing for the money. You believe that?"

"You could knock me over with a feather—Nibbs, isn't that why people publish? To make money?"

"Well—yeah."

"Okay then, so I don't see how it's some transgression—"

"Z, this is about more than money! *This is about documenting a legacy that goes beyond commerce.*"

"Why not just do your best work and then let it all play out as it will? If they're worried about that part of it, let them worry—you review the tapes. It's what you know, isn't it?"

He sat in silence but for the heavy breathing

that would have befitted a perverted nuisance caller. When it came to the subject of preserving for future generations a vision of the band in its most pure form, Brian was a dogmatic zealot, and in the wake of Rose's death had become obsessed, perhaps even insufferable, about such matters. "They just better have their shit wired straight. This is too important. We are the carriers of the primary experience—it won't be too long before we're gone."

"I know what we are."

"Do you?"

"Was I there?"

"That part was never in dispute."

I still don't know what he meant. Or how much harder I could have danced, how much more I could have believed in the cause. Maybe it never would have been enough. Nibbs himself certainly never quite got where he needed to be, somehow. But why?

-11-

I peruse Brian's review notebooks, opening one—by chance, mind you—to the entry for Greensboro Coliseum, May 10, 1993, the final show of that year's spring tour, and one of the last that Sally, Nibbs Niffy and the humble narrator at hand attended together. This, I recall, a fine fine show, which fell right before Brian finally started grad school to get his never-completed MFA, and long after Halsey and I had fallen in love.

Maybe my memory's off—I'm shocked and shaken to find that Nibbs has composed a terse, one-graph shiv to the ribs:

Rose, on the tail end of yet another food-and-drugs binge, sounds horrible on every song, a beached whale caterwauling on the rocky shores of Lake Eternity, begging to be put down. Pullen's base [sic] *lines are uncharacteristically lifeless, obvious, and tiresome; Jake's theatrics and offensively sloppy and ill-remembered cover of Dylan's 'Ballad of a Thin Man' stand as an affront to the aesthetic sensibilities of this reviewer in a manner that is difficult to describe without the use of profanity. The second set 'drums' improv segment, the shortest of the tour, is equally pedestrian.*

The collectibility of this performance, apart from sound quality, is to be considered suitable only for misguided completists.

RECORDING QUALITY: A+
HIGHLIGHTS: NONE

Subjectivity, thy name is fandom. So maybe I don't recall the show that well, but I swear what I remember was that it was decent, the finale of a strong late-period tour on which I'd seen maybe three shows to Brian's entire run up and down the east coast, pulling tapes and checking off 'gets' from his list of most-desired tunes. I was in the moment at Greensboro, I guess. An outlier of the larger context that Nibbs had grasped so fully and completely. The moment ends.

I dig out the CDs of the show that he'd made for me in the late-90s binge of CD-burning he'd gone on after the technology had caught up to the needs of the tape-trading network, and slip the first-set disc into my trusty, battered Discman I once used on my long walks around the bayfront property, or along the quiet two-lane running the length of the island. I decide to replicate those old walks, and dig out a pair of New

Balance to strap on the tender feet of a man who clearly does a fair amount of sitting.

The Edgewater County peace and quiet, the overhanging trees, the other houses lying quiet and still—this, a neighborhood of people like my folks, or else younger ones off working, maybe as far as Columbia. Closer to the interstate, the county has the look and feel of a bedroom community, with vinyl villages and the neon plastic nightmare that is the fast food corridor off the exit. Not here, not along the ridge.

As the music in my earbuds gets my juices flowing, I pick up the pace and pass an older house, one set back from the road at the bottom of the hill with a Caddy under the carport and an RV parked under a shed—more retirees. I wave. The elderly man tending his roses waves back, cheerful.

Indeed, the recording is impeccable, sounding as though Brian's microphones were well positioned. But the music! His review is so off-base: Rose seems to be in a good mood, her guitar lines clean and expressive, the vocal harmonies tight, the lyrics all remembered with accuracy—mostly, that is. No doubt in my mind that this is to be considered a keeper, an example of all that the band was still capable of in what we would now consider their senescent, modern period of decline. The old girl could still bring it. I probably said as much filing out into the Atlanta night, shuffling by the SWAT team lined up wearing their riot gear as though the F-Kids were storming the governor's mansion, not heading back to Jacktown to drink beer and eat lot food—veggies burritos, stir-fry, the fatty egg-roll dude who'd been selling outside the shows for twenty years—his career. F-Kids on tour knew his face almost as well as that of Rose.

Back inside, winded and chugging water, I say hello to Phyllis and go straight back to the reviews journal, re-reading Brian's bitter pan.

This time I note the date scrawled on the bottom of the page, which I presume is when he wrote the review, and I see to my horror that it is not an artifact of the time—this brief, ascerbic screed was composed only a few months ago, and long after the book project fell apart. Not fell apart—the book came out a year or two ago. Nibbs Niffy's reviews appeared nowhere in *Hit the Road, Jack: The Complete Taper's Concordance*, however. I didn't buy a copy.

I continue listening to the second set up in the guest bedroom, and far from belying my warm memories of the show experience, hearing the music only reinforces them. Contrary to Brian's assessment, the tunes crackle with energy, in particular the long jam in the second set, in which Linus Pullen's bass playing is anything but 'lifeless'—in fact, the interplay between Rose and him is organic, engaging and spry. Jake Sobel works his way through a raw and nasty 'Roadhouse Blues,' doing his best growly Morrison. Next, Jake and Rose pick out the delicate intro to 'The Ballad of El Goodo,' the bridge of which destroys me:

"*It gets so hard in these times to hold on . . . but there ain't no one going to turn me around.*"

In the second set, a long jam sequence—long by 1993 standards, anyway—includes a 'Nebula Rising' tease that prompts from the crowd a demonstrative, joyous eruption of approval. But 'Nebula' does not rise, though they would break out their 60s masterpiece of improvisational, spacey noodling later that year, a show I missed, like all of them on that tour, when we were busy opening Halsey's boutique in Charlotte.

Brian's review is bullshit! Why?

By the end of the last disc and a pitch-perfect 'Calm Before the Storm' encore, I am convinced that the Jack survivors ought to release every note of the show to the general public in pristine soundboard quality. After lunch, and with all due haste, I intend to fire off a passionate email to JOR Productions offering them this very suggestion.

Nibbs—what the hell is wrong with this show? What did you hear that I don't?

And then I turn the page over. In a handwritten note, very tiny at the bottom of the page, I can barely make out the words:

Last show with Sally Simpson.

Below the note there is a crude, sad-smiley face—one with an upside-down curve for a mouth, and a dot-dot-dash trail of tears leaking out of one eye.

Nibbs Niffy's secrets, which in this case weren't all that hidden from me, haven't so much begun to creep out of the shadows of his mind as become abjectly manifest. Halsey. If only I could explain to him that we loved each other more than Jack O'Roses. If only I could make him see. Even a blind man knows when the sun is shining, as the saying goes, but the long day has ended for my friend, and I don't enjoy the option of beaming any edifying light into his heart, nor of gaining his absolution. Not now.

Not ever.

-12-

The Ballad of Jack O'Roses
Verse 2

Driving home from the airport, the trip from Rose's memorial finally felt at an end, literally and otherwise.

I dropped my overnight bag and sat down in an old armchair—like most of my furniture, a hand-me-down. My cat, a loving and irascible Maine Coon named Oglethorpe, came bounding out of hiding, and in a display of tail-flicking feline indignation, promptly skittered back into the bedroom. Oglethorpe doesn't cotton to his master suddenly packing up and leaving town for almost 72 hours. You would think he'd be used to this kind of behavior by now, but you know cats. In any case, as well as he knows the sound of Rose's voice, I would never be able to explain to him the importance of my trip.

I looked around the disheveled living space that I called home, at the stacks of cassette tapes, books, magazines, the desk and computer, the posters on the walls, the trash that I forgot to take out, and the litter box that my friend Aimee had neglected to scoop for me this morning. Everything had a strange quality, as though I'd wandered into a museum of my past life. The only problem was that, if this was all in the past, I had no frame of reference for how I should feel about the present.

I checked the answering machine, which displayed an F *instead of a numeral—*F *as in* Full as Fuck *of messages. Most of them were condolences, many of which were thoughtful. A few came from people I hadn't heard from in years, acquaintances who knew me well enough to understand that, when they heard Rose Partland had died, I was hurting. These messages touched me, but my guts and soul smoldered, the whole terrible reality of the situation again hitting me like a sledgehammer.*

When I heard my mother's voice on the last message, I finally collapsed and broke down:

"Hey there—just thought I'd see if you're back yet. We're so sorry darling. I know you're really sad right now . . . call me when you get home."

You don't know the half of it, Mom.

Or maybe you do. We don't deal with death all that well in this family. My mother, in particular, seems to have a rough time dealing with the whole idea. I think that may be endemic to humanity at large, though. Death seems like a gyp—we're here for a short while, and such a long, long time to be gone.

I sat in my pathetic little living room, not more than a mile from where I'd been living for most all of my adult life, and only a few blocks from the dorm room where my life had really begun—my life with the band. I wondered if, as much as I'd traveled in the last few years, if I'd really gone anywhere at all—if I wasn't back to zero. I wondered if it had all been a big waste of time. How much energy had I put into following that stupid rock band around the country?

Into the collecting of the tapes, the articles I wrote for a fanzine called Scattered Petals, *the reviews of shows I'd seen, and tapes I'd made, or simply listened to . . .*

And now, thinking about the books I wanted to write about them.

Not books. The *book.*

Now there was an idea. This would be a big one, a group history as well as a look at the social impact that the band and its followers have had in the last thirty years. I'd done a bit of work on this piece here and there, putting together the history, doing the research on the facts. Easy enough for me to do, you see, as I have been employed as a librarian at the university since giving up on the MFA program.

The book was the answer. I would write the book that was going to let the rest of the world in on the big secret behind Jack O'Roses.

Monday morning came hard and brutal, and I went back to work. What I'd be doing, now, every day for the rest of my life. I was eager not to get to work, however, but to log onto my Southeastern account and check out the situation on the Jack newsgroup, at which I had not looked since the day Rose died.

Aimee, she-who-had-forgotten-to-scoop-the-litter-box, greeted me with a warm hug and a brush of a kiss against my hairy cheek. I held onto to her a little too long, probably, but I was sad and depressed about being at work—just like I always am at the end of a tour.

*"I taped all the stuff that you asked about—*VH1, 20/20, *and a couple more segments that you didn't.* Nightline *on Friday too. David Crosby was on that, and Ken Kesey. They both cried . . . I've just never seen anything like this."*

She handed me a VHS tape that looked as though it had been used and reused about a thousand times, the paper label on the side peeling off and betraying the existence of another, older layer beneath, a fading record of its past duty as a time-shifting device. Quaint, now, in this age of emerging technologies that make such crudities as magnetic tape seem like stone tools, consigned in their obsolescence to the memories of old men and the museums into which they will one day hobble.

"Not since Lennon, at least," I offered in the way of context that a non-F-Kid could understand, but did so unable to prevent sarcasm and bitterness from creeping into my voice. "A real pop cultural moment, this."

"That's what Ted Koppel said—the biggest music industry death since John Lennon." She looked a bit blown away by the comparison—Aimee, a Beatles aficionado. "I didn't have any clue she was so important."

"Thanks, Aimee—and Oglethorpe thanks you, as well."

"I don't think he liked seeing me come in the door instead of you."

"I bet he liked you putting that food in the bowl, eh?"

"He did indeed."

"In the end, that's all we need, isn't it? Food in our bowls?"

We shared a smile.

I pulled a few things out of my worn, black and gold nylon backpack, going about my usual Monday business and getting my desk neatened. I reached down and pulled the hem of my khaki trousers out of my gray sock, and yanked the end of my tie out of my shirt and let it drape down over my hard gut. I had to secure those dangerous dangling articles of clothing for the quick bike trip over from home, but sometimes I'd be embarrassed to discover halfway through the morning that I'd forgotten about my sock being pulled up over my trouser leg. I'm sure I got a pass on that, though—you know us academic types. A corpulent, stoned research librarian with one pant leg stuffed in a sock wouldn't cause too much of a stir around the Main Library at Southeastern.

I looked up to see Aimee still standing there, her arms folded, a look of concern on her face.

"Anyway, thanks. Did I say that?"

"You did."

A beat passed before she spoke again.

"It seems like Rose meant a lot to more people than only the F-Kids."

I felt a rush of anger, perhaps proprietary: "Oh, sure," I said, bilious. "Now that she's gone."

She seemed hurt by this, gave me a small frown and a shrug.

Now I'd had enough. I wanted to keep my cheeks dry. "I don't know that there's anything left to say, all right? Rose is dead, that's it, it's all over now, baby blue."

"Hey . . . I only want to help."

"Enough helping for now, okay? I haven't slept in three days."

Ironically enough, I was rescued from this awkward moment by yet more chitchat: A voice came booming from the doorway, a law professor named Buchanan with whom I was acquainted, and who knew of my F-Kid status. Buke had seen his fair share of shows, he claimed, back in the early 70s, although now he was in the closet about what must have been exultant and transformative experiences. But despite having seen and heard—first-hand!—these icons of rock making some of the greatest music the world had yet known, in his respectable middle age he'd now become one of those casual Flower Children, the kind who sort of wistfully remember the old days without being the slightest bit engaged in what was going on with the band at any given moment. Sure, I gave him a tape every now and then, but I don't know if he ever listened to them. Some of the oldschool F-Kids who turned yuppie can be that way—too busy with real grownup life to have kept the band in mind, too busy being captains of industry and law professors.

He held up the USA Today *from last Thursday, the one with Rose's obit on the cover—the top story, of course. Its sad portrait of the wan, disheveled Rose F-Kids had gotten used to seeing onstage made my blood run cold. "Well—if this isn't the all-time big steaming pile of bullshit. Rose Partland. I can't get my mind around this!"*

"To say the least."

"Well, now what, Mr. Godbold—will the boys try to go on without her?"

"Dunno, Buke—we'll see."

"Ah, hell." Buchanan had a look like he'd finally realized the enormity of what'd happened. "Never be anything like it again. But the art will live on."

"Nothing else to do but smile, smile, smile—you know us hippies."

"I do—I surely do."

Buchanan placed hand over heart and smiled at me with a solidarity that felt piteous and small.

A look passed, then, between the professor and Aimee—another smile, a secret one—and he pivoted on his polished leather heel to depart.

I turned back to my friend, the woman I loved who had spurned all my advances, both subtle and otherwise, and told her my head was splitting.

"I'm sorry I was short with you earlier."

"Don't be," she said with inordinate sweetness. "I know this is tough for you. Not been a good year, has it?"

It hadn't. The truth was the whole summer had been miserable. Any way you cut it, the tour that had become, incredibly, unbelievably, the Last Tour, had been a mess. There had been problems like you wouldn't believe—arrests, overwhelming crowds of people without tickets, hard drugs, even lightning strikes, as though God Herself had found a moment to offer direct portent of more ill will to come our way.

And then there was Drake Park, the last show I'd ever see. Nothing to say about that people don't already know.

I sat down heavily in my familiar, comfortable office chair. And as Aimee closed the door, a knot of emotion rose into my throat, no longer contained. I burst into tears, crying like some little boy who'd just been told that his mommy had died.

As I continue with the book manuscript, I find that Brian's again talking about writing a book within the damned book he's already writing, which is headspinning. On top of those layers, I'm now also leafing through his journals, squinting at passages, and looking for material about this Aimee, how he felt about her. Aimee, a new wrinkle—another great love, another rejection. In the wake of my rejection by Halsey—by Sally Simpson, as she'd also rejected Nibbs—I can only empathize with his heartache.

I put my friend's papers away and start thinking of getting a résumé together, of finding someplace to live in Charleston, and a job . . . but to do what sort of work I can't quite fathom. Hm. I'd better call Halsey, warn her to expect contact from potential employers regarding what will be, on paper, an embellished role for myself in her company.

Reality: with my extraordinary record of non-employment, I'll be lucky to get an assistant manager position at some fast food joint off a freeway ramp somewhere. Or, at an upscale fashion boutique, one that caters to the fatted bank accounts of aging, well-to-do women desperate to appear youthful, stylish, and attractive. Joy. A pair of jeans for you, my dear? Why yes, *yes,* those look perfect on you—like they were made for you! That'll be three bills and change. What's that? Oh my, yes, of course we accept the American Regrets platinum card; thank you and have a nice afternoon. It's no wonder they call running a credit card a 'swipe.'

My mind wanders: Was Brian's love for Aimee Pressgrove real? Or is she a literary stand-in for his lost love, Halsey Bedrich?

Intrigued, I decide to seek out this fabled Aimee, the mention of whom I find with great frequency in Brian's journals, as well as, I now see, his book manuscript. I go online, an excruciating process on Phyllis's dialup modem, and after the Southeastern University staff directory, finally, *finally* loads in, I find only one Aimee—Aimee Buchanan.

Buchanan. Buke. The law professor.

Ah ha—no fiction here, no metaphoric substitution of one woman for another: Aimee, like Halsey, another heartbreaker.

–13–

But it's not Aimee I ring up, not immediately, it's my ex-wife. And once I do, I'm forever sorry.

"I know this hurts, Z—I can hear it in your voice." This time I have her full attention, and get much more than small talk. Much more. "But I can't—and don't want to—lie to you. Anymore. I can tell by the way you sound when you call that you are not on the same page as I am. And now . . . you have to be."

As she explains, I'm shaken by her obscene truthtelling—but not surprised. A lover. Another, in her life. Behind it all. A rough stone of shock and anger has settled in my craw—Halsey hasn't only met someone, it's a someone that she's been with for some time, even while we were still an ostensible couple.

"At least everything makes more sense now."

"You know our friendship is important to me. It always has been. I guess that was part of the problem—we were great friends, but shitty married people?" Halsey's trying to sound sincere, much as she can, but it's hard with that eternally bored, flat California-girl patois of hers.

"No, sure—there's still no hard feelings. I'm a big boy," my voice breaking. What would I do, I ask her, with such feelings.

At last, I can't help but allow a patina of acrimony to creep into my words. "I—I should've fucking known."

"No, you shouldn't."

"You made sure of that, didn't you."

That gets her. A tiny admission: "I was a coward."

If I'd known, might I have put up a fight, gotten angry, insisted on more money? I don't think so—but Halsey's a calculating little shit, and in a hot flash of annoyance, I realize I've been had.

My father never encouraged pettiness, nor did he espouse grudge-holding or to embark upon campaigns of vindictive retribution over grievances minor or major, nor did he fail to teach me that there is knowledge to be gained in defeats as well as victories. I draw on this deep well of reason, chuck the anger out the window like the rednecks up the road who dump trash along the shoulder, and in an instant decide to let her duplicity go, wishing her well.

We make small talk about what I'm going to do with myself, to which I respond noncommittally. We discuss money—stocks and investments and whatnot. It's not unlike the conversations we used to have—dry, officious prattle about nothing, in other words—like a couple of accountants. Like colleagues.

Finally she asks me a question of substance, by which I'm both relieved and chagrined: "What about the thing with Brian's mother. The—what was it she wanted you to do? Read his diary?"

I'm now faced with the choice of using what I know to instill in my former lover the guilt and shame that cuts through my own soul like deadly razor wire, or letting that go as well. "What I've learned you don't want to know. Trust me."

"What, *what*?" I can tell from her tone that she's interested in the salacious details.

"He was in love."

"Oh *no,* Z . . . but she didn't love him back."

"Correct."

"And . . .?"

"You're wondering who it was?"

"Someone at Southeastern?"

"As a matter of fact, yeah." Either way one wishes to take it, whether Halsey or Aimee, I'm not lying. "Someone he worked with—a friend."

"That's the saddest thing I've ever heard."

"He lost Rose, yes. But he'd lost . . . this other girl. And the more I read, it seems like he'd had enough of loss."

"He used to be so much fun. I never knew anyone who loved Jack the way he did. Not even my folks," who'd taken Halsey to her first show when she'd been in her mommy's tummy, and innumerable West Coast runs through her California childhood. Nibbs had been green with envy at her Jack sheet, the classic shows she'd gotten to see as a kid. "Like he was the biggest fan I ever knew." Acknowledging that existence of many thousands of people like Nibbs, she adds, "And that's saying something."

I guess he didn't get a chance to grow out of it, like some people," I shoot back at her, caustic and hateful.

"They were just a band; you said so yourself." She chuckles. "You sound like him, suddenly."

Maybe I'm starting to feel differently," I say. "Maybe Nibbs was onto something. Maybe he was right and we were wrong. More than meets the eye, this mere rock band."

"You're high, aren't you. Lucky—I'm at work."

That part we'd had together, the weed. Long as there'd been something, right?

"What are you going to tell his mom?"

Through a wearied sigh I explain, "Brian's work, like his life, is incomplete—he blanked out big sections of his journals. Whole pages. Everything that he didn't want me, or *you,* or anyone else to ever know about."

Halsey doesn't know how to respond, says so.

"So, it's a permanent obstacle I can't overcome. Don't know how the hell I'm going to tell his mother about that part. She thinks buried somewhere in all this crap there's a grander explanation than I've been able to find. Rose doesn't seem enough, nor does being spurned by some chick."

I hear her sniffle. "It's so *sad.*"

I roll my eyes at her obvious, facile interpretation of the facts at hand. "So you already said."

"Oh, you sound so angry. That's the last thing I wanted. That's why I took so long to tell you about Clay. I didn't want to hurt you."

How charming, I think, that she believes I shouldn't feel angry. I know this Clay, a toothsome, lantern-jawed haberdasher of means that she'd met at a trade show, one who'd at times dined with me at my own goddamn dinner table, and with whom she'd gone on many buying trips. Had been served food prepared from my own kitchen, by my own hands. Oh, how they must have laughed at me, been pleased with their subterfuge. Clay. Not an F-Kid, as I recall.

"Sometimes people aren't meant to work out, and that's that. I'm no more upset than I already was."

"Good, honey. I'm so sorry, all right? It wasn't on purpose. It just happened."

"'The heart wants what the heart wants,' as Woody Allen said."

"Yes, hon—thank you for understanding."

The sensation of wanting to hold on overwhelms me, and I feel a sense of loss matched only by that day in August when the word came about Rose. I spit out a seed of abject bitterness, "Of course my self esteem is so rock-solid that there's no fucking way in goddamned hell that I'd feel anything other than relief at no longer being a yoke around your neck, and in the way of you and your handsome suitor and all your little trips and projects and—"

"Oh, Z, please don't sound like that—"

"Don't call me by my road name!" I shriek. "*Don't you dare.*" In a rush of self-righteous bullshit, squandering an opportunity to act in the fashion I so wished to when it became apparent that my marriage was finished—to rise above it all, to eschew pedestrian histrionics, to accept the truth like a man, to turn the other cheek, to walk away into the sunset with my head held high—I slam the phone down.

Epic fail: Instead, I start to blubber in acknowledgement that another benchmark has fallen: no Rose, no Nibbs Niffy, and now no Sally Simpson, like, for real, man. But I can't. Another lesson from my father: we don't cry in front of people. Not even ourselves. The pain dries up, slithers back down inside me, a hard black kernel I must keep sequestered.

But then a thought comes, the warrior thought, the final thought, the one I'd resisted but that must now be embraced, and I stop feeling sorry for myself: *He who travels the fastest, travels alone.*

SECOND SET

Calm Before the Storm
(Oglethorpe/Partland, ©1970 JOR EL Publishing)

We knocked him down
He made no sound
He grew a beard
To cover up his frown

He was future-bound
He turned around
No longer able
To throw his weight around

His honest eyes
were his best disguise
He won the game
But didn't get to keep the prize

So is this it?
Or just the calm before the storm
Abstract thoughts refuse to take form
A lonely bee, just trying to keep warm

Just trying to conform . . .

–1–

When I call Aimee Buchanan's work number at Southeastern, she's suspicious, but a moment or two of explanation and assurances that I am who I say I am, however, seems to not only tamp down the flames of her caution, but pique her curiosity.

Brian, she says, used to talk about me all the time. How he seemed to miss me, and my wife Sally.

"I wasn't surprised when I heard," she says of the grim news about our mutual friend, speaking in a measured cadence of an accent I can't place. "I know he wasn't happy before Rose died, and flat-out miserable afterwards."

"As were all of us . . ."

A defensiveness, as well as more direct hint of a drawl lurking in her words. "I *tried* to be there for him, even after he quit and moved away. He resisted it, ignored my emails, et cetera. I wasn't sure I'd ever see him again. And so . . . I didn't," she adds with a sad, resigned chuckle. "Oh, Godbold, you ninny—no, 'nitwit.' That was his favorite. You nitwit."

"I'm sure you were a fine friend to him. Not an easy task with someone like our boy. Take it from me—when he got wound up, he could be a force of nature."

She laughs. "I expected you to call him Nibbs. To you that was his name, wasn't it?"

"Yes, it was." I think about the Chuck Palahniuk book I'm reading. "But in death, an F-Kid has another name," I paraphrase, "and *his* name is Brian Godbold."

Her voice now comes weak and introspective. "That's certainly who he was to me. Not the other one."

We make small talk; I ask if she wouldn't mind meeting for coffee, that I'd like to ask her about Brian's life here in Columbia after Drake Park. We ring off with a date—not a date, a meeting—around four-thirty down in the Old Market.

I drive into town early, securing a corner booth in the bustling coffee shop. I try to page through more of Brian's manuscript, but enervated by the prospect, I flip through the alt weekly instead.

I twirl the spoon in my latte and scribble a few lines in my own notebook, a fresh Moleskine that I'd found among his effects, still in the shrink wrap. How the light of the bedside lamp had shown across the plastic, my face reflected and distorted therein.

In a hot rush I'd pulled the shrink wrap off and tossed it into the wastebasket, where in the silence I could hear it crackling and expanding.

I didn't write anything in the notebook that night, but now I've started carrying it around and jotting down thoughts—little pithy observations, even a poem or two, tripe and nonsense that'll mercifully never be seen by the unsuspecting eyes of innocent readers. Most of the notes that I have made are about Brian's work rather than whatever pops into my head. Don't know how or why I've chosen to adopt this new hobby, but I have. Thought about keeping my own journal, for once.

Maybe I already have.

Before Aimee's appearance, a lull in the activity at Maxine's, but idle of the afternoon is soon interrupted by the air-brakes of an arriving delivery truck, and the next wave of students and faculty and shoppers ordering their personal variety of blended caffeine fixes.

You pump yourself full of that crap all week long, I note, *and then on the weekend guzzle booze to balance it all out. And F-Kids are the dopers, here? Very very very interesting.*

I feel a great incongruity, now, between my presence and that of the students and bohemians who populate the college neighborhood at this hour, and I question my worth as the caretaker of my dead friend's memory. I remember the golden innocence of our time living on campus, of trading tapes and hanging out and him schooling me in the ways of Jack. Meeting Halsey. A lifetime ago.

I consider riding over to Redtails Stadium, later, and sitting in the parking lot for a while, closing my eyes and reliving that first show, on a July afternoon that'd been so hot people's flip-flops were melting. That's when I climbed aboard, so to speak, though not in the way I finally grokked the true psychedelic, transformative experience Jack was selling—only later, and after a few other shows, would I be fully transported, at Ventura, by the sea, when Rose pulled back the curtain for real and let the shimmering prism of starlight shine through to me. Ventura. A story to counterbalance the horror of Drake Park.

But then Aimee walks in, pretty as a picture, and for a while I don't think much about Brian, Jack O'Roses, or anything else but this striking, gloriously demure and intelligent flower of a woman.

For two strangers with nothing in common but a dead mutual acquaintance, we get on quite well—despite being here to discuss Brian, she's warm and bright and curious about me. Or that's the impression I get, anyway. She's so lovely, this tall, angular librarian, early 30s, fit, unadorned by makeup and not needing it in the first place.

Perhaps, he thinks, too lovely—Nibbs Niffy slaps me upside my head and says: *She's married, you nitwit.*

Since the late great Brian is the reason for our meeting, and looms over our conversation, she asks for historical context regarding the relationship. "So you met him at a Jack O'Roses concert here on campus, when you were students?"

"Yeah—my first show was here at the stadium, summer of '87." I tell her about the heat, the flip-flops, the songs they played. About meeting Brian, finally, but not at the show, instead on campus.

Aimee, resting her chin on one bony set of knuckles, wears thick-framed glasses that catch a glimmer of reflection from the spoons nestled alongside our cups. "You didn't go to the concert with him?"

"No, and I don't remember seeing him, either, not in that mass of sweaty hippies—40,000 people there that day. But that next week, I was be-bopping across campus and saw him wearing a Jack shirt. How could you not see that tie-dyed hulk lumbering around? I struck up a conversation, went from there."

"Since I knew him from work, I didn't see the tie-dye side of him much. But yeah, he's a big boy—he stands out whether he's trying or not."

I ask her if she's into Jack at all, if they had that in common. I'm also thinking, now, of her hubby, Buke, the erstwhile F-Kid.

"I love the older stuff, the country-rock period, the acoustic songs. Brian made me some tapes."

"He must've given you some '83 Radio City stuff—was it old Rose or young Rose?" Among F-Kids, a line of demarcation, after she got hooked on the white powders and became fat angel Rose, with a smokescarred voice more reedy than strong like it'd been, and less dexterity and inventiveness on guitar or piano leads. "Or was it summer 1970 stuff, when Gram Parsons was hanging out with the band? Those are the two periods when they were doing acoustic sets. You can tell the difference."

"The older stuff, I think." Aimee's singing voice comes to me, delicate and divine: *"Twenty-thousand roads, I've been down, down, down, and they all led me straight back home to you . . ."*

Goosebump city. "Everybody always hoped that one day they'd bring the 'Grievous Angel' back, but Rose never would. You could always dream, though. That was what kept us going over and over—waiting for that big breakout tune, what Nibbs would have called a 'get.' That was one of mine. That I never got, unfortunately."

"So, you obviously had a good time at that first show, I take it?"

"Oh, I had a good buzz going. And yeah—hot, hot show. Like, literally. Rose made some crack from the stage about seeing a ' mosquito the size of a freakin' mockingbird'. When we first met, that bit was what

Nibbs kept going on and on about—'Rose actually said something to us!' She never spoke from the stage, at least not after I started seeing them. He hung on every word, even if it was only a tossed off joke."

"Didn't y'all become roommates?"

"No, never. Best buds, though." I ponder the deep, dark past of 1987. "Maybe I saw him around some before that day, but I'm fairly sure that was the first conversation we had." I shrug. "Who can remember these arcane factoids?"

"I'm good at that stuff. My old friends, they're always laughing about how I can remember that so-and-so wore a pink sweater to the football game where it started raining on us in the second quarter that time the sky looked all purple and red at sunset, that kind of crapola that clutters up my head. People tell me I ought to be a writer. To me, it's just remembering a bunch of useless detail."

"What will you remember about today? About meeting me?"

She smiles. "That you were such a good friend to Brian. And that you had on a navy blue Ralph Lauren polo shirt, khaki pants, and old, worn Birkenstock Arizonas that need to be re-soled." She wrinkles her nose. "And that probably stink. A little."

I nod. "No need to find that part out. But, I am going to test you on all the rest one day."

"*Ooh*, I'm good and all, but I'd better take notes, then."

Is she flirting with me? What is this?

I start to tell her everything about the last few years, and the narrative of Brian's life, as I understand it, becomes inextricably intertwined in my own sorry tale of personal woe—before I can stop myself, I'm talking about Halsey and the breakup and the whole wretched oh-I-don't-know-what-to-do-with-myself routine.

She commiserates with compassion, her expression of deep empathetic understanding, the kind that comes only from shared, bitter experience—she's divorced too, from Buke, a kind of ah-ha moment that changes everything. We swap cheating spouse stories. We have common ground.

I tell her about both her, and her ex's, appearances in Brian's 'Ballad' manuscript; she's gobsmacked, says so.

"The worst part for me is that when I found out, he tried to make me feel . . . old-fashioned. Unsophisticated. 'These things happen,' in that cavalier way he tried to blow it off. But instead, I just felt cheated on." She suffers a wave of self consciousness. "So, what are going to do now that you've moved back down here?"

Ack. "Three little words: I-don't-know."

I tell her that I have an accounting degree, but never got my CPA license, about my post-college and post-Jack life, about Halsey's boutique empire taking off, setting up and opening the various stores, all successful, the house on the bay shore, blah blah blah. "She'll have one in every high-end shopping center in the country soon, I'm sure. Sally's—I mean, Halsey's pretty driven and ruthless."

Curious, she eyes me. "Why'd you almost call her Sally?"

I explain that Sally Simpson was Halsey's Jack-tour road name, taken from the Who song on *Tommy*—the tune about one of Tommy's most fervent of teenage girl disciples and the fervor his appearance creates in the crowd full of worshipful Sallys.

"I never got into The Who. I'm more of a Beatles girl."

"Who isn't?"

"So, you're a Beatles girl, *too*? That's, like, totally bitchin'."

Aimee—when she makes jokes like that one, her eyes twinkle, a charmer, a southern girl, she admits, from the western mountains of North Carolina, above Asheville. I'm glad I called her.

"So . . . what happened with your wife? Work came between you?"

Nonchalant, a bored, water-under-the-bridge affect of disinterest: "We grew apart; she found someone she liked better. Same old story—you've heard it a thousand times before."

"Honey—I've lived it."

Is this a cosmically good break, or what? I'm beginning to believe that this is the start of a beautiful friendship, and it's all I can do not to verbalize the cliché.

I now pepper her with questions about the period after Rose died, when Brian began to withdraw into himself to the point that he'd finally quit the job at Southeastern. She offers concise but descriptive anecdotes about Brian's state of mind, but after a certain point, Aimee reports that she didn't talk much to him anymore. "I got married to Buke that fall, and after that Brian really started acting pissy."

I have to decide to lay it all out, now, or let sleeping dogs lie.

"It's because he had multiple heartbreaks to contend with. Rose . . . and my ex-wife. And you, too. A little bit."

Her pleasant demeanor hardens into a shocked grimace. "*Excuse me*?"

"Aimee, I don't know you all that well, obviously, so I don't know if it's my place to say any of this, but I will: Brian had a thing for you. I think—well, I've already said it. There's no thinking it. He wasn't devastated or anything, but I know he liked you and wrote very sweet things about you, and when you married Buchanan, it was something of a knife-wound for our old boy."

"Oh, god—don't say that. That's not right. We—we were just *friends*."

She doesn't understand how I know what I know. "I have his journals."

Aimee blanches at the notion. "So, what," in her unsettled state her natural hillbilly drawl creeping in, "you had me come down here to make me feel like I done something wrong? What is this crap? Don't you think I done had enough of my own heartache?"

"Aimee, I—"

She bursts into tears, sudden and shocking, a rain shower that ends as quickly as it began. Flustered, she digs in her purse for a tissue and blows her shiny, red nose.

My cheeks burn, and I feel mortified and misunderstood. "I thought you'd want to know. If you cared about him. I didn't—that's all it was."

She's pissed, now. "I do. And I did. But the idea that he was sitting there thinking about killing himself, and thinking about me . . . he never even asked me out!" Aimee puts her face in her hands, then looks up, stricken and faraway, racing through her forest of details, looking for trees. "Or, did he. That time outside on the steps when he had on the blue tie with the mustard stain, and he was rubbing the bike grease off the cuff of his pants and said, he kept hinting, but he didn't ask—Ash," as I had introduced myself to her, "he never asked me out. *It's not my fault*!"

Heads turn. Aimee flutters her hands, tries to calm herself, apologizes.

Brian, you big lug—you never even tried with this one, either? A coward of this magnitude, I think, deserved his loneliness.

"You weren't the only one who broke his heart. Far from the main one, truth be told. I think you were just a side-trip."

She laughs, but in anger rather than mirth, exaggerating the hillbilly in her voice. "Wellsir, that don't sound too good neither, do it?"

"Not especially. Look—he loved Halsey. She was the one. That was the first heartbreak. I'd say I stole her from him, but like you, he never really made a play for her. Only dreamed about it."

Her face, distant and hard. I've lost the thread of our chemistry. I said too much. "Is that true?"

"What?"

"That you didn't steal her from him?"

And now I wonder what, exactly, Aimee Buchanan—or Pressgrove again, I assume—was told by Brian Godbold, about how he felt about her. And about me. But I don't ask. I don't want to know.

In my non-answer, she knows. She goes to wrap up our coffee meeting, smiling and cordial, but stiff.

Out on the sidewalk, the light's begun to fade, and chittering, delightful birdsong fills the air—the overgrown red-tips lining the sidewalks are filled with a migrating flock of cedar waxwings stripping bare the clusters of red berries. Aimee seems interested, watching the activity with narrowed eyes.

I worry aloud about being shat upon, to which she offers no acknowledging chuckle, only a dry, thanks and I'll see you around type-farewell.

This cannot stand. “I feel like we’re ending on the wrong foot. Let me make it up to you.”

A small shake of her head. “I just got out of this thing, and all. So did you.”

“Let’s not think of it that way. It won’t be a date-date. And I promise that we’ll talk about anything and everything but Brian, okay? Movies, current events, Gore v. Bush, nine-eleven conspiracies, whole bit.”

“Ooh, no,” she says, wagging a finger at my nine-eleven reference. “Too soon.”

The last exchange we have: “Hey, Aimee—do me a favor: call me Z from now on, huh? If you would.”

“That’s what Brian always called you.”

“It says more about who I really am, I think.”

A measured softness returns to her pretty face, and I feel better. “Z, it is. Gimme a shout sometime.”

-2-

I go home, watch TV, try to read Dad's Charleston newspaper, but I can't concentrate. A certain Nibbs Niffy keeps whispering around the edges of my consciousness, won't let me rest. *Give a guy a break, would you?* But the crusty old tour rat won't. I decide to inspect the redactions further, to see if I can discover anything of note hidden beneath the black ink, or if it's even possible to do so. Halsey, yes; Aimee, certainly; Rose, inarguably, but all this black splatter is obscuring another secret—I've seen plenty of passages, pre– and post Drake Park that are fairly explicit about losing Sally Simpson to me, and those aren't redacted.

So, I tear individual pages from the notebooks—as I do so, I feel as though I'm desecrating my friend's corpse—and then stand on the sofa, holding each over a hot halogen floor lamp. I stare at some pages lit from below for so long, straining to make out words and phrases, that the sheets begin to turn brown in the middle from the hot lamp, but I fail to make anything out. Brian, or at least these pieces of him, will remain hidden—his penmanship has already been enough of a challenge. In the later handwritten journals, after his plunge into the depths of addiction, his writing approaches a kind of graphomania: page after page of racing, scribbly lines that present as illegible as the redacted sections.

I abandon this exercise in futility and poke around through boxes until I find an artifact fraught with personal meaning: his 1991 summer tour diary, buried at the bottom of a stack of what appear to be nothing more than random Jack O'Roses press clippings, magazine articles, and other various and sundry memorabilia. This diary, a record of what would turn out to be the only complete tour that the terrible trio would do together, coast to coast, stem to stern, the whole shebang, was an early incarnation, I now realize, of his dream of writing the Jack story.

I glance through the worn spiral notebook, the one with the cracked, green cover and the Jack stickers and the entries in his scrawling penmanship, here vastly more legible than the redacted notebooks—in those days Nibbs rarely drank, could be counted upon to be the sane and safe and sober one. But for the psychedelics, of course.

In those days, with the two of us finishing up junior year at Southeastern, Halsey, at the beginning of the tour still only a friend, had been itching to ditch her unsatisfying life as a struggling college student in any way possible, and it had been she who'd talked us into doing the whole tour—an air of 'no time like the present' ruled our decision making about how to spend our summer. Nibbs, of course, had already planned to do the whole east coast segment. I'd been the one who had to be talked into the crazy idea. I'd planned to get a job that summer, as my dad had been pushing me to do. That got put on hold.

We'd worked hard on our studies, most of the time; we were ripe for reward. By then Brian was fully immersed in his life as an F-Kid, wore his eccentricities and proclivities on his sleeve: he organized a pot legalization rally that sparked a contentious series of editorials in the paper, including one he'd written, which if memory serves was the only writing he'd ever gotten published; he marched around campus barefoot, even all winter long, with his huge chest stuck out and the thick mop of wiry hair pulled back into an enormous ponytail, striding into traffic and extending a thick arm, expecting vehicles to stop for him; he suffered neither critics of the band nor fools, two designations that to him were a measure of stark equivalency. Nibbs was F-Kid royalty, at least in his own mind.

Halsey—who truly was Sally Simpson during this period, seemingly as devoted to the band as Brian—had had academic difficulties, to be charitable, and though she wouldn't quit for another year, she was already making noise about dropping out. After having a long distance argument with her parents, the cryptic nature of which has long since disappeared from the recesses of my mind, she declared that school was "bullshit" and "a waste of time and my parents money. We are going the fuck on tour. Fuck it."

Halsey—Sally—a cutie-patootie, barefoot sprite of a free-spirit, with hair wraps and gauzy dresses and hemp necklaces, who could party hard and look back over her shoulder expecting you to keep up. We'd met the previous semester at a Jack listening party Nibbs had started hosting at a hippy-friendly bar in the Old Market, one now long closed. Had all gone to the fall tour shows that'd come through the area, a couple of runs within driving distance—DC, Atlanta. Had hung out, had gotten high. She'd been dating some dude when we'd first met, but they'd since broken up. We'd gotten drunk and screwed one night after Nibbs had passed out on in the couch in his off-campus apartment, the same one he'd described in *Ballad.*

The next day we'd both felt awkward. I could barely remember it, a squishy meaningless fast coupling. "I like being friends," she'd said, and though I didn't agree—I was in love with her by then—I pretended to accept that it would only complicate the tour.

The three of us had walked across campus to mail off our ticket orders at the university post office, Brian leading the way like a general off to battle. The notion of dropping out sounded romantic to me, and I said to Halsey that if I wasn't so close to completing my accounting degree, I'd withdraw in solidarity alongside her, in protest of empty values and useless knowledge. Which was my way of saying that I'd follow her anywhere.

"You're sweet, you know that?" She pecked me on the cheek, lowered her voice so that Brian couldn't hear. "And I had fun last night."

A competitive process, the ticket mail order, one that hadn't yielded tickets to all the shows, so we'd had to go through the new service they called Ticketmaster to fill the holes. Nibbs had it down, had proxies, including his mother, either calling or standing on line at various on-sale times. Every show had sold out but two, the biggest stadiums. Jack O'Roses Summer Tour. The very idea felt like the greatest adventure ever. Nibbs had made a believer out of me.

With the semester completed, we headed west in Halsey's Vanagon for the Memorial Day weekend start of the monthlong tour, three shows on the band's home turf, at an amphitheater that'd been built, essentially, for Jack O'Roses, and at which they played a number of what constituted hometown stands throughout the calendar year. “The West is the best,” Nibbs often preached. At Ventura, my Jack-epiphany show, I’d lived his aphorism firsthand, so that first travel day I felt balanced and ready for some great times, and tunes, from our house band.

Nibbs and I got off on the wrong foot, however: I told him I felt that I was finished dosing, that I’d done enough acid, that the drug had taken me as far as it could, and after the transformative experience I’d had at Ventura two years before, to try to go further was simply a waste of good LSD. I felt that the pathways had been laid, and that I could traverse them without the drug that had shown me a new way of thinking about life, and myself. Acid had changed me, and that had now changed my relationship to the drug. Had made me respect its power. He disagreed vociferously—called me a pussy, and a tourist, a wannabe—but I was not swayed.

No wonder: Nibbs in those days treated the substance like a rail commuter does coffee and danish: he’d tab before his long class days, which were Wednesdays; on an ordinary Sunday, he’d dose to go to the park and throw the Frisbee around, when all I wished to do, at best, was burn one and chill out; we’d decide to go to a movie, but he’d want to drop and wait for the effects to begin, which caused all sorts of inconveniences with regard to theatre showtimes and transit.

I began to see his casual use of the sacraments as an apostasy.

To be honest, much of this disapproval is in retrospect—I had the feelings, but I didn’t have the words, not then.

After a time, he’d come on his own to see that he was going overboard a bit, and dialed it all back. It all added to his legend in F-Kid circles around campus. That next semester it got back to me that Nibbs Niffy had 'dosed every day for an entire year,' or some such hyperbole. Too much, in my opinion, yes. But not that apocryphal amount. The stuff of rumor. Of myth.

My other reasons included that the band seemed to be in decline, and rather than gloss it over, LSD only seemed to enhance this knowledge—with so many clams and miscues from Rose, even while tripping, I couldn't lose myself in the music. The band was interfering with the trip. Something was amiss.

At New Year's in Oakland the previous holiday season, which the three of us had flown out for together and stayed in Marin at Halsey's parents' spread atop a grassy hill which overlooks other, similar estates, I'd noted through the haze of my revelry that Rose once again appeared to be in an unhealthy state—as she thrashed at her axe or pounded upon the keys of her grand piano, the chin would rest on her chest, her head cocked at that weird angle when she sang, with the half-squint, half-scowl that made her look like she was either doing a Popeye impression, or else suffering mild pain; a shock of gray-streaked hair lay pasted across her shiny, damp forehead, and a complexion possessed of a grim pallor, a cast of illness, of embalming fluid. No mystery, if one allowed oneself to see it: Rose was using. Was hooked, again, on the white dust.

I wasn't that worried, not really. She was built to last, Rose Partland. Larger than life, as a taper who'd scored a VIP pass described her after going backstage. The notion blew my mind—I didn't want to meet Rose. I didn't have anything to say to her I hadn't already said by gyrating and supplicating myself before the altar of her artwork.

As the tapers broke down after the show on

the 30th of December, the warmup for the big three-set New Year's blowout, I asked the lucky VIP badge holder about his backstage adventure:

Easy Eddie, a squirrelly, nervous type wearing a Blue Öyster Cult T-shirt—an ironic commentary, I thought—said he'd had only one quick chance at face time with our leading light, our living legend, our Rose.

"And?"

"Okay," he said, painting a picture with busy hands and the wide, dazzled eyes of a guy who'd been to the Other Side. "I'm so freaking scared, right, that I'm gonna puke—it's unreal, man. It's like—she's walking toward me, and it's as though you're standing you're looking at a damn Disney character come to life. Yeah—a life-sized cartoon. The hair. The dress. The glasses. And tall—Rosie's tall, just a big big woman. Rosie's big, dude—bigger than your ass, that's for sure," ironic coming from a guy Eddie's size. "Yeah, she is."

We got it, we got it," Nibbs blustered, dropping his fifteen-foot mic stand into its own footprint, the shotgun mics mounted on a T-bar looking burnished and wicked and expensive. "But what was said?"

"I'm getting to it. When she brushes past in the hallway I call out, 'Rose, Rose, over *heah*, babygirl!' And so she stops and shoots me a look like: *Yeah, pal?* And the only thing I can come up with off the top of my head is what? What else: my stats. I says, 'Rosie, out of the seventy-five shows you've played on tour this year, I made it inside at fifty-four! Fifty-four,' I repeat, and hold up my hand for a high-five. 'What you think about that, Earthmother?'"

"And her reply?"

"She snorted and cackled and said, 'Guess what, ace—I was inside at all of 'em'!" He slapped his thigh, danced a jig. "That you were, Fat Angel. S'all I could say to that. That you were."

Nibbs asked, "Eddie—you get your high-five?" Grinning, Eddie put down the black, snaky microphone cable he'd been coiling. "Shake the hand that shook the hand."

Neither of us wanted to; the act seemed too close. Or so I thought I could see in Brian's eyes. Rose's sweat, her DNA, there on Eddie's olive-skinned, lined palm.

"Nice," I said. "Sweet."

"Piece of god," Eddie replied, dead serious.

He and Nibbs went back to stowing their gear, there in the cavernous and smoky old basketball arena, the young men careful and dutiful in handling the tape decks and microphones and cables and the tapes they'd pulled, while the rest of the F-Kids, including Sally, had already gone back to rage in the parking lot until security finally manhandled the movable feast out onto the streets of Oakland. The New Year's Run would be over the next day—time to go home, to go back to school. The real world. Wasn't so bad—mail order for spring tour would be in two weeks, and the summer tour on which we were about to leave had come only two weeks after the end of the spring run. Glory, at hand once again before we could blink our eyes.

But we had patience, of a kind. We could wait for the real thing. We had the tapes. Nibbs, I believed, could go without dope for the rest of life, and maybe the shows themselves, so long as he had the tapes. I had no idea how relatively soon, in the grand scheme, anyway, the F-Kids would all have to face that. I thought we had all the time in the world. Seemed that way on tour that summer. Especially after Sally and I gave in to the feelings, and forever changed the dynamic inside her tour wagon, that rickety not-so-old VW.

-3-

I skim through the tour diary, in which Brian describes our transit from the adventures at Bayfront Amphitheater south of San Francisco, to blissed-out nights on the beach after the Ventura shows, which simply *smoke*—not like '89, but still good stuff—to the lows of the California leg in the conservative, southern part of the state. Those shows had a perfunctory, greatest-hits vibe, the most expensive beer I'd ever seen in my life, and packs of privileged, straight-looking, middle-aged yups who didn't exude the same kindness that their northern California brethren did. Get us out of the OC, we thought, and so we, and the band, headed east.

In perusing the entries, I find that Nibbs reviews not so much the musicianship or the song selections, but instead the details of our travels—what we do, what we say, and what he records as disappointment after disappointment in our behavior, which he says is driving him 'nucking futs.' Well, Nibbs, futs you—I had the time of my life on Summer Tour '91, and neither your pitiful death, nor the eventual dissolution of my marriage to Sally-slash-Halsey, can take that away from me, sir.

I dwell on the pages that describe our trek

eastward, in particular the Colorado stopover, wherein I'm reminded of our visit with some hipper-than-thou friends of Halsey's we met up with in Boulder.

Jack O'Roses 1991 Summer Tour Diary
of Nibbs Niffy
[excerpt]

[. . .] *I'm sitting outside in some amazingly crisp and clean air, enjoying a pizza with fresh ingredients, including tofu instead of red meat. I've thought about going vegetarian, like so many of my brothers and sisters on tour. For a southern boy like me, where the rivers run red with barbecue sauce, having the option of tofu is so progressive that it seems like an extravagant luxury.*

So, too, do the vistas and natural environment inspire me: The peaks rising to the west, the hummingbird that was attracted to my bright tie-dye as we hiked a steep trail, the sound of the moose (or whatever it was) baying down the side of the mountain from our campsite, and the swing by Red Rocks, for a quiet moment of reverence and lamentation over the fact that Jack O'Roses has forever outgrown the beloved, but small, venue, a sacred place where Indian war councils once met. Nothing's for keeps, though. There's always a chance.

Much as I love the surroundings here, I have to say I won't miss Sally's friends much. Z, too, seems to be eager to get moving. I wonder if he's simply jealous? Sally hasn't paid much attention to him since we got here—these dorks are poseurs, big time. I won't have their pitiful derision. I simply won't have it.

He wasn't wrong in his thoughts about Sally's friends. She was way, way distracted by her old high school chums, who'd come to Colorado for college, failed, stayed.

Well, not both of them, only the guy, Derek—Halsey's friend Nance had been all set to graduate that fall with some kind of biology degree. They were now living around the fringes of the campus neighborhood, hiking, getting stoned, enjoying life. But they had a regal sense about them, real nose-in-the-air Colorado outdoorsy types, with all their Gore-Tex and Patagonia crap, and an attitude that, for having come from a backwater like South Carolina, we were unsophisticated rubes whose presence was barely worth acknowledging.

What got Nibbs, though, and me, too, was that Sally's buds were both uniformly above-it-all concerning the Jack O'Roses experience in which we were willfully immersed. Derek, a rock climber, all sinewy and tanned and glowing, had Been There, but had returned with an attitude. "Yeah, yeah—when I was a teenager and into smoking dope all day, I listened to those dinosaurs. I grew out of it though," he said, derisive. "Rose Partland's washed up—she can't remember the fucking words anymore."

I can remember as though it happened yesterday how Nibbs had snorted and bitched and stomped around the rest of the afternoon we were stuck hanging there in the apartment with those folks. How he'd told Sally that her friends were tools, and dorks, and full of shit. How Sally had gotten angry, been silent the next day as we'd packed the Vanagon to head out for Bonner Springs, an amphitheater outside Kansas City, and then Drake Park.

Images from the rest of the tour flash through my mind: Lying around all afternoon at the campground outside Drake Park, Nibbs reading a humanist manifesto called *Beyond Good and Evil*, and when it wasn't that he kept his nose buried in Brautigan's *A Confederate General from Big Sur;* Sally, held rapt by a collection of Bret Easton Ellis short stories, a volume that Nibbs derided for what he termed the author's "vapidity masquerading as stylistic conceit, suffused with an overwhelming concern for trivia in place of genuine emotion"; nearly getting pulled over in Ohio right after puffing a number, but managing to get off the hook when someone blew past the cop on the other side of the freeway at a hundred miles an hour, saving our narrow white asses, which was the moment Nibbs started codifying certain road rules—his fear of arrest extended only to one consequence, and one consequence only, which was being detained and potentially missing the next show; succumbing, the two of us, and making love in the tent, in a hotel room bed, and in the back of her van before the Raleigh show at Carter-Finlay, during the afternoon of the last show of the tour, while Nibbs went to hook up with his taper buddies, Easy Eddie and Chico and Martin; how every time we came together I fell into her eyes, and thought that I didn't even care if went into the show that night, didn't care about anything except her soft moaning and supple body next to mine.

I remember driving home to Columbia, almost a month after we'd left, with a sense of optimism and a lightness of spirit that, frankly, I'd never before felt—but it wasn't from the shows, the tripping, which I'd mostly stuck to not doing, and the music. It was Halsey Bedrich. Once home, I told her every chance I got that I loved her, to which she would smile and squeeze her blue eyes and give me little kisses. She didn't go back to school that fall, but I did, and so did Nibbs, but he'd been different, then. I couldn't see why.

And, of course, we came home to a much worse distraction than what I'd come to understand was Brian's jealousy over Sally: three days after the end of the tour, Matt Alvin Christopher, himself a replacement in the early 70s for the band's original keyboardist, was found dead with a needle in his arm, and everything we'd experienced, and all our hopes for the future, were in the space of a brief news-blurb we heard on CNN now called into question. This was a time when we thought to ourselves, will they call it quits? Could Jack actually end? Unthinkable.

As Rose herself asked in song: *Is this it? Or just the calm before the storm?*

The answer, of course, was no—within a couple weeks after they buried Christopher, a new keyboard player, Lenn Circosta, was auditioned and hired, and the fall tour went on like nothing had happened. We were too relieved to send our fall mail orders to consider the deeper philosophical implications of this decision by the band, and by Rose. All we could see was that their cosmic ballgame wasn't going to be called as a result of rain, nor of death—not of the 'new guy's' death anyway, which is how certain F-Kids still felt about Matt, despite the incontrovertible fact that he'd been a vital and crucial member of the band for over fifteen years.

So, that next tour began only six weeks later, and we went to the first shows at the pro basketball arena outside Cleveland. In the parking lot, Nibbs saw a rainbow in the sky that told him everything he needed to know about the whys and wherefores of the decision by Jack O'Roses to soldier on the wake of a fallen comrade. "There he is," Nibbs, an avowed atheist, said. "Matt says yes. Yes to all this."

So Circosta, the new synth guy, did his thing and it was okay and then after a tour or so, nobody much worried that Matt was gone—half the time Rose played the grand piano anyway, the keyboardist only there for color, and the occasional harmony or lead vocal.

Nibbs talked Sally and me into dosing that night, that it was the most crucial Jack show any of us had yet seen in our touring lives, and thinking that we was right, we all got puddled, had the time of our lives—not like Ventura '89, but a fat trip nonetheless. Because they were breaking in a new guy, the band had been rehearsing like crazy, which they never did, not at that stage of their long career as rock legends, and it showed: That night they played and sang like they meant it—one uptempo rocker after another, Rose sticking her finger in the air and belting it out like the Earthmother of old, and the cherry on top? A long and dreamy 'Nebula' in the second set, complete with the oft-elided third verse, that made us all feel as though we had been privy to a momentous and cosmic occasion. Rose seemed to be saying: *Not even death shall hobble us, shall slow us down. We are eternal.*

I put away the sad and progressively fragmentary tour diary—as Sally and I had fallen in love, Nibbs had become sullen, had begun drinking tons of beer, had withdrawn from us.

Suffused as I am with nostalgia for those halcyon days of young lust and what I'd considered love—if such love ever existed the way I once thought that it did—I sit struggling with the desire to again call Halsey.

To ask her if she'd ever truly loved me. If any of it—our marriage, our friendship, the 1991 Jack tour—meant anything.

Does that matter? Did it, then? The answers do not come, or if so, are best left ignored.

I decide not to go back, but forward—I ring up Aimee, who seems cautiously pleased to hear my voice. Feeling the same about hers, I know I made the correct choice, and we decide to meet again—this time, I hope, for our own sake, and not that of Brian Godbold.

-4-

Excerpt from the peoplepedia.com entry for 'Frank Oglethorpe'

[Post caretaker and moderator: Brian K. Godbold/joroses420@aol.com]

Francis Allen Oglethorpe, born in 1939 in St Louis, Missouri, was the son of a Marine Sergeant killed in the battle of Iwo Jima (not one of the flag-hoisting iconic figures, however). Young Frank grew up amidst poverty, but then upon his mother's remarriage to the young scion of a manufacturing concern, his life changed for the better.

His stepfather Norman Milliner's heavy manufacturing company, already solvent with war profits from its government contracts to produce several important components of Flying Tiger aircraft, was set to become even more wealthy as the defense industry continued to boom in the post-war years and Cold War era to come. This allowed the formerly working-class Oglethorpe survivors to enjoy opportunities and plenty unlike anything they had previously experienced.

Frank, an athletic but quietly intellectual boy, medium of build and light of foot (throughout his childhood he played at the running back position on football squads) claimed to have been negatively affected by his mother's remarriage in 1947, even as the union obviously lifted himself, his mother Doreen (Oglethorpe) Milliner, and his three-years-younger sister Noelle out of their heretofore impoverished state. The memories of his real father Colin "grew hazy, but even as a young child, the sense of my true father's heritage was never far from my mind." [Conversations with Jack O'Roses, pg 104]

Oglethorpe spoke of feeling 'imprisoned' and 'stifled' by his stepfather, and later wrote that he was 'intellectually disgusted by Milliner's sense of privilege and lust for more of everything, even as he already had, through fortune of birth, more than any one man could need.' [Ibid, pg 107]

There is anecdotal evidence to suggest, however, that young Frank took to his new bourgeois lifestyle with aplomb. According to acquaintances and classmates, throughout his adolescence he was known for appearing in the finest of clothes, upon the most sublime of bicycles, motor scooters, and later, in top of the line automobiles. It is said that he often flashed (and spent) money, especially on young ladies of society. Far from rebelling against his stepfather's privilege, the record suggests that Oglethorpe enjoyed, if not reveled, in his status. [Peoplepedia alert: citation needed]

Another family tragedy changed him forever—the death of twelve year-old Noelle, in a boating accident on the Mississippi River, and in front of a teenaged Frank Milliner's horrified eyes.

Afterwards, he gave up on sports and began running with a 'bad crowd,' as one of his later school reports noted; to the consternation of his parents and teachers, his grades suffered, and in spite of obvious intellectual engagement.

It is during this period he dabbled in petty crime, suffering an arrest for vandalism that scandalized the family.

After becoming acquainted with a group of musicians playing the local jazz circuit, he discovered marijuana. "That was the moment everything changed for me." [Conversations with Jack O'Roses, pg 106]

Despite his teenaged rebellion and disengagement, Oglethorpe did in fact graduate from high school, although as myriad outside interests began to take hold in his senior year, his grade point average had plummeted. He became quite taken with rhythm and blues and its nascent offshoot sub-genre, rock and roll. He began to sport clothing mostly associated with the stereotypical juvenile delinquent as depicted in photoplays and television shows of the era.

Oglethorpe, who upon his eighteenth birthday had returned to the surname of his biological father, was no typical street hoodlum, however—the façade he cultivated was perhaps in response to the knowledge he'd gleaned of his biological father's rough-and-tumble upbringing, of which his mother had described on numerous occasions to her ever-curious son.

[Peoplepedia alert: citation needed]

Despite his tough-guy countenance, Oglethorpe ran with an enlightened crowd of musicians, writers and other artists, and was encouraged by the same to delve into what would have then been considered the vanguard, confessional fiction of iconic literary writers such as Henry Miller, William S. Burroughs, and Jack Kerouac.

Oglethorpe himself began writing, although only fragmentary evidence remains of what he once called "the embryonic scribblings of a small-minded nincompoop from nowhere. As God's cold rain ran down my collar, cleansing me of past affectations and childish notions, I burned everything I'd ever written up until that point, every word, every scrap, in a garbage can outside Longshoreman's Hall in San Francisco, on New Year's Day in 1960: Year zero." [Reluctant Avatar, pg 32]

Oglethorpe ended up in San Francisco under circumstances typical of the time. By 1959, a nearly twenty-year old Frank had been given an ultimatum by his stepfather about either attending college, entering the family business, or else learning an honorable trade, at which point Oglethorpe decamped from Missouri for the west coast, a direction decided, he said, "by the flip of a coin—heads was New York, tails was California. I didn't even know where in California I was going at the time, until a saxophonist I met one night at a club in Denver told me that San Francisco was the place to be." [Hey, Brother: An Oral Biography of Haight-Ashbury and the Summer of Love, pg 203]

A further complication: a dalliance with a young woman of means from another prominent local family threatened to keep him in Denver indefinitely, a pregnancy scare mentioned in his autobiography Roses By Other Names. In that text he insists that the actual reason he left Colorado was that "I'd become enervated and bored by the provincial, redneck attitudes of the locals, who could have passed for extras in a John Ford oater [Western movie]." Either way, he ended up at Fisherman's Wharf in San Francisco, cut off from his family's wealth and down to his last twenty dollars.

Oglethorpe then 'made the scene' in North Beach, and inspired by poets like Allen Ginsburg, Michael McClure, Lawrence Ferlinghetti, and Richard Brautigan. He began writing anew, and reciting poetry in the coffee houses of the Bay Area.

Never a success in this regard—only one slim volume of work was published from this period, and then only a few copies printed, an extant one of which sold at auction in 1999 for nearly $10,000—he nevertheless made friends easily, embarking on a series of love affairs with both women and men. [Reluctant Avatar, pg 38]

After moving farther down the peninsula, Oglethorpe managed to eek out a modest living working at a bookstore in Palo Alto, a college town with a burgeoning bohemian scene.

"What," Oglethorpe asked in his autobiography, however, "was to follow the Beats? No one knew,

because they didn't yet realize the necessity of moving on." [Ibid, pg 39]

Through contacts at Stanford University, he came to participant in the famous Stanford LSD experiments, met Ken Kesey, got involved in the south bay folk scene, and from there his story is a relatively well known one: acid, politics, and ultimately art, in the form of songwriting and band management, that led to a serendipitous encounter in 1964 with two young folk singers from Georgia named Rose Partland and Jake Sobel.

Partland and Sobel, transplants from Atlanta, Georgia and calling their act The Itinerant Travelers, had attracted a following of "attentive and reverent listeners who'd deemed their harmonies to be of a sublimity rarely seen in a genre that'd become overrun with Dylan and [Phil] Ochs imitators. Rose and Jake had more—they had tunes, and they had chops—Rose Partland, every body in the scene seemed to know not only who she was, but why they knew who she was—she was a virtuoso. The two of them just needed better words—my words." [Roses by Other Names, pg 44]

Bassist Linus Pullen and drummer Paul LeMoy were already gigging in a jug band Oglethorpe managed, and once the core group of musicians began playing together, Oglethorpe sensed that the foursome shared philosophical and musical underpinnings that could lead to bigger things. The addition a few months later of rhythm and blues aficionado Jeff 'Skutch' McKellan expanded and enhanced the band's eclectic and inclusive musical background.

At that moment in pop cultural history, bigger things meant The Beatles, and rock & roll. Dylan's electric rebirth the next year convinced Oglethorpe that the future was in amplified music—as well as amplified consciousness.

Apocryphal stories abound about how Jack O'Roses obtained its name, in spite of what appears to be an obvious reference to Jake and Rose themselves. The most frequently repeated explanation is that at one of the many LSD parties at which the young band played—now merely called the Travelers—an attendee produced an unusual deck of cards featuring elaborate rose-themed designs. After prompting by amateur magician Pullen, Rose allegedly pulled a card at random from the middle of the deck—the Jack of Roses, as she purportedly called it.

At Oglethorpe's insistence, and after a slight modification, the band had a new name, and a rock legend had solidified into its classic configuration, and bound for untold glories to come: Jack O'Roses would tour for thirty years, and become the biggest-grossing live act of the rock era, the band's repertoire of over 300 tunes making them the most prolific recording artists of all time. [. . .]

From what I've read, in Brian's wiki-entry and elsewhere, Oglethorpe's always had a keen sense of his own legendary status, and clearly, rightfully, considers himself instrumental in the success of Jack

O'Roses. This is true, in one sense, because without his financial help—Brian's entry neglects to mention the eventual reconciliation with Oglethorpe's stepfather, which helped finance his early Bay Area ventures and adventures, including fronting all of Jack's early expenses—the band might well have floundered and never taken off quite in the manner that it did.

I think of him often, old Frank Oglethorpe, sequestered away, it's said, in Australia, like J. D. Salinger still furiously writing, but never publishing—novels, stories, poetry by the ream, as legend has it: Oglethorpe, hunched and tanned by the relentless sun, typing away on his own enigmatic exegesis that may well end up being some kind of final word on the band that goes far, far beyond his autobiography, which I haven't read all the way through because I found the tome to be frustratingly light on Jack details that aren't already well known.

I've also heard him described as impatient and irascible when confronted by admirers, which doesn't sound like too much fun. I hope it's true about his writing—now if that's not the person to make the definitive literary statement about Jack O'Roses, who is? Not a dead nouveau hippy, that's for sure. Oglethorpe, for obvious reasons, is someone I'd like to meet one day, a real link not only to Jack O'Roses and the 60s, but to the Beats themselves. Never happen now. And maybe it shouldn't—as with Rose, what would I say to this esteemed elder?

I copy and paste Brian's peoplepedia entry and shoot it over to her work email. Since the nice lunch we enjoyed last week, Aimee and I have been swapping notes, chatting online, playing getting-to-know you. We haven't talked about Brian much; what is there to say? But as a way of opening the gates of conversation about him, I make this gesture, and hope that bringing our mutual friend up doesn't make her uncomfortable. I shouldn't; why I feel compelled to do so is anybody's guess—a lingering sensation, perhaps, of unfinished business.

In turn, she's been forwarding me links to music that she likes besides Jack O'Roses, and I'm pleased that it turns out that Aimee enjoys P. S. Jones, to whom I find myself listening to with great frequency—Jones's different styles and voices offer variety, and not unlike the best of Oglethorpe's classic-era Jack lyrics, interesting Dylanesque story-tunes that reward attention and consideration.

A multi-instrumentalist like Rose Partland, a similar plaintive reedy warble to her voice, a fragility, an honesty, a facility with slipping in and out of musical styles—you've heard her various tunes on a variety of satellite radio stations, from light rock to jazz standards to modern alt rock—like Neil Young, P. S. Jones does tours sometimes with a hard-hitting backing band, as well as alone on stage but for an acoustic guitar and a baby grand; last year she cooked up an all-female bluegrass combo that knocked everyone's socks off at Merlefest, a modestly-scaled music festival in Wilkesboro, North Carolina every spring; that fall, she had a number one country single. A contemporary—in her mid-30s, a late bloomer in the pop music world—I can truly say she's my favorite musician since Rose.

I suggest checking Jones's website to see if this interesting songbird's playing in the area anytime soon, that if it's convenient, how we could perhaps go to a show together. Last year Jones did a co-headlining tour with Gillian Welch, the both of them making new Americana music like during the country rock Jack era. Something along those lines would be sweet.

Aimee says she'd groove on such an outing. Music lover, down to earth, seems to be open to the idea of hanging with me—man, am I getting to like this girl, or what?

–5–

On another visit to the Old Market and the downtown Columbia area—I've begun thinking of staying here instead of moving home to Charleston, maybe buying a townhouse or bungalow close to campus—I manage to make some new friends with a couple of F-Kid wannabes who sit down next to me at the coffee shop.

Sophie and Chance—short blonde dreads and a skater-punk vibe from him, skinny granola hippy girl all the way with her, warm, blissed-out sweetness coming off in waves, youthful light dancing behind their relaxed eyelids seem like good people. I'm not getting anywhere looking through the real estate guides—are they out of their minds? Three hundred thousand for a renovated bungalow?—so I strike up a conversation with the two, who are understandably wary at first.

Both, I find, are sophomores at Southeastern and veterans, I discover, of an extensive summer Panache tour that'd taken them across the country—twenty-first century tour rats. I knew it.

They sit rapt as I discuss my own adventures now dating back well over a decade, when the two of them were but children—Sophie, looking a little too clean under the trappings of her hippie outerwear, tells me that when Rose died, she heard the news while away at summer camp! I feel moldy and ancient.

Chance, however, is *extremely* and *totally* and *totally deferentially* impressed with my statistical knowledge of the shows I've seen, the songs, the bust-outs, the surprises, the duds, the mindblowing experiences that came on the best nights. And this is me only BSing, fudging a bit on some of the facts, which I don't remember too well in the first place—this kid would have been staggered by Nibbs's recall of Jack minutia.

Their band, Panache, an act that's in its way a successor to Jack in that they have a following, play a different setlist every night, have a commitment to spontaneity and the possibilities inherent in the improvisational spirit of the moment, is a strong substitute and successor for the lost and scattered Jack scene, while carving out a quirky and specific personality all its own. I've seen Panache a couple of times, once a year or so after Drake Park with Nibbs Niffy himself, when I felt obligated to meet him at Merriweather Post Pavilion, the shed that's about forty-five minutes from what we now think of as Halsey's spread on the bay shore.

I dig them: There's a playfulness bordering on satire with Panache, and more of a Zappa influence than the Americana that so colors the Jack catalog. With that atmosphere and vibe in play, tons of younger F-Kids, cheated out of touring with the real deal, latched onto Panache tour. In less than a year after Rose's death, the band had gone from theaters to arenas—a grim but lucrative inheritance, for fans who happened to love both bands, a melancholy largess.

"So—I need a show," Nibbs had said, calling to beg me to meet him, saying he'd sport the ticket and the beers in the lot and whatever I needed to get my freak on. “Any show, even these little fucks. I need to walk the lot. I need to be with the peeps, however many are left.”

I dug what I’d heard on tape of Panache. Said, sure. We went. I drank a few beers in the parking lot crawling with heat, the kids all furtive and sketchy in their big shorts, hand signals, and the ‘pharmies’ that seemed the drug of choice among these Reagan babies, as Nibbs called them, a generation raised on pills and meds for their every nuanced shift of mood or attention span.

The music? Terrific, the band tighter than a gnat’s pee-hole, as I said. Drunk and stoned and tired, we walked out of the sloping, forested venue and into the grassy parking lots, vastly different from Drake Park’s corn fields. No duck pond. No tear gas and helicopters. Good music played well, and a lot scene that felt familiar, but in a positive way. I felt fine and dandy, but still distant from Nibbs, who I could see was no longer the same person with whom I used to go to shows.

Standing by the car, I said I thought it’d been a fine show, but this, an opinion he pooh-poohed. “I find the value and purpose of this whole scene full of nitwits completely and utterly questionable. Look at them—these little mofos all act like they invented the wheel.”

I shook my head. “Look at it this way: Rose always said what, Nibbs?”

“She said a lot. Narrow it down, spud.”

“Well, that’s not exactly true. About her saying things. I’m not sure I ever heard her say much of anything . . .”

“You know what I mean, tater tot.” Nibbs, the whole afternoon offering a variation on the old road names, mine having an inexplicable and evolving potato theme. "Narrow it down," he said, dreamy and distant. He'd smoked opium, and eaten a bag of mushrooms, but had never seemed to get off.

"Remember in that one interview? She said that in her eventual absence, she only wanted one thing, and that was for her legacy to be something that could be expanded upon, something that wouldn't fade away—she wanted to create a model that could live on after her."

"And . . .?"

Deliberate in his obtuseness, I thought, but to what end? "Look around you!"

I recall that as we wandered around the grassy parking lot filled with buses and vans, people cooking food, bartering, selling, buying and living a life, at least for a few days or weeks, that was to a certain extent, if not off the grid, then at least a little ways off the beaten track, Brian saw what I meant, and his face grew slack. There were some tweakers and junkies and sixteen year-olds staggering about—but had it not always been that way on Jack tour, too? This was good. But it was no longer his. I could see the confusion in his eyes.

Had Drake Park been his, though? Or mine? No. An aberration.

"It's not the same," he said. "None of this is the same." We walked by the fatty egg roll guy. I bought one, drenched it with Sriracha. Tasted the same as it had on the Jack lot.

"Nibbs: Rose's template, whatever its flaws, survives and thrives. *How can you not be glad*?"

"I don't know why I never thought of it that way," he said, reflective. "Something essential. Missing here. I can't—I don't know." Thoughts unclear, words half-formed.

"I figured you'd done nothing *but* think about it, *señor*."

"Did you, now."

"Yeah—and I think you're overthinking it, now, and missing the old girl so much that you can't see the positive aspects in terms of the social legacy that's in play out here in the lot." I watched guys eating food they'd bought, wearing shirts they'd purchased. "Rose lives here, in every one of these people."

"Oh, listen to you. The music from these guys lacks emotion, and depth."

Nibbs, in curmudgeon mode. Enough already, and I said so—he'd made up his mind. Fuck the truth. Eschew the obvious. Be a dick.

He cruised over and set about buying a beer from a dude, and a veggie burrito from a cute girl with dreadlocks down to her dirty, bare feet, the soles calloused and blacker than printer's ink.

"Hey, now," I heard him ask, "you ever get to see a Jack show?"

"Nah, nah," she said with a low stoner's laugh. Her eyes, two dancing, kaleidoscopic pools set amidst a gamine, girlish face full of dark freckles. Her entire being seemed alight, and alive, with positive, psychedelic energy. She looked around with wonder, giggling, mesmerized as the flicker-flash of fireworks from the other side of the parking lot caught her dilated eyes. "I would've if I'd been old enough, brotherman—I was just a little little kid, then."

"Three years ago?" he shouted. Nibbs, having a moment—impossibly, and in the blink of an eye, he seemed to realize we were aging into our mid-thirties before this charming hippie girl's beautiful, stoned eyes.

She shrugged, laughed at him. "Veggie burritos!"

she called out, singsongy, refusing to meet his eye. “You know what somebody told me? The only time is right now.”

“You think?”

“That’s the rumor I heard.” And hawking her burritos again, and again.

He turned away with an odd grimace and we strolled on our way. A drum circle getting going, people calling out for ice cold beer and ice cold nitrous oxide, hissing tanks everywhere, balloons on the ground like colorful, spent rubbers, kids sitting down, falling down, stumbling around—this felt like Drake Park, suddenly, and my little hairs all stood up. “Let’s cruise,” I said as a couple of mounted police galloped by, and I could see the ice blue rollers of cop cars all up and down the sides of the highway leading away from the venue. “I’m getting the willies.” Nibbs, subdued and faraway, agreed.

We motored out and back across the bay bridge. Nibbs spent the night there on the farm, the last time we ever enjoyed such intimacy. We never talked, the three of us. We never talked about Drake Park, the two of us, not the whole weekend. Halsey had been gone. On a buying trip. Nibbs and I cooked out, drank beers, smoked dope and watched movies. He quit Southeastern not long after that trip, but he hadn’t said anything about it then. And he hid his harder drug use from me, I now realize. Neither here nor there, now.

Now that I've proven my street cred by having seen and described my few Panache shows, Sophie and Chance clue me in to a music festival that's happening nearby in about a month, one with a relaxed atmosphere of fellowship and fun that sounds totally groovy. This, an event I believe I'll suggest to Aimee that we attend.

The Hogstomper Hootenanny, the kids tell me, is a private music festival that's put on twice a year, spring and fall, and located, ironically enough, on some gently rolling Edgewater County farmland only fifteen miles from my father's house. The land's owned by a "guy more like your age," who the kids say is a devotee of the paradigm laid out on Jack tour—music, community, cooperation: there's a kitchen set up, and there are no tickets to buy, only a hat to pass around, with suggested donation of twenty bucks per head to help pay for the kegs and generators and to give the bands some scratch for their hard work. No cops, no security, no rules other than an encouragement to camp so as not to give the local gendarmes any late night easy pickings. Sweet.

I need this Hootenanny—with everything that's happened this year, a chance to blow out the tubes sounds perfect and apropos for a man like me, of so little obligation and responsibility, but with a surfeit of lingering emotional baggage. Fits right in with my life of aimless soul-searching—go and party with a pack of teenagers out in the sticks, under a benign Carolina sky filled with glittering diamond-points of light, one of which might be Rose, and another that could be my old, lost friend, forever joined with his idol in the endless, violet velvet void. Here's hoping they've at last found some measure of peace together.

-6-

My father laughs when I tell him about the Hogstomper Hootenanny, then shakes his head and admonishes me in his gentle, polite manner for continuing to waste my life on such activities.

Especially ones, he notes, "That I thought you'd surely outgrown by now, son."

"It's enjoying music—why should that be something to grow out of?"

"There's music, and then there's noise."

"So it's an accounting of taste you desire? I've heard that's a tough row to hoe."

He agrees, and sets aside his disdain for another discussion about how long I'm planning to stay, which I defer until later.

We go on to discuss the events of the day such as the upcoming presidential election, which despite being challenged by Bush III, as the wags are calling Jeb Bush, should this time be Gore's for the taking: in the ongoing wake of nine-eleven, his approval ratings are through the roof, and for the first time since perhaps Pearl Harbor, the country feels united in its solidarity against the brown-skinned turban-wearing enemy of the people and threat to the union, the beacon to the rest of the world of all that's right and good, as we are.

Cynics like the conspiracy theorist friend that very day have dared to begun to whisper that nine-eleven, if not planned outright by the government, was at least allowed to occur to ensure Gore's solid reelection, which sounds monstrous even by my own skeptical standards about all things political. And legacy frat boys shall lead them.

As for my role as custodian of Brian's legacy, this task lies moribund and ignored—partially out of laziness, partially out of ennui, but also thanks to the inescapable feeling I get whenever I read his journals that, somehow, he's accusing me of crimes committed against either him, or Rose, or someone, I've given up on scouring his literary record any further.

So, instead of trolling Brian's words for meaning—for truth discernible through the cloudy opacity of phrases like *I made the call but did not call the tune*—I spend many hours fending off the questions of what-next and take power walks around the quiet subdivision in brilliant, warm Carolina autumn, my body feeling good and strong. I've started following my own diet instead of eating Phyllis's food. That kind of cooking will kill you.

On this particular day's walk, I decide pay a visit to Will Wrightson, the elderly neighbor a half-click up the highway from the entrance to the subdivision, in his older country house, at the turnaround point on my walking circuit.

Mr. Wrightson is a generous sort, and in the weeks I've gotten to know him has never had an ill word or gesture about anybody or anything; he's told me that I remind him very much of his own son, lost years before to a tragic automobile accident. As a result of our cordial relationship, I feel little trepidation in asking Mr. Wrightson for a favor: the use of his RV for the Hootenanny. As it turns out, on my visit to him today he's charmed by the romantic nature of my plans for the vehicle, a classic Winnebago Warrior that has a neat little kitchen and bedroom, musty but neat as a pin on the inside, and in desperate need of an exterior wash and detail.

Wrightson isn't familiar with the gathering to which I'll be taking his chariot, but "dang if that don't sound like a fine time to me. You say there'll be a bluegrass band? Well, I dee-clare. I didn't think you young-uns was into all that. I run over yonder to The Dixiana every now and then," a tavern in downtown Tillman Falls, "to hear some pickers they got there that rip it up on Friday nights."

"Sounds very very cool," I tell him, and I mean it—one of Rose's side projects in the 70s was a bluegrass band that recorded one album, a record credited by many as turning on an entirely new generation and demographic outside of the South to the country music genre, this F-Kid included. "I love me some bluegrass, y'all."

"I could tell you had you some good taste, son," laughing and pleased. "Come inside and let's get ourselves a cold drink," which we do, albeit quietly—his wife Loretta, ill with cancer, he says, and sleeping upstairs.

So, Mr. Wrightson is happy to let me borrow the vehicle without further elucidation regarding the Hootenanny, and is also emphatic in his refusal—the reaction on his face is one of mild insult—when I offer to hire the conveyance from him at whatever the market rate might be to rent such a vehicle.

"You just put back whatever gas you use, dump the septic tank, and we'll call it even," he tells me there at his kitchen table.

I argue that I don't see what's 'even' about me taking advantage of his generosity. "I have plenty of money."

"Be that as it may, I know your folks from church, and having no doubt that you're as good a person as they are, consider this a courtesy and a favor and leave it at that."

I thank him; he blows his bumpy, veined nose into a handkerchief with a thick old man's hand, his arms liverspotted and sunbaked. "We don't hardly use it no more, not since Loretta got sick. Just bring her back in one piece, son, is all I ask." He smiles and clasps my hand. "And have yourself a big old time listening to those pickers. You ever drive one of those before?"

"No," I say, sheepish. "Back when I was into camping, we just piled into an old van and slept under the stars. Is it automatic?"

"Oh, heck yeah. C'mon then, let's run her up the road a ways. I predict you'll get used to old Bertha here right quick."

Like my father, in a moment of extreme self-consciousness after getting high on some Sour D I scored from Chance and Sophie, I become somewhat concerned about my future.

I think it through: I'm not exactly spending a great deal of money, and the settlement from Halsey is enough to last me for quite a while—so long as I remain the frugal thirtysomething, overgrown son living upstairs.

But everyone in the house knows that it can't go on like this—Phyllis' constant bromides, platitudes, and scornful commentaries regarding the moral turpitude of liberals, the new breed of hardened, determined, and outright successful terrorists they're calling Islamofascists, gays, drug users, pornographers, abortionists, activist judges, and other such destroyers of the republic have become an idiotic mantra of nonsense that I am increasingly unable to tolerate.

But it's not only dear sweet befuddled Phyllis: In the wake of nine-eleven, madness seems to have swept through certain corners of our society. The Patriot Act, as I try to explain to her, is an evil document, and an admission that the terrorists have already won, but she scoffs and tells me over and over how none of this would have happened if George Bush hadn't had the election stolen from under his Texas cowboy nose, how close to God he and his brother Jeb are, and how he'd be looking out for us all and would ever do anything that wasn't blessed and ordained by a power greater than all of us combined, and thank god he and his brother will have their sure hands on the tiller of government come January, when we'd be rid of that pot-smoking commie Al Gore.

The sad truth is, though, that Gore, facing not only a turbulent and unusual reelection season but also a hostile Republican congress, may have to swallow this so-called Patriot Act. I'm soul-sick—the legislation represents a new level of constitutional degradation. But I can't get that across to her, unlike Aimee, who's with me on all matters political.

As for Rose Partland, I'm sure she'd have hated the Patriot Act worse than she'd loathed Nixon. I suspect that many of our esteemed leaders are becoming opportunistic power-crazed libertines rather than statesmen . . . but not the President, bless his heart, who seems to many as stalwart and strong as the California Redwoods he wants to protect.

Appearances deceive—who knows if Gore has anyone's best interests in mind? After all, the President's bowed to rightwing pressure and begun saber-rattling about another larger than life comic book villain besides Usama Bin Laden—voices are calling for America to rally its allies and take out Iraqi dictator Saddam Hussein. But that would be a war of choice, not of necessity or retribution. Wouldn't it?

In the face of such madness, all a peaceful F-Kid can do is put on a show, and dance such troubles away . . . which is precisely what I think we'll do on our peaceful Carolina hillside, at our Hootenanny.

–7–

October zips by, a hazy dream-sequence of inactivity, and a time worth remembering only for the occasions in which Aimee is involved, lunches and strolls around the campus that are growing in frequency.

Then Halloween comes—I always think of the great 1993 Atlanta run, one of the last, best times I had at Jack shows—and the next weekend we find ourselves at this Hootenanny-thingie, comfortably ensconced within Mr. Wrightson's aging chug-a-lug Winnebago, which belched and farted its way across the county to the festival site, a lush, secluded idyll of a hillside a few miles from the river that forms the eastern border of the county—only knowing that the Sugeree River Nuclear Station is three miles away colors my experience of standing there and taking in the gorgeous farmland, a last gasp of summer's green before the senescent onset of autumn.

Aimee had to be talked into the adventure, but it didn't take much arm twisting—I can tell she likes me. Feels comfortable. We've held hands; we've smooched and cuddled a bit, but nothing more intimate than that. I only hope that she's starting to feel about me the way I do about her, or this is going to turn out to be a carbon copy sequel to the great aborted Nibbs Niffy-Aimee

Pressgrove romance novel.

As the mild, golden afternoon, languid and bittersweet, rolls on by, the Hootenanny already feels like a home I've forgotten I once had: the sound of Rose's guitar issues from the boom-box I brought, sweet music that you can hear outside too, pumping out of the PA as the sound guys set up for the first band; the smell of kind bud; the sound of a drum circle from farther up the pasture; the patchouli I've slathered under my armpits, like we used to when the campgrounds didn't have shower facilities.

My new hippie friends Chance and Sophie join us inside the RV for comestibles, combustibles and conversation; Phyllis has made us a basket of sandwiches and snacks and about four-dozen of her best cookies, which Chance at first thinks are ganga-laced, and disappointed to find out otherwise.

"This reminds me of the old days here, boy," I say through a cloud of blue smoke, passing a squat, red travel bong over to Aimee, who hesitates until I give her a reassuring, you-don't-have-to-if-you-don't-want-to shrug.

"Oh, why not," she says. "Just to piss my daddy off, one of my uncles used to let me puff on his little wooden pipe. I didn't never really get high-high, though. I don't think."

I catch Sophie and Chance exchanging a mildly condescending look: *These old muggles are such a trip!*

As if to confirm their suspicions of our decrepitude, I lapse into grizzled geezer mode. "I'm telling you what, this RV's the bee's knees compared to the olden golden days—we did it hardscrabble back then, me'n the crew on Jack tour. We slept in a van, down by the river!"

"Do tell," Chance says, winking at me. "Let's hear some stories."

My mind is clear, but I can sense a thick buzz creeping in from this heady stash Chance has brought—a tingling at my temples and a slow, pulsing sensation across the top of my head, a comforting launch pad for the long night ahead. "No luxuries for us back then, baby, just the cold hard ground. Peanut butter and honey sandwiches—you were *lucky* if you found bananas to put on 'em." I lean forward and extend a finger in Chance's direction. "Walked six miles to a show, once, through a blinding snowstorm. Uh-huh. Got lost, and in desperation we ended up eating a VW pop-top full of spinners from Santa Cruz."

Sophie's looking at me like I'm from Mars. "Do what, now?"

"Oh, it was bad. They didn't find us," I intone, "until sometime that next spring tour. Those of us left alive, that is," I add, laughing malevolently.

But a shadow falls, and I clear my throat. "And then there was this one old show that I walked six miles back home from. But that wasn't no fun. Not a good time. Not a good tour story."

Aimee releases a lungful of smoke—an enormous plume—and the others laugh as she coughs up a storm.

"Sure you did, old timer," she gasps through a raw throat. "And Rose was a hundred feet tall if she was an inch."

"Preach on, sister—now you got it. Go ahead and hit that again." She does.

"Whoa," Aimee says with a wheeze, passing the plastic waterpipe to Sophie. "I'm, uh . . ." A long pause as she seems to grope for words. "I'm good."

Every time we hook up for weed I turn Chance onto some kind Jack shows from my collection, and at the moment he's searching for unheard gems in my binder of Nibbs-discs.

"What was your favorite show again? I know you told us that day we met you at the coffee shop.. ." He trails off, voice quiet in that stoney way, when the smoke is drawing you inward, and the vocalizations of your ideas come out smaller than they seem inside your head. "Bayfront? Or Ventura?"

"Wellsir, it was first night at Ventura, summer in the year of our Lord Rose Partland 19 and 89. That was the big one for me . . . that was the breakthrough."

I think how disappointed Nibbs would be that I didn't mention the complete and accurate date, so I do. "July 7. Most important day of my life until that point. I saw decent shows before that, and better shows later, I think, but that day something else happened for me, beyond the music and the scene and the whole circus." I gesture up toward the heavens. "Through the looking glass, but for real."

"Panache got banned from Ventura," Sophie says with sad regret. "Red Rocks, too . . ."

"When the hell did this happen?"

"This summer, dude . . ." Chance seems disgusted. "Bunch of wooks rushed the gate."

"*Banned*?" Aimee is shocked, her eyes already turning red. "From playing a concert there?"

"Yep—now we'll never go to Red Rocks again."

"Aw," Sophie says. "Don't say that."

I get a shiver, remember our visit to the venue on the 1991 tour, our feelings of loss that we'd never see Jack play there. "Gatecrashing? Sounds like Drake fucking Park."

Chance loads a fresh, green bowl. "That tour lot lizards came out the fucking woodwork, like a plague—I didn't know who all those people were, suddenly, on

Panache tour."

I shudder anew as a wave of heat washes through me—the brutal sun of Drake Park, the panic attacks I suffered that awful day, as Nibbs and I forced our way through the desperate throng around the entrance gates to get in the taper line, with a very dark vibration hovering in the Indiana air like heat coming off asphalt. "Anybody get hurt?"

"No, no, not really, but people started throwing beer bottles at the cops," he says, rolling his eyes. "Dumbasses."

"Jesus!" Aimee, beyond mortified. "What kind of band is this? Metal?"

"No," I say in reassurance. "Nothing like that. Panache is good people."

It wasn't a mystery to me what was happening in the Panache scene: the same people who killed Rose Partland had begun to mass there. Bad apples, spoiling the bushel. "And what happened at my beloved Ventura?"

"Man, I don't even know. California—you'd think out there . . . I mean, it wasn't even sold out, but you still had lot lizards crashing the fences. I just don't get it."

Enough of this grim talk. We pass the bong; the CD ends. "Here, let me play you guys something cool." I pop out the disc, an early 90s second set, and after rummaging around in the case of shows I replace it with a famous set from '70—*okay, okay,* I say to Nibbs' ghost, *October 4, 1970, you exacting bastard.* The night Janis died.

"Listen to this show, an excellent statement of the period. It's got everything, the long jams, the Skutch spotlight segment—it's a thirty minute 'She Caught the Katy'—other cover songs including the *de rigueur*

Dylan stuff, a mind-melting 'Nebula' that pretty much traverses the entire breadth of the known universe in just under twenty-eight minutes . . . this is the real Jack O'Roses to me. The realest version. A band that, in truth . . . I never got to see at all."

Now I do sound like Nibbs, and as the music begins, my heart clenches at his absence. For the first time, maybe, I feel what's been missing, an emotion I'd buried beneath the anger and annoyance that welled up in me in the wake of Brian's suicide, a feeling I haven't had since August of 1997: grief for my friend, grief for the scene. I wonder if he isn't speaking through me, now, somehow. "On this night, right before they went onstage, they were told that Janis had died. That's why it was such a great show."

Aimee, skeptical. "They played a great show because Janis Joplin died?"

"Sure—they're musicians. That's how they worked out their grief. They knew the music could heal them—and us. They played a great show that night not out of disrespect, but out of love for her. And everyone gathered there with them."

The music flows out of the RV's factory speakers, each note carrying volumes of emotion and depth, the melodies and improvisations and plaintive lyrics demonstrative of the band members' own yearning, searching desire for the big answers.

"I read about this shit, y'all—oh wait wait wait, check this out . . ." Chance is excited, flipping through a trade-paperback Jack biography he's got in backpack, until he finds the photos section, and one particular page.

"Here—check it out: a pic from the show we're listening to!"

He hands the book to Sophie, who says, sadly,

"Awww," before passing to Aimee.

She nods and frowns a little, and gives me the book, which is open to a famous picture, a dramatic black and white shot of Rose Partland belting out one of Oglethorpe's lyrics, the stage lights illuminating the tear-streak that extends down from the corner of her eye. Sweet Rosie—young, slender, her hair still dark, her face smooth, devoid of the deep lines that would cut into it only a few years later, the deaths of people like Janis and Skutch McKellan probably responsible for a more than a few: lines on the mirror, lines on her face. *Partland says 'goodbye' to her friend Janis*, the caption reads.

"Heavy," I say as my own waterworks threaten to kick into high gear, closing the book with quiet and careful reverence. "Listen to this stuff. What a show to have seen."

Chance puts the book away and produces a packet of tinfoil from the backpack. "Anyone interested in doing some chocolates?"

"Oh my god—*I freaking love chocolate*," Aimee says, high and overcome with munchies. "Gimme gimme gimme."

"Chance, maybe you should tell her what kind these are . . . it's not Reese's Cups."

Once she's informed that her beloved sweets are a carrier for psilocybin mushrooms, Aimee looks a bit wide-eyed, demurs. "Oh, goodness no. But y'all knock yourselves out."

I'm concerned about what Aimee, who is by her own admission no stranger to organics, thinks about me tripping with these kids. I consider how I gave up acid after 1990, the disdain from Nibbs, how, like I said before, I managed to find my way back to stoned, psychedelicized consciousness using only the neural pathways already forged. How the mushroom high is easier to control and regulate. “Standard dosage?”

“A gram each.”

Aimee, shrugging: *go for it.*

I eat only half of the chocolate, saving the rest, gauging the trip. Nibbs, snickering at me from beyond. *You pussy.* Whatever, dude. All things in moderation’s a lesson you might have tried glomming onto, big boy. And if you had, maybe we’d be here, together, having fun like old times. But you didn’t and we’re not, so get the fuck out of my head.

Nibbs, silent in response, skulks shuffling out of my thoughts. For a while, anyway.

–8–

We wander en masse down the hillside toward the stage area, a wooden shed where techies are putting the finishes touches on the front of house setup. Guitars are tuned, keys tinkled, drumheads diddled. Music awaits us!

Behind the stage is the community kitchen set up under a smaller and more decrepit shed. The cooking area, like the stage, is alive with activity: a middle-aged woman with dark wiry hair pulled back in a bandana stirs a giant pot of chili; a younger crunchy granola chick and a teenaged boy twist up veggie burritos and other wraps; a couple of guys dump a bag of ice over a keg of beer sitting in a large plastic tub.

"Smells wonderful," I say to the chili-lady, who beams love and positive energy to me.

"It's not ready just yet, angel," she says. "A little while yet to let the flavors blend."

Chance pulls out his glass chillum and pulls a quick hit.

"No, no," the cook says, her happy face mildly troubled. "Not back here—lots of kids running around."

"Ooh," Chance says, embarrassed. "My bad."

We move on. I don't really want any food anyway—the chocolate 'shrooms, eaten a half-hour ago, have made my stomach feel thick, though thankfully not nauseous. "What's back in the woods here?" I wonder aloud.

"There's a crick back yonder," a redheaded teenage boy walking by us says in his rural, hick accent. "Y'all ought to go check it out. It's real purdy."

"I think we'll do just that."

Indeed, a path through a thicket of hardwoods leads down to a gurgling stream full of mossy rocks. Sunlight dapples—there's no better word—through tree limbs brushed by a fall breeze. This part of Edgewater County is beautiful: rolling hills, farms, the lake country.

Aimee, still stoned, examines flora, including what she says looks like a mountain rhododendron, one that reminds her of the woods near her North Carolina childhood home, and moves deliberately and quietly, looking for the source of her beloved birdsong. My trip is coming online. I feel unfettered, alive.

"Check this out," Chance calls from a few yards off the path where he's found a decaying, abandoned school bus covered in mold and several years' worth of dead leaves and twigs. "It's somebody's ride!"

But this, no ordinary bus—painted up in swirls of day-glow colors, with intricate, stoned artwork reminiscent of vintage R. Crumb gracing the panels, this might have once been a school bus, but became somebody's righteous and totally awesome tour wagon.

I climb inside to see a single bed, a rusted camp stove, magazines and paperback books scattered around, and Jack posters, some half hanging and others fallen altogether. A smell of peat and mildew, a hint of burning sage, the echoing of a drum circle long finished, the ghosts of F-Kids lolling in the dusty spiderwebbed corners. "This baby saw some shows," I call back over my shoulder.

"I got it for a song from this kind brother, back in '82," a voice says from behind me.

I pop back out of the bus to meet a man who turns out to be our host for the evening: "Antonio D'Alessandro," he says, the rest of the introductions going around. "Tony."

Aimee, returning from her birdwatching peregrination. "D'Alessandro—like the Italian restaurant in Columbia?"

"Yeah—that's my family."

"You don't look very Italian," Chance says, narrowing his eyes.

Tony shrugs, chuckles. "Go figure—Dad used to say I was the milkman baby."

True to this, Tony's a blonde, gone-to-seed pretty boy, his light hair now wispy, graying, and in full retreat; his stomach, probably once washboard tight and tanned after being down at the beach all summer, now causes the bottom of his Baja pullover to hang over the waistband of his worn-to-shit Guatemalan drawstring pants.

Of the old, rotting bus, he says, "This tub used to be my crib for a while, till my old man passed."

"I'm so sorry," Aimee says.

"Wasn't all bad—after he croaked, my sister Opal said I could finally move back up into the house."

I jerk a thumb back at the tub, as he calls his old tour machine. "You take her on the road much?"

He produces an ornate glass bubbler out of one pocket, and before passing the pipe to me takes himself a hit. "Fuck yeah," he answers through his smoke. "Bought her before spring tour '84, rolled all up and down and across, too, till that fucktard Bundrick tried to kill Rose. Instead of her dying on us, it was only my ride that did, though, thank god."

I gestured to the faithful old bus, put my hand on her rusty side. "Maybe she took one for the Fat Angel."

"I reckon it was time for her to give up the ghost—the bus, I mean."

"Yep. 'Time's come again to collect its due'," I quote from 'Came a Day,' "'and there's nothing we can do'."

"All things must pass."

I thank him for putting on the Hogstomper Hootenanny. For keeping the vibe alive.

Tony replies, "We got to keep this thing going. I mean—when we get up there? If we don't carry the torch, Rose is gonna be pissed as hell." He starts back out of the woods, glances back. "Just don't chump out when the hat gets passed. Got to pay the piper and all."

Back on the hillside we discover that, with twilight upon us, the first band is now onstage and playing, and they sound good—good music, played well. What else an F-Kid to ask of one more Saturday night?

The shed-like structure, appearing hammered together for this one and only purpose, is large enough for the average garage band and its gear. A basic light rig is turning, simple combinations of red and green and blue, and controlled by the sound guy off to the side who's set up his board under a white, ten-by-ten pop-up tent.

People mill about among tiki torches to either side of the stage. Further up the hill, a cluster of tents have sprouted like rare, colorful fungi following a rainstorm, and a few more RVs and buses are pulling in and parking—a steady stream of headlights creep over the crest of the ridge. When I squint hard enough I can see Tony running back and forth and waving a flashlight, gesturing and pointing and barking out instructions.

A group of guys off to the side are building a modest bonfire out of scrap wood and felled tree trunks they've dragged out of the forest. I nudge Chance in the ribs and while Sophie and Aimee spread out a big blanket we go over to help.

"This is great, man. I appreciate the buzz," I say.

"Well, thanks for letting us crash with you later, dude."

Oh, shit. These kids assume they can stay in the RV with us! "Um—no tent for you guys tonight?"

He scatters an arm-full of small sticks near the base of the woodpile, gives me a confused look. "Well, nah, bro—when you told me about the RV . . . I assumed . . ."

"Of course, of course—it's cool," I say in reassurance. "I just wasn't sure. Plenty of room."

Wellsir: So much for the psychedelic post-show tryst with Aimee that I'd planned.

But maybe I'm only trying to recreate history, a misguided attempt to hold onto the past. After a great show, under the stars, that's how it came together between me and my ex-wife—a head full of lovely pictures and the sound of the band still ringing in my ears, her face, flushed and damp, our bodies melded into one under the great Mother American Night, Sally naked and entwined with me both spiritually and physically and grasping me and scratching my back and meeting every thrust and peering into my eyes, deep, as though we were sharing something special, which we were. Meanwhile, Nibbs, wandering lonesome around the campground sucking on a balloon, a smoldering resinated number, and a bottle of blended whiskey instead of his preferred psychedelics. Nibbs, probably listening to us screw.

Don't go there, dude. Not tonight.

This is Aimee, I remind myself. Not Sally, and not Nibbs. This is right here and now. *This is where you are, the moment is right now, and this moment is eternal—let go of the past, Z. Let go.*

Let me, I say to my dead best friend. Show me how.

–9–

The moon rose, over an open field . . .

A dusky, pockmarked disc, engorged and oblong, creeps over the tree line like a forlorn jack-o-lantern shown up late for Halloween. As the music flows, the moon marches upwards in the sky on its eternal arc, paradoxically glowing brighter as it shrinks in perceived size. I am whole and alive: energy ripples through the ground and into my body, the stars above a great grid in the sky, the lights on the musicians slowly morphing and melting from one hue to another, shimmering off the guitar bodies and the faces of the mostly young men playing them.

Aimee and I have been dancing together on the blanket for what seems like hours; my trip is going strong—to nudge the journey along, I went ahead and ate the other half of the Chance's chocolate mushroom treat.

"These guys have some chops," I say to Aimee, who agrees, nodding, eyes redder than roasted peppers. "They're really bringing it."

"So are you," she says, casting her eyes around, an awkward look on her face. Her hand darts out and takes mine. "Handsome man."

Warmth, from her hand and through my entire body. Yes. Yes to this. Yes to Aimee. Yes to it all.

The band, jamming through a long improv segment, a descending chord progression that seems oh-so familiar and that drifts into a melody, hinted at first by the rhythm guitar player, and then picked up by the lead guy and the bass, very much the way Jake, Rose, and Linus might have done it—as though owed to telepathy.

The familiarity becomes clear, and the hair on my arms and the back of my neck rises: they're going into what's known among the Nibbs Niffys of the world as the Mercurial Jam, a rare bit of music that Jack O'Roses played most frequently in the early 70s, but revisited on several memorable occasions in the modern era, including one auspicious instance I'd enjoyed the honor of experiencing: my beloved Ventura '89 show. The band hadn't even named the melody, this so-called mercurial piece of music—it was the F-Kids, in particular the tape collectors, who'd christened the jam as such.

A voice reminds me: *They played it six times in '73, four in '74, just once in '75, and only three times since then, one of which was July 7, 1989.* Were he here with us now, Nibbs would not only be telling us how many times, but also on what dates and within what tunes the Mercurial Jam had occurred—but he's not here, he's not coming. In any case, I got one. The last one. They never found their way to that special place ever again, not after Ventura.

Not unlike me, come to think of it.

Awash in the energy and the memories, I begin jumping and flailing my arms; so, too, does Tony, who's standing over beside the stage. As many of the hillside dancers realize what the band is doing, a ripple of recognition also rolls through the audience, and a modest cheer wells up—acknowledgement from those who know the score.

But this is no mere tease: The musicians, an act calling themselves Tin Foil Hat, go on to develop the jam in a much more complete and thorough manner than Jack O'Roses probably ever did. As the music peaks, the lead guitarist begins lightning-quick runs of notes—not unlike the way Rose might have climaxed the jam, sometimes matched and twinned by Jake—and I'm suitably blown away.

Of its own volition my body begins to spin around, my eyes streaking across the dancers, the tents, the bonfire, a simmering crackling living being all its own—the fire calls to me.

"Come on," I insist to Aimee, grabbing her hand. "Over there—let's go!"

I pull her along and race across the hillside to the bonfire, where a ring of dancers are shaking and grooving, the flames licking the night air speckled with swirling embers streaking across my vision. Hand in hand we dash around the fire, skipping and cackling with joy—Aimee lets go, sees my joy, joins with me, childlike. I'm running and laughing, but only until it becomes crying—HAH HAH HAH—and then laughing again, and then sobbing.

"Whoa whoa whoa," Aimee says, planting her feet and flinging me around to a stop. I tumble over, nearly taking her with me. I'm winded, gasping, no longer laughing—my breath's gone; the jam's winding down, and I'm on the ground.

Aimee's bugeyed, freaked, falls to her knees beside me. "Z—are you all right?"

Getting my air back, bringing myself into a moment of clarity, tripping hard but realizing I'm okay and have only fallen down, and I begin laughing again—halting at first, then full on wind-sucking howling, which Aimee joins in, rolling onto the ground beside me. Aimee, beautiful, stoned, glowing red-gold from the flickering flames, lying across my legs and caught up in my euphoria. I hold her, kiss her.

"Get a room, y'all," I hear somebody yell over the music.

Under the harvest moon, on a South Carolina autumn's night out in the middle of nowhere, Nibbs may no longer live, and Jack O'Roses will never give another concert, but in that moment I understand that Rose Partland survives, and maybe in some tangential way this means that my friend still does, too. Now, the band leaves behind the Mercurial Jam and goes straight into another number, one delicate and beautiful despite its unfamiliarity, probably an original song—the conversation that Rose started goes on, here, there, and everywhere. We go back to our blanket, gather again with Sophie and Chance, and dance away the long and cool autumn evening.

-10-

The Hootenanny ends up being a fantastic night, but thanks to the kidlets, as we call Sophie and Chance, bunking with us in the front part of Bertha, not nearly as fantastic as I'd planned. All good things in all good time. Aimee—she's into me. There's no doubt. She's an old-fashioned girl, however, and seems to like to take it slow. I can dig it.

As for the music, last night made me feel something that I haven't in perhaps ten years, not at Panache shows nor any other Jack-inspired acts that I've seen since Drake Park. The scale of the Hootenanny, so local, so personal—tribal, even—strikes me as profound a legacy as any pop band could hope. Rose's life and work, vindicated.

Will Wrightson is impressed with my ability to back the RV underneath its shed, and more so with Aimee, who is demure and mortified by her disheveled, sleepyhead appearance.

As I open the door of the Explorer I've left parked there, he leans over and whispers. "Looks like a keeper."

"We'll see—for now, only a dear friend."

"Sure, sure," he says, winking.

Driving down the tunnel of emerald that is my

parents' street, Aimee's quiet, then clears her throat and blurts, "Hey: I had a great time. That was—different. All the other dates I've gone on since the divorce now seem terribly ordinary."

"I hope you mean 'different' in a good way . . ."

She considers this. "You got a little out there for a while. "

"Laughing laughing fall apart, as I recall."

"Something like that." Her expectant look says: explain yourself.

A flood of self-consciousness. "I needed to blow off steam. Was that okay?"

She muses upon the question, her mouth downturned. "Am I getting attached to a person who's out there . . . all the time?"

"No," which is true enough. "This was like homecoming for me. A special occasion."

Ton of bricks: attached? Did she say that?

"Okay." She pats my hand. "I'm really glad we became friends."

"Me too." A stab of panic that 'friends' are all she wishes to be. "Like—super glad."

"To be honest, I don't have many people in my life I feel that I can trust. You? I feel like I've seen the real you, somehow—you trusted me enough to cry."

"And to do drugs—for all I know, you could be a cop. Deep cover."

"Oh," she says, scooting over and leaning on me, hush hush, right in my ear. "I think there's some deep cover in your future, all right—I expected it last night, in fact."

I'm pulling into the Zemp driveway, curving concrete and brickwork and manicured landscaping—so I blew a chance. I am more interested in this trust talk, the lack of confidants and buddies.

“Why don’t you connect with people? Where are the friends?” I could be talking to myself.

“I’m—private. I pull it inside.”

If she thinks this is a confession of dark secrets, she’s got a ways to go before I’m dissuaded. “I’m that way, too—maybe too much.”

“My husband couldn’t handle that side of me.”

I put the Explorer in park, unhook my safety belt, and give Aimee a flirtatious tilt of my head. In a Harvey Fierstein-esque growl, “Oh, I’ll handle that side of you before much longer, little sister—don’t you worry.”

She gives me a faux-shocked look, slaps my hand. “There you go.”

I lean over, kiss her—deep and emphatic, a dance of tongues, no reluctance on her part; a sigh once we break apart, a lingering hand on my leg. I touch her face. She smiles.

“Now,” I say, presenting my incipient tumescence with a cease and desist order, quelling my lust with thoughts of the heavy Southern meal that awaits us, “let’s go meet my folks.”

-11-

I'm cleaning up the hard drive on Brian's laptop—I suppose I should now think of the machine as belonging to me—and preparing to compose a résumé and cover letter when the guilt, the feelings I said I was finished with, washes over me anew.

I open up one of the chapters of his unfinished book at random to find some of that insight into the band he sought, rather than of the fan writing the book—or so I think at first.

The Ballad of Jack O'Roses,
Verse 5

Jack O'Roses as a big-ticket show business concern was always about defying expectations, belying and outlasting the critics, the lack of mainstream radio success, the genre-defying experimentation, all in the service of turning convention on its pointed, blessed little head. It is perhaps this iconoclastic approach to the work that was in itself part of the group's undoing: at its most obvious, the band's endless touring along a path of their own making had as much to do with the loss of its de facto leader, and by extension the loss of the band itself, than the drugs the pundits wanted to blame for Rose's unfortunate, premature demise.

In an early 1980s interview in a once-leftist and progressive broadsheet paper turned slick magazine, she summed up quite incisively her disdain for any sort of political or leadership stance, other than that of a songwriter leading an unlikely, unwieldy group of musicians out of the forest and into the trees:

PARTLAND: We'd moved north, late summer of 1970. We set up the band office in San Rafael, Jake and I had the house in Stimson Beach, and we was golden, baby, just golden. Songs flowing out of our souls like quicksilver.

But anyway, so we're talking about booking the next tour and the album and getting Columbia Records paid off—finally—for all the studio time in '68. Real down-to-earth stuff, mundane as hell, living and loving and making food and smoking grass, all of it necessary for our continuing experiment, as Pullen likes to call it, our effort to soldier on and wallow our way into whatever's coming next.

But the thing was [here Partland leans in and gestures with her ever-present unfiltered Camel] that there's this continual trickle of people showing up, some we sort-of know from the Haight, some from other places that we sort-of know, and still more that we don't know from Adam. And it was like they were going, okay, so what do we do now? As in, so the 60s, whatever that was, are over, Altamont has happened, Janis and Jimi are dead, we're still across the sea killing people—ours as well as theirs—and Nixon sits there, this immovable force up on his pedestal, sending in shock troops to mow down college students . . . and there were these kids, and older cats too, all looking at me like I had some insight into anything beyond how to manage my own life.

I kept saying to them, Jesus H. Christ, don't look at me, man! What the hell do I know, or any of us? We can barely get our PA working on some nights, Oglethorpe's wanted on some bogus grass charge, the accountants have to be paid so they can figure out if we've got enough bread to make payroll through the next tour. What the fuck do we—do I—know about anything, except the music? I'm just a guitar picker, a piano-banger. That's what I'd tell them, anyway, and then these folks would sort of hang around for a while, ghostly, on the fringes, and then drift away . . . I'm telling you, it went on like that for years. It's never stopped, in a sense. [cackling with laughter] They'll be sitting there around my fucking grave, waiting for me to let them in on something that they already know.

REPORTER: But your following, the F-Kids, aren't they the genesis for you guys being thought of as hyper-symbolic stand-ins for a whole moment in history, of that entire era?

PARTLAND: Well, I'd always hoped they were coming because they liked the fucking songs, the jams, the vibe. Good music, played well. Still reaching for that ineffable thingamabob—Jake calls it IT, Linus calls it the Other, I call it That Place . . . we all have our names for the headspace we're trying to get into with our little circus act.

But I don't know what we have to do with the times in which [the group was] born, and certainly not in any tangible way beyond the art and the experience itself. The thread we're looking for goes back—way, way back, man, and it goes beyond politics and warfare and elections and all that earthly bum trip shit.

That's part of it—I don't get up there and preach some political line or offer social commentary because of those people I told you about, they who've kept waiting for me to do so. That's not my job; that's not what we're after. And if you think we ought to be doing it—us!—then I think that's just pathetic. Us? [laughs] Forget about it. If we're the ones to lead, then things really are truly fucked.

REPORTER: But having the bully pulpit, think of the good someone like you could do.

PARTLAND: If I want my lifestyle or approach to making art to inspire someone in some way to apply similar principles to, say, running for political office, or writing letters to the newspaper and their congressman, or going into business, or serving the community . . . well, then that's nifty. But that's all you, you know, not me—I'm a Taoist, to lead I get out of the way. It's all there in them—I can't give it to anyone, they have to find it on their own. [. . .]

In 1988, on the summer tour, when I first did more than a couple of shows in a row (I did six that tour, not consecutive), there were a ton of political shirts and stickers, parodies of the process—but let's face the fact that it's difficult to parody that which is already farce and artifice.

I bought a PARTLAND FOR PREZ button and another similar item, a tie-dye of pale pink and gray (an odd combination) that featured a screen print of a familiar image, a scan of a beatifically smiling Rose, an image made famous on the back of the seminal 1973 four-disc live album Across the Great Divide (Columbia Records 14578). *In that photo she has a look on her face you didn't see often enough in 1988, an expression that seemed to say, "I know something you don't, and not only that, but I'm having an absolute blast with this knowledge."*

In the context of the shirt, with its slogan PARTLAND IN '88, TOWARD A SAFER AND SANER AMERICA, *her face is a perfect symbol of a quality lacking in the political process: humanity, and humility, in all its yearning complexity. Instead, the engine of our supposed democracy is a process that is more about millions of dollars, commercial jingles, sloganeering, fear mongering, the stoking of xenophobia about some of our own citizens, politicians riding in tanks, politicians wearing service uniforms even though they never served in the military themselves, posturing, pandering, and in short, everything but giving the people a true voice in their governance . . . in this context of foolishness and chicanery, the notion of having a humanistic, gentle spirit of a guitar-playing, piano-tinkling Earthmother for a leader doesn't seem that crazy after all—not so much a parody as a plea for reason, a cry for help.*

Help.
Help.
We need help—then as now. But there are no Roses to which we may turn. Only fools and hollow men.

Brian's cries for *help, help, help* yank me out of the narrative. I know by now that this is the real purpose of his manuscript, much more so than compiling a definitive biography of his favorite band—a plea for that help. To get clean. Other chapters wallow in his drug addiction, his attempts to kick, his failures.

No, rather than leave a document for historians and archivists to ponder, he's trying in this manuscript to recover his soul from a bleak, empty place that was inescapably shadowy and suffocating: a world without Jack O'Roses. A world in which someone like Rose Partland—or Nibbs Niffy—can, in an instant, simply cease to be. And in which he'd turned to palliatives and remedies that could only make matters worse, in the end, if seemingly better in the short run.

And then, the journals: why, in all that obscuring, redacting ink, are these words left for posterity to ponder: *I made the call, but I didn't call the tune.* 'Calling the tune' doesn't have anything to do with whether Sally loved him, or whether Rose lived or died.

Nibbs always wanted to call the tune.

A voice, whispering: *All roads lead to Drake Park.*

As the tragedy still played out in the news cycle, I recall Halsey's I-told-you-so headshaking after we pulled in from Indiana late the night of July 4—we'd driven across the bay bridge to a fireworks display. Nibbs had gone straight upstairs to the guest bedroom and shut the door. We wouldn't see him again for twelve hours, and then only to say goodbye.

"What. The. Fuck," my wife asked as we sat on the upper porch and looked out at the thin, pinkish band of summer light still visible on the horizon of the bay. A doe and her fawns, barely visible in the crepuscular half-light, foraged along the line of reeds next to the shore. Geese, flying over in a V. A placid antidote to what I'd suffered at Drake Park, my home, and I felt glad to be there.

"It was—hellish. The death of everything good about the scene."

Scoffing. "'The scene'."

"That was a community ripped apart, like when a fucking tornado comes through. I don't fully understand why, exactly. But it happened. *Sally*."

"I told you not to go. How—embarrassing. To be a part of such childish foolishness."

"Don't remind me."

"Poor Rose," she said, sniffling.

I described how Nibbs, a silent, quivering mass of unsettled, barely contained rage, sat in the Jetta listening to the announcement that, with Rose in the hospital 'under observation' and in 'serious but stable condition,' the final show of the tour was, by obvious necessity, to be canceled.

Nibbs, mewling and screaming epithets; how he'd pled with God to let this be but a bump in the road, and not the last Jack show ever. How Rose had one more life left in her—at least! How it couldn't be over.

"Ten years is not long enough," he kept saying, meaning how long it had been since he started seeing shows. "Ten years will not do me, Rosie. I need more." He wouldn't get it.

Did Halsey cry when Rose died that next month, in a rich person's rehab where she'd gone to kick the dust one last time? I don't remember. Like poor Nibbs, I think I've blocked certain memories out. All I remember of the day of the our Earthmother's death was buying a bottle of vodka and tonic water, listening to tapes and hearing her soul crying out in every delicate lead line, every heartfelt lyric, every gentle chord tinkled on her baby grand. Torture.

"You knew she'd keel over one of these days," Halsey said, tipping back her own cocktail, a Sea breeze heavy on the ethanol. "There were always the rumors she was back on the dust again. Now we know."

"'Now we know'," I said, mocking. "Now we don't have to wonder anymore when we'll hear that Rose died."

"Have you talked to Brian?"

"Not yet."

"Well, go and call him, Z. Call him right now."

I did. He didn't pick up. I left a message, paraphrasing my own epiphanic wisdom. *Well, now we don't have to wonder anymore when it will happen . . . now we know*. I didn't talk to Brian for some time after that. Not for some time.

I close the file and put away my dead friend's work, try to drive him from my thoughts, try to meditate on the front porch, but with birds chirping and neighborhood dogs yapping, it's no good. I'm nagged about the meaning of making a call, but not calling a tune. No matter—I won't find the answers today.

Besides, P. S. Jones is on Austin City Limits right now. Her voice and songs soothe me, like old Rosie used to. Thank god for the P. S. Joneses of the world, what few remain. They are necessary angels, these songbirds.

-12-

It's after eleven on election night, and I'm goofed on Chance nugs; Gore has his reelection in the bag—they called it only seconds after the last west coast precincts closed. Wolf Blitzer says the prevailing wisdom seems to be that, when the country's at war, you simply don't change horses in midstream. And at a mere two months past nine-eleven, we are, as they keep reminding us, engaged in the war for our culture and our lives.

I'm relieved. Anyone who Phyllis and her bible study group supports the way they supported the Bush Boys is a politician to be feared. She wouldn't look at me earlier, stomping off to bed, my father close at her heels, shaking his head and saying we'd be attacked again before the holiday season, now.

Munchified, I'm frying up a skillet of garlic, onions, peppers and mushrooms for a vegetarian Philly cheesesteak I've decided I must consume, and this despite having eaten a decent Phyllis-style home cooked meal only hours before. I'm spastic and squirrelly, making noise, dropping things, a little shaky inside, heart beating a little too hard—potent stuff, this new dope. I smoked a fat bowl, too fat. I'd been feeling anxious. Been waiting tonight for a call from Aimee that never came. Been thinking about packing up my things and moving down to Chucktown. Been getting the vibe that if I don't, soon, my dad's going to present me a bus ticket and a handshake.

"Tobey?"

I'm startled out of my skin by my father's voice. Groggy, cinching his robe, he's probably been asleep for hours by now, emerging from the gloom of the family room.

"Sorry—did I wake you?" A stupid question.

"No—I was reading. Kept smelling things." Working his eyebrows. "Wanted to make sure the house wasn't burning to the ground."

My cheeks color—their bedroom, almost directly above the front porch where I often have a quick late-night puff. "Just scrounging up a midnight snack."

He goes to the refrigerator, peers inside, selects a carton of 2% milk and pours himself a splash to wash down a few of Phyllis's ever present cookies. "Lord, but I wish she'd go back to whole milk. This tastes like dishwater."

"Better for you—milk fat clogs up the pipes."

I take a serrated knife and slice open a hoagie roll, hollow out one side and fill it with a mix of shredded cheddar and provolone, slide the bread into the toaster oven.

"What's got you so hungry this late?"

"I—don't know. Long walk today."

He stands sipping watery milk and waiting for a real answer.

"Feeling indulgent? That what you want me to say?"

"I'd like it if I were allowed to ask you something."

I set the timer to medium-dark and close the toaster door. "By all means, father."

He casts his eyes down to the tips of his slippers,

then back at me. "Are you depressed, Tobey?"

"Depressed?" Stirring my sautéed veggies one last time, turning off the burner. The smell of the natural gas always takes me back to college, to the dumpy place Nibbs lived in, the gas stove. Getting high and making food late at night. Like this. "Not as such."

"'Not as such'?"

"Not clinically. Not . . . what are you getting at?"

He seems pained. "You don't seem very motivated. Phyllis—she's concerned. And so am I."

"Concerned."

"About your future, son."

I feel ridiculous, like a teenager confronted about taking a year off before college. "Join the club."

"So if you're so concerned . . . why don't you do something about it?"

"About my future?"

"Yes."

"You want me out of here."

"No . . . but yes." He sits down at the table. "The toaster's smoking."

I panic and yank the door open—cheese is melting down onto the glowing orange coils. "*Fuck*."

"Tobey Zemp!"

I go to pull the bread out of the toaster over, in doing so burn my fingers. Crumbs and cheese everywhere. A ridiculous mess, my sandwich has become a project about which I now feel so self-conscious I want to dump the whole mess into the disposal.

"Sorry. I'll clean all this up. After I eat."

"Sorry is what you ought to be for cursing in Phyllis's kitchen—I don't want to hear any more filth out of your mouth. Do you hear me?"

"Dad—you're talking to me like I'm a child. How

old do you think I am?"

"How old are you?"

I think about this. "Thirty-six, give or take."

"And yet I'm having to talk to you like you said—as though you were still a child. How do you think that makes me feel? Son—you'll always be my child. That's simply the way of things. It's a connection that's unique, a love that can't be dimmed. One day, maybe you'll know how it feels. I never understood why you and Halsey didn't have children . . ."

"Too busy being capitalists."

Ignoring the remark. "But it's not too late for you. You have a lifetime ahead. If you want to have a life, that is. Living in your father's house, at your age, isn't a recipe for anything, though. What about that girl?"

"Aimee?"

"Yes. Aimee. She seems lovely, and sweet, and smart."

"Yes. She is all that."

He folds his hands together. "So—what do you think she sees in you?"

"What—you mean a man with no career, no ambition, living in his father's guest room off his wife's alimony, an overgrown Benjamin Braddock floating in the pool with no discernible longterm plan for his future? That type-deal?"

"Pool? What pool? Son—I can't even follow what you're saying anymore."

"Never mind."

He opens his hands. "We want you to be happy. That's all. Will that woman make you so? Will that sandwich make you happy? Or simply give you a stomachache eating it this late, or perhaps bad dreams?"

"I didn't think about the consequences. Only how it would taste."

"Consequences. Now there's a good word."

There's little more to be said, not really—nothing but empty platitudes, and reassurances that I doubt he'll buy.

I offer one anyway, a half-lie, an excuse I've been using with myself, too: "I promised Brian's mother I'd finish going through his papers. I feel . . . an obligation to that. To her. Once I'm done with that, I'm going to get moving on something. Anything. I'm thinking about getting a master's. Perhaps teaching."

"That sounds wonderful."

"Reasonable enough?"

"No," he says. "Not that part about wasting more time reading a cowardly, dead man's nonsense. But I can respect a person who keeps a commitment. To be sure."

My father gets up, creaky, and puts his glass in the sink. He turns to me, his eyes wet. He's never been much of an emotional man, not cold, but decidedly cool. In this instance, however, he comes to me, puts a warm, strong hand on my shoulder, holds my gaze. "Don't live inside this gloom. Forge your way out of the morass. Get your life started. Again."

I realize how good this advice is. How much time I squandered—not only on Halsey, but on myself. A wastrel, living on her coattails. And now, coasting along, like he said, on the words of a dead man. A man who'd been my friend, yes, who'd opened my eyes to a vast and engaging world outside my experience. But indeed, all now receding into the past. We used to joke, Nibbs and I, about getting a Doc Brown DeLorean so we could go back to experience all the classic Jack shows we'd been too young to catch; in this instance I'd rather use such a fantastic machine to skip forward a bit. See what waits for me down the road.

"All I need," I say in service to my inner thoughts, "is a destination."

"Ask God," he says. "Ask him where you should go. One way or another, you'll receive an answer."

"Sure, I'll give it a shot." I shovel steaming sandwich innards into the hoagie roll. "I'll ask the universe what it thinks I should do."

He squeezes my shoulder, as close to a hug as I'm ever likely to get. "Pose your questions, and rest easy—but arise and make it a new day for yourself. This is all that we ask."

I'm left alone, the nighttime lying heavy and sullen and still over the mess by which I've so besmirched Phyllis's kitchen—the indulgence of my late night sandwich-makings begs attention, and so with quiet deliberateness I wrap up the sandwich to save for lunch, clean the toaster and countertops and the sink, and quite pointedly ask no questions of anyone, much less the universe.

In bed, finally, I drift off dreaming not of my troubles, but instead only of indescribable and glorious music, of strolling a great meadow and hearing a voice from on high calling to me toward a towering stage and PA stacks covered in tie-dye and a million F-Kids, grooving and in the moment and fully alive—the voice is not of God, not of the universe, but of Rose Partland, and as always I dream yearning with the singular maddening notion that *if only if only if only I could remember and sing this music in the light of day, oh! All would be forgiven and all would be made right.*

But morning is full only of birdsong, until of course I put on the first show of the day, a Rose funk-rocker from the late 70s.

I sit down with steaming coffee to email Aimee, in whose direction I believe I've been aimed—whether caused by overactive gonads or cosmic intervention, the one idea I feel I can grab ahold of is that she's where I need to be. Universe, make it so, if you'd be so kind. Let her be the real deal.

–13–

I shouldn't have had such anxiety—a few minutes after sending a mushy, whiny email, Aimee calls me, sounding bright and cheerful and happy, and wondering when we can next see each other. I tell her I have nothing but time, and we make plans for dinner later tonight, at D'Alessandro's.

I do take my father's advice, however, so far as to go early to Columbia and meet with a financial advisor, to at last discuss how best to invest and protect what monies I have at my disposal, which is substantial enough an amount, but not eff-you forever money, especially not if I'm going to buy a house or a condo somewhere and put down a reasonable down payment.

The enthusiastic young man, an overfed whiteboy a couple of years out of the frathouse named Seth Lachicotte, gelled of hair and reeking of some obnoxious men's fragrance leeching from the stiff starched color of his Ralph Lauren shirt, keeps yammering about future income, and I have to remind him that there isn't any, not yet.

"Okay okay, once you get your career back on track and you know what you've got coming in to work with, the question is, how well do you want to live? With the money you've got right now, I can point you in the direction of investments," Seth says, lowering his voice, "that can have some truly stupendous rewards, but those are the risky ones. This is a nest egg you have here, but it could be a whole henhouse, if you get my drift, whether you get a job someplace or not."

"How *well* do I want to live?" I consider this. With Halsey, I was living about as well as anyone needs to, and it was as empty as any experience I've had. "What does 'well' mean?"

"That's what I'm sayin'," he says, laughing, adjusting the bluetooth in his ear. "That's the central question of our times, friendo. You could go buy yourself a camper and live in the woods and grow your own tomatoes and, you know, live for a long time off what you have. Sure. If that's what anybody would want to do, which it ain't. That much I can tell you with a certain degree of certainty, Mr. Z. Or you can invest wisely now, and build on it once you have a regular income again. But for now, you can do a lot with this money. Trust me."

I leave after deciding to park most of the money in a CD, which leaves Seth enervated and disappointed, but also granting that, in a world where nine-elevens can happen—the stock market was closed for days afterward while the pile still smoldered, and had required mechanisms to kick in to keep from tumbling thousands of points upon reopening—the safer bet was sometimes a wise enough choice for an investor like me.

"Like me?"

"Someone without clearly defined wealth goals." All traces of his good humor seem to have vanished—his is now an air of disapproval. "Not an easy task to advise someone in that—position."

I don't blame him for being disappointed. For

a man whose next money is coming from god-knows-where, however, the safest place short of a mattress or rusty Folger's can buried in my father's back yard will have to do for these pecuniary spoils of my defunct relationship with the fair-haired Miss Halsey Bedrich.

I meet Aimee for our early-bird special dinner at Tony D'Alessandro's family's Italian joint, and while the food and wine are excellent, dinner and our stroll afterwards isn't that fun—Aimee's nervous and withdrawn and crabby, which she attributes to girly trouble. I think it's more, somehow, but I can't put my finger on what on earth it could be.

-14-

Over the next couple of weeks Aimee and I spend oodles of time together: Movies, intimate dinners enjoyed while tucked into the corners of sushi joints and tapas bars, taking in a local theatre production of a recent Edward Albee play, walks along the riverfront trail by her apartment complex. Handholding. Whispers. Smooches, and trips around bases. Aimee, encouraging me whenever I talk about getting another college degree, in expanding my horizons rather than looking for a cubbyhole in which to while away the workday.

Today, on a bright, crisp autumn Saturday only days before Thanksgiving, we've embarked on an easy hiking excursion through the Congaree Swamp National Park, an old-growth nature preserve twenty miles southeast of Redtails Stadium, on the other side of the beltway. We've left the boardwalk for a looping trail set amidst bald cypress and champion gum trees, river birch, tupelo, ash, and loblolly pines almost as big as the redwood trunks I'd once seen in Muir Woods north of San Francisco. An ancient stillness exists in this place, one that instills the same sense of peace in my soul—that, and Aimee's presence, which seems a gift.

As we stroll through shafts of sunlight we talk about Nibbs, and how I'm no longer reading. Instead, I'm putting my time into researching the idea of grad school at Southeastern—but not to get an MBA or some related accounting nonsense: as I'd once planned, I want to get a degree in English, a course of study that, on my father's advice, had been abandoned, a major like that of my best friend—Brian and I became fast friends not only because of Jack O'Roses but also because we were both bookish, articulate middle class kids who'd gone to decent high schools with engaged literature teachers. On many a stoned afternoon we talked not about Rose and Jake and the boys, but Kurt Vonnegut, Henry Miller, Tom Robbins, the Beats, an absurdist debut novel he loved by some guy I'd never heard of named David Foster Wallace.

"I've wanted to write a great novel for a long time," Brian told me one smoky, hazy night in his dorm room.

"So why don't you?"

"Because I haven't lived a great life yet, don't know what I want to say, et cetera et cetera et cetera. Soon enough, spud."

I've let Aimee read select bits of Brian's manuscript and other documents like his account of Drake Park, and as we stroll and commune with nature, she questions me—again—about the sordid details of that misbegotten weekend from hell. "You say his is a reasonable account of that day. What's with the weasel word?"

"Weasel word?"

"'Reasonable'?"

A fast shrug of my bony shoulders.

"Okay—so when are you going to tell me what really happened?"

"When I figure it out, I'll let you know." *When I call the tune, the one Brian missed.* "Instead of Drake Park, why don't I tell you a different story . . ."

A little smile. "Ventura? That's the other big one you've been saving."

She knows her Z-shorthand: Ventura equals heaven, Drake Park the simmering bowels of hell.

Before I begin, Aimee pauses, a finger to her lips—she's peering through a small set of birding binoculars, searching for the source of nearby chirping and tweeting. "I can't find who that is singing to us. Where are you . . .?" She finally spots a wren flitting happily around. Satisfied, she touches my arm and we continue walking.

I give her the shorthand version of my Jack shows leading up to Ventura: the Redtails Stadium gig, on the tour that summer after they'd their first hit record since the early days—'Came a Day.' How the tours and shows got so much bigger than they'd been throughout the early 80s; how the older tour veterans called all the new people like me 'daytrippers,' an insult one notch above 'tourist.'

"Rather than some relic of a touring act that a few thousand burnt-out hippies followed around, in the course of a season Jack became the biggest party around. That's the way they'd sold it on MTV that summer right before I first saw them, a live broadcast from the Meadowlands about a week before they played Redtails Stadium. 'Came a Day' was on the radio every time you turned it on—Jack became hip. Hip enough that I went and bought a ticket, my first."

"Everybody loved that song—I remember catching my pop singing along to it in his truck, and that's a man who hates rock and roll."

"True—a top ten, four-wall hit record. Check.

But the thing was, for me it wasn't the song: after the assassination attempt and the health scare, well, it was like Rose had come back from the other side. Nibbs Niffy made me understand that people like me were now given a chance to get on board."

I get a catch in my throat as I relate how Nibbs had sold the idea to me: "Like God wanted to make sure Rose lived long enough to get one more generation hooked on Jack O'Roses, and all the joy and freedom the band had to offer. To make sure it stuck, as Brian put it."

"That's a bit of a stretch, isn't it? God being interested in the Jack O'Roses legacy?"

"Exactly—it's hard for me to imagine God being interested in much of anything we ants are pursuing down here, but a romantic, mystical notion nonetheless.

"So anyway, by the spring of '89 I'd been with Brian to maybe a half-dozen shows, nearby tour stops like Greensboro and Atlanta, and all the way down to St. Pete for a two-night run in a small arena there. All good fun, all mindblowing, but I was lacking something critical, as Nibbs so astutely pointed out, which was a West Coast run—the Earth-motherland, as he called California."

I tell her how excited I was when we mail ordered for Ventura, which was a three-day weekend in June at the County Fairgrounds, my first trip out west for any reason, much less a stand of Jack shows. How my Dad raised holy hell about all this concert-going with 'those people,' as he referred to the tribe. How I didn't care.

Details: flying into LAX and renting the car and being talked into a red convertible by the perky blonde rental agent, and then the drive up the PCH following a stony afternoon at Venice Beach, where we hung with some real hardcore travelers—bus people living off the grid, as much as one can while riding around in a vehicle that requires fossil fuels to run. They became our best friends for a few hours, after which we made our way up the coast to the guys we were staying with in Oxnard, a few clicks south of Ventura.

“So those were some real followers?”

I nod. “I mentioned to Nibbs how cool those cats were at the beach and all, but he just said that we were nothing but custies to them.”

“Custies? What the hell is that?”

“There’s a school of thought that divides the family—the F-kid family—into two main subsets: Custies, and, well, Family. The old, you’re either one of us type-deal, or you’re them: a custie—as in customer.”

Aimee gets it—authentic F-Kids versus Tourists. “So by then, what were you?”

“Which was I? You tell me.” I’m not sure I ever felt quite like Family, in the capital-F sense, not in the bus-people sense. Didn’t necessarily look the look, didn’t talk the talk. Nibbs, either, at least until he let his hair and beard grow out. “We were in with the tapers, a completely different breed in themselves.”

“Did those family-people make you feel like—oh, what is it. Fellow travelers?”

I get her reference: sympathizers, but without the bona fides. “I thought some of that Family shit was more affected than genuine anyway—a goodly number of those folks were what we called trustafarians, prep school refugees loosed upon the land with daddy’s platinum card fronting the tour for them.”

“True elitists, then. The trusties versus the custies,” she says with a giggle. “That’s the way it was in the 60s, too, you know—how many of those who became hippies and radicals did so because they had Daddy’s money to fall back on?”

I don't know, and tell her so—I was born in 1970, after all. But I can well imagine the phenomenon—from what I know, poor kids got scooped up and sent off to fight in Vietnam, not tune in and drop out.

We stop so that Aimee can take a photograph of an enormous tree felled sometime in the past, "probably by Hurricane Hugo fifteen years ago," she informs, which of course I remember in vivid detail—Brian and I ate mushrooms that night and watched the campus get blown to hell by the monstrous, historic storm.

I tell Aimee about the guys we stayed with in Oxnard all weekend, who turned out to be what I would call *ubër*-tapers, gearheads wielding an unbelievable stash of topflight recording equipment: not one, but *two* state of the art Sony D-10 DAT decks, microphones by Schoeps, analog to digital converters, and custom-built, shielded cables that cost "more per foot than you want to know," as I was told by Brian's friend Chico, a middle-aged real estate attorney who was manic about the whole process of recording the shows—"archiving" them, as he put it.

"The other dude, Bates Mahoney, but who called himself 'Country Gravy'—a great fucking road name, I must admit—also had the best pot I'd ever smoked, at least from what I remember."

A pedantic digression goes on for a few moments about tapers and gear, until I realize that this is what would preoccupy Nibbs about such a narrative, not me. Aimee herself notes that this digression is making The Ventura Story seem like all preamble, and little story.

"So, after many adventures on the beach all afternoon, he elides in one felled swoop, we're inside and the band finally comes out, bravely, I might add, since the stage faces the setting sun. Rose had on dark glasses, and a flowing tie-dyed dress. I had this weird visual tic going—the sunlight was reflecting into my eyes off the frame of my own shades, this strange sensation that I kept noticing, until finally I took them off . . . and realized that I was starting to really, really trip hard. I mean, coming on *heavy*." A shudder creeps up and down my back. "I'd really gotten puddled."

Aimee snorts with laughter. "Excuse me?"

I hold out a cupped hand, lower my voice. "Liquid LSD—a big blue glurt someone I didn't even know gave me for free. I slurped it right up."

"Jesus—sounds dangerous."

"Yeah. Maybe. But he was good people. He was family. Country Gravy vouched for him, and that'd been good enough for Nibbs Niffy. So anyway, this is heavy stuff, I'd taken more than I'd ever tried, and in a small, troubling manner, on the inside I was starting to freak.

"I verbalized this fact in a series of grunts and clicks and hand gestures, which Nibbs understood with perfect clarity, allaying all fears and concerns: He talked me down, as much as he could, by discussing what they might play. He had his little setlist bible he carried around, sat studying it like it was the book of Revelations, like guessing what they'd play was his equivalent of the opening of the Seventh Seal. Ever the statistician, ever the librarian, that was Nibbs. To me it didn't matter that much what they played—at that point there were still plenty of songs I hadn't yet seen them do, so it wasn't hard to impress me.

"He pressed me for what I thought they'd open with—trying to get me to call the tune—so I rattled off the first four songs that came to mind, the four most recent ones that'd been running through my head. I didn't think about what was possible, only what I wanted to hear. And he laughed. Nibbs laughed at my picks, a couple of which were rarities.

"'Dream on,' he said. No way would they play those tunes."

"Oh—you guessed right?"

"Yes: one-two-three-four, right out of the gate, one of which, 'Day Without a Daydream,' hadn't been played for over six years. You want to talk calling the tune. Ho ho," I said, puffing out my chest and clomping around in a martial strut on the path, "if I wasn't Family before, I was then."

"Impressive."

"But the music, it began to matter less *what* than *how*, and seemed both transportive, but also tangential to the meat of the experience—I thought I knew what being high was, but before this trip, I hadn't known squat. My view of the concert stage was from within this sweeping, circular vortex of color and image, with the band at its center, and Rose herself at a different kind of center, simply radiated energy, a kind of purple, crackling light. The banners that hung behind the band that summer were moving ever-so-slightly in the ocean breeze . . . or perhaps not moving at all. I perceived the musicians as standing at the front of a great, infinite hallway lined with those tie-dye banners rippling gently in the air.

"And at the end of that hallway was a tiny pinpoint of light—probably a reflection off LeMoy's bass drum, or a mic stand, but to me that was the beginning of life, the secret to it all: That little inkling of starlight winking at me delivered huge, revelatory epiphanies, a thousand of them every second, and every second lasting a thousand lifetimes. I thought I was a hundred feet tall, looking down on the band. I thought—"

She grabs my hand, squeezes tight. "What?"

I thought I'd departed my physical self and

become a being capable of unlimited, infinite movement, existing in simultaneous harmonic convergence with every atom of the entire known universe—with no agenda, mind you, no sense of purpose or self. Not like being God. But to know how it must feel. Infinite sight, and infinite insight as well . . . a word came to me, and it formed in the sky over the stage, and I yelped and jumped and reached for it as it reached for me. The word was 'all,' in great pillowy letters. ALL."

Aimee pulls away and performs a spooky, trippy dance along the path. "Hoo-doggie—that sure was some dose you got."

"Yes. But then—"

"Let me guess: You actually levitated and touched the hem of the great floating 'ALL'?"

I chuckle. "No—the first set ended, and the harsh hot stadium lights ringing the fairgrounds came up. And I found myself wrenched back into a tactile and present reality, one wherein I found myself tripping balls." We both explode with laughter. "It was kind of grim—until Rose came back onstage. Once the music began again, I felt safe. Had a blast—like I was coasting on air. So, yeah. Levitating, in a way."

I remember the comfort I felt when the lights fell and the band came back out. How they played a long and dreamy second set. How I felt cradled in the arms of the music, breathing in the salt air and sensing minute vibrations caused by both the waves lapping against the beach a hundred yards away, and the multitude of swirling and dancing feet. A newborn, resting my head on the Earthmother's ample tie-dyed breasts, drinking of her. The starlight-child.

I describe all this as best I can, and conclude thusly: "I saw another forty or fifty shows between Ventura and Drake Park, but never another like that.

The feeling stayed with me through that weekend, and the rest of the summer. After that trip, everything looked different. By the time I went with Nibbs to the RFK Stadium gig later in the tour, I knew I was home, a feeling that carried me a long time."

"Until Drake Park?"

"Drake Park was like being cast out of the garden."

"Z—you're crying."

"So I am," I note in a flat voice. "Errant tears sneaking out of their confinement, is all."

She puts her arms around me. "Let's head back."

We get Cokes and a packet of Nekot cookies from a vending machine in the ranger station, and linger for a few minutes to experience the nocturnal personality of the swamp beginning to emerge—a whippoorwill sings mournful somewhere out on the oxbow lake a few hundred yards into the park, where earlier we'd seen a noble alligator cruising along the placid, opaque surface of the water; I could swear I hear an owl hooting, but Aimee says it's something else.

We hold hands on the twenty-minute drive back into Columbia, a journey that takes us past the dark and looming structure of the venue in which I'd first seen the band—as we pass by Redtails Stadium, a dark silhouette of concrete and steel against the lavender sky, I hold up a hand in salutation, a power-fist of acknowledgement, the place where it all began.

I catch a glimpse of the structure again in the rearview mirror, and then I take Aimee back to her apartment on the river, where, for the first time, I am asked if I'd like to spend the night. I would like this very much, I tell her, and so I do.

Sitting in Aimee's apartment the night before Thanksgiving, a show spins quietly in the background, a delicate sequence of guitar interplay between Rose and Jake from late 1974. The music—a conversation between old friends, lovers, even—is patient and relaxed; themes are suggested and explored, drifting elegant and unhurried until segueing into a structured tune, this low-key choice a perfect accompaniment for an evening of tender embrace following our meal of take-out Chinese and Sauvignon Blanc, and also provides a lovely accompaniment to our lovemaking.

Across the Congaree River, rocky and low in this dry season of ours, the modest cityscape of downtown Columbia twinkles. I've been all but staying here with her for the last two weeks—a new phase. I've yet to compose that résumé, however. Nobody's pushing me to—I don't see my father or Phyllis very much. By design.

As the CD fades out and silence descends, we lie together in the damp afterglow of what was a moderately successful adventure in intimacy—Aimee, apologetic, has already explained that she's always had a hard time. With apologies to *Annie Hall*, maybe I'll suggest smoking a bowl beforehand. Always seemed to help Halsey, who also has difficulty in achieving release.

"That was—lovely." She strokes my belly just above the tree line. "You feel so good. But—"

I tense up—her words sound like the run-up to: *But I don't want to get serious with anyone right now, not on the rebound, not for the wrong reasons.* "Oh, shit."

"It's just . . . I keep having this strange guilt."

"Guilt? I thought you said it was a clean break."

"Yeah, no—not about my ex."

It doesn't take me long to figure it out. My cheeks get warm. "Brian . . .?"

She doesn't answer—she doesn't have to.

I sit up on the edge of the bed, my back to her. "How do you think I feel? This whole nightmare—his mother thinks I was his best friend, when all I did was make life worse for him."

My voice breaks at the end, and in that moment I realize I've never cried for Brian. Maybe for Nibbs, but not for Brian. And yet—the tears still refuse to come.

Aimee sits up, draws me close, puts a cool cheek against my center of my back, her long hair tickling my ribs. "Z, I love being with you, but is this just a way for us to feel better? If not about Brian, then . . . what? After all, we are the rebound twins. That's dangerous."

"Hush your mouth—I feel a real connection with you. And I don't say that lightly—it hasn't happened too often for me. Maybe—maybe not at all."

"Same here, angel."

She touches my face. We kiss, long and loving.

"So," she asks. "You want to try?"

I think about all the implications of the question: the permutations of *try*, the layered and diverse tapestry of possibility inherent in the simple word. "To do what, exactly?"

Her hand slides down my stomach. "Again," she says, demure. "You want to try . . . again?"

And so that is what we do, this time with better results—a new angle, Aimee in control, grinding, her jaw set and back arched. Crying out, collapsing. Success.

The next thing I notice is the gray light beginning to creep in through the blinds, and then it's another Thanksgiving Day, a holiday celebrating family and the land of plenty, one on which I feel happier—indeed, more thankful—than I have in a long time.

THIRD SET

Day Without a Daydream
(Partland/Sobel/Pullen/LeMoy/McKellan,
©1974 JOR EL Publishing)

Point me to the Fountain
Point me to the riverbank
We took the ferry
And a couple of Bloody Marys we drank
My mind was blank . . .

It's a day without a daydream
The day the world was spun
It's a clock without a face
The day two became one

I ran to the almond tree
When your distress call came to me
You were wrapped up in certainty
They pulled curtain back for me to see
So much to see . . .

It's a day without a daydream
A loss of symmetry
It's a clock without a face
The day two became three

Outside the hydrant's sprayin' water in the street
Don't look down now—there's air beneath your feet
Three days and thirty years got thirty lashes, and some
tears
So many, many tears . . .

–1–

This otherwise ordinary December weekday finds the headlines again screaming, the cable pundit shows in overdrive, the country now in a celebratory mood that goes beyond the mere enjoyment of the first holiday season since nine-eleven—we've already received a present, a gift that feels like victory, like vindication:

BIN LADEN CAPTURED ALIVE
IN AFGHANISTAN BY SPECIAL OPS—
No Americans Killed in Raid on Compound

A huge victory in Gore's new War on Terror. The perp's now being held somewhere and sweated down, I assume, by some tough, tough hombres. Score for us, with broader war now likely averted.

The Limbaughs and Karl Roves and Vice Presidential candidate Dick Cheneys of the world had predicted this would come before the election, to ensure Gore's heroic status and high approval ratings, but it didn't, not for another month. On a Monday morning, no less, first thing while we were all sipping our coffee and rattling our Post & Courier and ignoring each other at the breakfast table.

Top of the news cycle—like nine-eleven had

been. They really know how to play this stuff. Almost like show business.

Even bigger: The President, it's reported, is to make a speech, controversial and earthshaking, that leaked copies of which acknowledge that the actions of terrorists like Usama Bin Laden have their roots not simply in purely ideological and fanatic terms, but in large part due to our own incursions into their world in the name of profit, in the name of petroleum, in the name of a hegemony that is "no more our birthright than it was any other nation in the history of the world whose influence began to spill over its borders," as he plans to say. "Nine-eleven, we now are beginning to realize, was the event that needed to happen if we are to not simply prosper, but survive both the end of fossil fuels, as well as the damage caused by their use."

Whoa. Sea-change.

And then, more boilerplate Gore talk that we've all been hearing since '99: renewable energy, a Manhattan Project style scientific push on fuel cells and fission and yadda yadda—that part we're used to hearing out of him. Big talk; hot air. None of it will come to pass. He's owned by the petrochemical giants, like they all seem to be. And by they, I mean we, of course.

True or not, I have to admit that Gore has turned in a performance that inspires confidence, feels like change. When was the last time anyone could say that about our ostensible leaders?

Somebody's going to shoot this guy.

On leadership: What can we say about Rose Partland, the F-Kids' 'reluctant avatar?' As Nibbs quotes Rose herself as saying, of her bandmates and I think, maybe, of all of us in the audience as well:

"I couldn't lead anyone anywhere—the people

who'd follow me already know me too well, that the only place I'd lead them would be in a circle, from here to there and back again. But remember, like the man says, the journey itself is the reward . . . the journey's all we got, man."

We are a couple. I've all but moved in. Introduced as 'the boyfriend,' now. Me likey.

I'm so bona-fide, in fact, that I'm being paraded in front of Aimee's family—I've been talked into spending Christmas Eve and part of the Day itself in the mountains of western North Carolina. Why not?

Christmas Eve is charming and fun at Aimee's childhood home, what had once been little more than a mountain cabin. Tucked well off the highway on a winding road that turned to dirt before we finally got to the property, the cabin's a structure that through the decades has been augmented, updated, repainted, repaired and otherwise mutated into a comfortable, large residence.

As we pull up the steep driveway, a light snow is falling, a magical sight to a lifelong, low country South Carolinian. Maybe I should move to the mountains—very different up here from what I'm used to.

"If you need me to translate," she tells me as we get out of the car, "just touch the side of you nose or wink or something."

"Translate?"

"Took me forever to get rid of that accent . . . you'll see."

She isn't kidding. I can understand her folks quite well—for the most part—but some cousins and uncles speak in a rumbling deep-Appalachian patois that's at times damn near impenetrable. I manage to muddle through without winking or touching, though I squirm uncomfortably under the questioning of her father and an older brother, working men who seem suspicious of this gentle-voiced, smooth-handed, unemployed college boy.

The menfolk stand around outside, me braced against the chill while a couple of young kids build a pyramid of kindling in a fire pit out behind the house, on a rise overlooking a scenic valley—how wonderful it must have been to grow up here, I think, but Aimee claims that its dullness and isolation all but made her suffer social anxiety.

"We never much cared f'that other one," her brother says of Aimee's even-more college boy of an ex. "Like he always talkin' down to all us."

"Well, you won't get that from me." I play up my Charleston drawl. "I'm as southern as they come—listen to me."

The question asked next is the tough one. "So, what line you in, Mr. Zemp?"

"I'm—in a transition phase."

"Do what?"

Aimee's brother laughs, as do I—turns out it is they who need the translator, not me. He puts his free hand—the one not holding a PBR tallboy—on my shoulder, a brotherly gesture. He's a beanpole like Aimee. They could be twins but for the age difference, him somewhere north of forty. "I'm guessing he means he's in-between vocations. Beau—I been there."

"I used to work for my wife, and once we split up . . . new career track, as-yet determined. I might be heading to grad school, get into a new line."

Her brother grunts, smokes, nods. "You out to make an honest woman of my sister?"

"Depends—is she dishonest?"

"Highly doubt it," Aimee's father says. "Thing is, I just hate to see her make another mistake with some freeloading good-time Charlie from up yonder at that university. Especially this quick."

Gulp. "We're just . . . friends. Good friends. I've coming off my own bad trip." I regret the word choice. "I mean—bad marriage. We're trying to take things slowly," a bald and brazen lie if there'd ever been one.

"Well, I just hope you ain't planning on just living off her. That's all I care about. I can't," *cain't*, "stand the thought of no peckerhead taking advantage of my girl."

I'm starting to take umbrage. "Aimee's a good friend. That's the important part to me."

"So's you keep saying." Her brother kills the beer, chucks the can into a rusty 55-gallon trash drum. "Hope you ain't full of beans."

I'm let off the hook when some old timers pull out bluegrass instruments and proceed to rip it up for an hour or two. Clear liquor is shared by nearly all standing around the fire but Aimee and myself. I know almost every tune they do. Rose would be pleased.

We sit down to a traditional dinner, exchange gifts, and I endure small talk and questions and suspicious looks from the older relatives. Aimee herself seems anxious about getting going, and after consulting with me, ditches the plan to stay until Christmas morning. Her mother seems downright weepy that we're not staying the night. But Aimee insists, and we saddle up and head all the way back home, a drive on which she explains that, as a divorced woman with a new boyfriend in tow, she had to endure too much of a grilling to relax and enjoy herself, and honestly began to feel that she couldn't breathe there in her own childhood home.

I apologize for adding to the stress, but she holds my hand and insists that she's not keen on those family gatherings anyway. Only one more to go in Edgewater County, and then we'll be free of familial obligation—we have shows in our future, after all: Jake Sobel's band Pallet Jack, playing a New Years run at the Fox Theatre in Atlanta—a show! We're going to a show!

–2–

Of course, my own relatives asking for details about the Halsey situation isn't much more attractive than Aimee's grilling from her people, and it is I who suffer through Christmas Day on Shady Lane in Tillman Falls.

The Zemp household, warm and alive with folks and relations milling around munching on finger foods, though for once it's thankfully not Phyllis and the assorted members of her bible group, a set of people with whom I've managed to avoid interacting. Everyone tells me I look like I've put on weight; an elderly aunt says both Aimee and I look 'peaked,' that it worries her to death the way young people like us sit tap-tapping in front of those computers all day long.

I have to admit that by contrast Lil, my long-lost citygirl sister, looks hale and hearty and years younger than her early 40s. As a younger sibling, I watched Lil put my father through his paces as something of a teenaged wildcat party girl, though she settled down and did well in school and career. Not the black sheep, no; for this we have another candidate.

She's with a beau I don't seem to know, another in an apparent series, she whispers, a handsome character tanned and toothy, and whose cashmere sweater and slacks have the cut and drape of clothing much more expensive than anything I've ever owned. Since she's in publishing I make him for a writer, but it turns out his is a trade no more glamorous than that of a dentistry practice, albeit an upmarket Manhattan one—Mary Tyler Moore is a patient, he says, and he once had the honor of doing emergency root canals on both Henry Kissinger, as well as former UN Secretary General Boutros Boutros-Ghali. I feel like I've met a real rock star.

While I fill her in on my non-life since the divorce a season ago, Lil greedily inhales carcinogens on the screened back porch. We lament how we barely talk anymore; I point out that we never really had. Lil's a private person, not close to the family. Like me, in other words, only a slightly older version.

I'm shivering—it seems colder down here than in the mountains. "Aren't you chilly?"

"Back home I have to smoke up on a fucking thirtieth-floor balcony," she says, waving her cigarette around. "This's nothing."

"So, how's publishing? Things happening for you?"

"A dying business; a dinosaur. But they need me, because I know how to sell these things. In fact, I'm being wooed right now by Knopf, but keep that on the q-t."

"Who would I tell?" I hug myself against the nip in the air. "Full of secrets, you are."

She brays obnoxious laughter. "If only it were that dramatic."

"You don't even sound like yourself anymore. You know that?"

"You know how it is for Southerners, especially in a place like the city. As though we've an inherent deficiency . . . as though we're corn-pone stereotypes like in some movie. Sometimes when I've had a few too many, a 'y'all' will slip out, and it just mortifies me."

"That's silly."

"You have to be careful—coming from South Carolina, people have preconceived notions."

I can't disagree. We did start the Civil War, after all.

I ask about nine-eleven, where she was that morning; she holds up a hand. "I can't think about that day—the smoke. The people walking uptown, quiet, all covered in dust. Like a zombie movie. I saw the tower come down."

"We all did. What do you think happened?"

"What is there to think about? Those fucking fascist towelheads attacked us. I hope they're sticking hot pokers in Bin Laden's eyes right now."

I ask if it's that simple; she replies that if Gore hadn't stolen the election in 2000, that none of this would have happened, and now that he's back in office it'll probably happen again.

You know what they say about politics and religion in otherwise cordial conversations, so I change the subject by going on to tell her about Aimee, how lovely our relationship is so far, also about how the split with Halsey was definitely the best outcome.

"There was a third party. That I didn't know about until afterwards."

"Ah. Ouch."

"Yes—I've had a few shocks this year."

"Aw," my empathetic sister says. "Phyllis told me about your friend Brian. What happened?"

"Ate some pills, drank some booze, didn't wake up. Like fucking Jimi or Janis. Classic." I realize how bitter I sound. "A damn shame. A huge waste."

"He do it on purpose?"

I shrug—the last place I want to go right now is a discussion about how I'd scoured his papers for an answer. I'd rather talk Bush v. Gore again. "He was depressed. But I don't know. No one does."

"So . . . what now?" Lil's always made me feel guilty about my apparent lack of motivation to do something—anything—of note with my life. "Did you get anything out of all those years you put into Halsey's stores?"

"Oh, sure. I can coast for quite a while."

"Especially living here for free."

"True that."

Without asking, without self consciousness, I pull out my trusty Sneak-a-Toke™, a small golden bullet of a pipe with a rubber stopper to insulate tender lips from hot metal. Watching over my shoulder, I fire up a quick hit, and drop the self-contained pipe back into my pocket.

"Jesus—are you smoking dope? *Right here on Alston and Phyllis's back porch*?"

"You're standing there smoking *your* weed. Where's the harm?"

Smiling cruelly. "No wonder you don't have a job."

I sneak another toke. My dry mouth crackles. My eyes feel swollen. I'm high for real. Feels good. "It's not this. It's that . . . I don't have a job because . . ." I adopt a Jeff Spicoli cadence. "Because I don't, like, have one, not that I got like fired for being *stoned*, dude . . . what were we talking about?"

Lil busts a gut, hugs me, turns motherly. "Just be careful. It's still illegal, even in New York—especially since nine-eleven. Used to be you could walk around the village sharing a joint, and nobody gave a crap. No more." She casts a furtive glance inside. "Here, give me a quick hit on that."

Pleased, I hand her the pipe. "Hit her easy. It's packed to the hilt."

She inhales; her eyes grow wide and she coughs. "Holy crap—that tastes like the real deal. Here, one's plenty."

She hands me the pipe back, and it goes into my pocket glowing warm against my thigh. "It's good. Maybe too good . . ."

"Now you tell me." She lights a fresh tobacco stick. "So anyway, if you're going to stay here in the South, why not back home in Charleston? Or Atlanta—Atlanta's *hot*. Did you know Elton John lives there now?"

"Elton *John?* What that hell does he live in Atlanta for?"

"Big gay scene," she says with mild incredulity, as though I should be on top of such hipster knowledge.

"As it turns out, we're going to Atlanta for New Year's."

"Really? For an interview?"

"No—Jake's playing the Fox. Feel compelled to go, for some reason."

"Who the fuck is Jake?"

Most outsiders—the great unwashed—are quick to associate the iconic Rose with the band, but have little idea of the other members' names. I explain about Jake Sobel and his side project—now his only project—and about how I really need a taste of that old magic, if it's still out there.

She rolls her eyes. "What, going 'on tour' again? I thought you grew out of that."

"I did," a frank admission. "But you know, it's for Brian. I want to go for him. I know he'd have been there at these shows, and if I go, maybe a little bit of him will be there."

"Mystical. Heavy. Groovy, brother." She mimes the toking of a joint. "Wow . . . say, gimme another hit on that thingy."

"Asshole."

"I wasn't kidding—c'mon, give me another quick taste."

As she smokes again, this time with more caution, my sister launches into a monologue about this acid casualty of a homeless person she sees on the walk every morning into her building on Sixth Avenue, some old timer with bare crusty feet who always wears a tattered Jack shirt, singing quietly to himself as he shakes a Styrofoam cup for spare change from those inclined to indulge such pitiful behavior.

"I used to worry about you, that you'd end up on the street somewhere like one of those people. I was glad when you grew out of it," she says. "Acid's bad news—look where it got your friend."

"Not acid—Brian, like Rose, got into the wrong drugs, the wrong headspace. Tripping at a Jack show was the only truly spiritual experience I've ever had."

"Heavy," she smiles. "And totally totally groovy. But still just a rock band. Not worth giving up your life for. Somebody should've told your boy that."

Adrenaline squirts into my gut. My heart thuds, heavy with grief and guilt. "I suppose they should've."

Britt, her charming suitor, emerges out on the porch with a cocktail in his hand, but from living with my pious family I know he must surely have brought the liquor himself. "Monty, baby, your dad's ready to serve dinner. Don't want to miss the blessing," he says, stopping in his tracks. "Holy moses—smells like I'm the one missing out on something."

"I didn't think I ought to come grab you."

"*You fuck-king cunt*," he sings, and they both explode with laughter. "One quick taste, if I may."

I produce the implement and he smiles in recognition. "Ah, fantastic! I had one of these in college." Knows what to do. Hits, a little too hard. Coughs. "Christ Jesus." He hits it again and asks through a strangulated voice, "Anybody got a sugar-free breath mint?"

I offer him a packet of Listerine tabs I keep handy. My tummy rumbles. "Let's go eat."

Before she slips inside, I grab my sister Lilliana Montgomery Zemp's arm. "'Monty'?"

She shrugs. "It's what they call me back home."

Well, well—another sneaky little name-switcher in the family, but she'll always be Lil to me. Now I understand the desire on the part of my father and stepmother to cling to 'Tobey'—there's a comfort in familiarity.

Harshing my mellow, inside Britt drapes a cashmere tree limb around my neck, and asks in a stoney, stentorian voice that booms out hollow in the cavernous two-story great room of the Zemp manse, "So, Ashton—I understand you're between gigs. What line of work you planning to get yourself into, my man?"

A hush drops; all eyes turn to us. Aimee looks at me with her own intimate brand of curious anticipation.

I clear my throat and say the first word that comes to mind: "Plastics."

Britt cocks his head like a dog. "Plastics?"

"Plastics—it's the next big thing."

A murmuring sweeps through the family, a wave-ripple of approbatory head-nodding. "Go get 'em, Tobey," an uncle calls out.

"Mm," Britt says, contemplative, clearly not that familiar with *The Graduate*, which'd sucked me in on

TCM yet again last week. Sounding like a politician on the stump, he continues, “Long as you have a direction—it’s a new age in our country. This is no time to not know who we are.”

–3–

Christmas is over, and I'm sitting alone in this Aimee's apartment, scratching down thoughts in my notebook, scribblings that lead nowhere and seem to mean nothing. Trying my hand at a poem; trying to write a short story, about two guys on tour following a Jack O'Roses-like rock band, but the characters just seem like Nibbs Niffy and Z, which offers me no particular insight into either of us, living, or dead.

I look for inspiration: I spin a hot show of what they call primal Jack O'Roses, the 60s flowering of freeform psychedelia—Rose is leading the band in a stunning, swirling jam, deep within one of those spaces they created at the Fillmore East or West. Gorgeous, then frightening, then resolving again into melody, and another style altogether, one of Skutch's thirty minute R&B rave-ups, climaxed to a thunderous conclusion. They are LEGENDS of rock, I think, like on the VH1 documentaries about the classic behemoth acts, the Floyds, the Stones, the Who, the Beatles, and Jack.

After the live album made some noise in 1969 they toured relentlessly, straying from their mainstays of San Francisco and New York, playing colleges and becoming etched, indelibly, in the minds of many with the times, and the vibe, and the whole freespirited, stoned era.

But the iconoclasm of the South from which Jake and Rose had come would be as crucial to this band as the San Francisco LSD scene: As Nibbs—Brian—writes in his manuscript, once he finally stopped writing about himself and got around to telling the history of the band, in about chapter eight or so:

[. . .] *In an interview, Rose mentioned going home to Georgia in 1969, jamming with the Allman Brothers and hooking up with Duane on both a romantic and a creative level, and how reconnecting with her Southern roots showed her a way to grow musically that she hadn't previously realized was possible—the blues. Country. Gospel. She had an ah-ha moment—the synthesis of these styles, more so than mere appropriation. More than just copping licks.*

The supposed romance with Allman, whether true or not, was most certainly short-lived, as Jake and Rose were married a month later on New Year's day, 1970, when the band took a long-deserved vacation in Hawaii. When they got back, they began prepping for their tours—and the rest of their lives—by moving north, to Marin. The end of an era, for them, for everyone.

This was how Jake described the moment of truth, the moment of their union as a married couple: "We looked into one another's eyes at sunrise on a beach of black sand, and swore that with the dawning of a new year—a new decade—we'd spend the rest of our days together, until we were too old to play music anymore, and all we could do was sit on our front porch and pick banjos and watch the grandkids making their own music, that we were the only ones who could trust each other fully, who had come from the seed and the roots together—I'd known her since we were in high school. But it didn't exactly work out that way, did it? Didn't matter. Onstage, we stayed the best of friends through it all. And had a beautiful baby girl, too. That's what it's all about right there, not some concert we played or a song we wrote. Addie's our finest contribution to the firmament, to the culture." [From the Rolling Stone *interview with Jake Sobel, published on the first anniversary of Rose's death, the August 9, 1998 issue.]*

Following a quiet year in 1971, Rose wrote more than two dozen new songs with Oglethorpe, her spouse Sobel, and of course the band as a whole. Jack O'Roses then exploded out of its brief, post-1960's hangover dormancy with a pair of new albums that were released within six months of one another. With endless touring and a modicum of radio play featuring several cuts from both albums, despite none of the songs charting any higher than the mid-30s, the band's popularity increased exponentially. Already Jack O'Roses was being designated as more than a rock band, but as torchbearers for an entire cultural epoch, one of many burdensome yokes Rose Partland would decline to accept, if not outright decry as incorrect, or even offensive. In her words, Jack O'Roses resisted symbolizing anything other than whatever it seemed to be at any given musical moment—no more, no less. The albums were critical favorites and, by Jack standards, sold fairly well: Bluejean Baby *featured artwork centered on a chubby, jean and tie-dye clad infant Adelaide held up to the cosmos by hands that one was safe to assume were Rose's. The record introduced the band's take on the country-rock sound popularized earlier by some of their contemporaries like Gram Parsons to the record-buying public, and received the best reviews of their career thus far.*

Bluejean Baby *was followed in October by the eponymous, live tour-de-force* Jack O'Roses, *known among F-Kids by its unofficial name* The Green Man Album, *owing to the artwork on the front which featured a Green Man face (most people think it is a combination of all the band member's faces) within a blood-red, fantastically blooming rose. More new songs were debuted on this three-platter concert album, another unusual tactic for a major label act—no 'official' studio versions of these songs would ever be cut.*

By 1973, the band played stadiums around the country, but as the stage setup became bigger and bigger, still continued to struggle financially. It was worth it in one sense: their sound reinforcement equipment always lay on the cutting edge of concert technology.

It is in this time of great activity that Rose and other band members began using cocaine more so than the psychedelics on which they'd cut their intellectual and artistic teeth, though the problems of such drug abuse would not manifest themselves, at least externally, until much later.

Some sources suggest that Rose first tried heroin during this period, perhaps during a guest recording session with Eric Clapton for an album that's never been officially released; others claim that she first discovered the drug in smokable form on the lauded Europe '74 tour, which is still regarded as perhaps the best run of shows that the band ever played. Either way, once she began, opiates would be a problem for Rose until literally the day she died, of a heart attack while in drug treatment.

Later in 1974, though, the band seemed to be

at the moment of its greatest success—that summer they played the biggest concert ever, a rock festival outside of Atlanta that Jack O'Roses co-headlined with the Allman Brothers and Led Zeppelin, with some estimates putting attendance as high as one million concertgoers. But that fall, Skutch McKellan, suffering from end-stage alcoholism and despondent over being unable to reconcile his damaged, volatile relationship with his wife, put a .38 in his mouth, and ended the Skutch rave-ups for all time. "It can never be the real Jack O'Roses again now," Rose famously said. Yet they kept on keeping on, for another twenty-three years.

At the time, of course, F-Kids report that it seemed for a long, dreadful moment that autumn that the band might be gone for good . . . but they went back on tour that November, issuing a press release about the hiring of session musician Matt Alvin Christopher on keys, and Jack O'Roses went onward and upward as though nothing had happened. They'd do it once more after Matt OD'd. They'd not try after Rose, of course. They rest of them weren't fools.

I'm trying to get in the mood for the two Pallet Jack shows on the 30th and New Year's Eve by poking around in Brian's files, which I've kept on the desktop of the computer in a file I've marked MORGUE. Aimee should be home from a doctor's appointment she said she had to get in before we left tomorrow morning—she hadn't been specific about what kind of doctor, or what malady, and I hadn't asked. Couldn't be anything too terrible in a physical sense—I'm starting to feel as though I know her inside and out.

I don't know why I'm bothering with Brian's writing—I always come across some passage such as the Skutch-suicide and get yanked out of the book and back into the bleak reality that its author did the same stupid thing, in much the same state of mind: over the loss of a lover, although in Brian's case one as untouchable as Rose Partland. To read more of this 'work' is but an excuse to wallow around in the mushy skull of my dead friend instead of my own unexamined life. No good excuse to do either, actually.

This time last year, Brian—Nibbs—was getting ready to go the Panache shows in Miami—just to have 'something to tape,' he claimed—and when I laughed at the suggestion that I attend along with him, he'd gotten really steamed.

"It just reminds me that the scene has passed on by for me, now. Just burn me a set of discs, if you would, after you get home. That'll suffice."

"Oh, bullshit, Z. Weren't you telling me at Merriweather Post that you can get to some of those same places with this band? "

"Look, dude, that's not it. I'm just past it, alright?"

"Past what, exactly?"

"The whole thing."

"What the fuck does that mean?"

At first I couldn't muster an answer, mainly because I was struggling with the particulars: it wasn't as though I didn't still party a bit—I did and do—and it wasn't as though Halsey and I couldn't stand a few days apart—we could, obviously—and it wasn't as though I didn't dig Panache's music—I did then, and still do. Just not enough to saddle up and make the trek. That's all I meant. That, and the fact that Nibbs Niffy scared me. The Nibbs of Drake Park had not been the same person with whom I went to Ventura, and almost seven years after Drake Park, he'd only gotten worse—he'd gained about a hundred pounds, looked waxy and shiny and yellow around the eyes.

But I only told him the first part of my reasoning, to which he replied with more rancor than humor: "What—pussy got you that tied down?"

I ignored his crudity. "It's just not my scene, man. None of it."

"Oh, I bet some of it's your scene. But you don't have time for fun anymore. Or your *friends*—Jesus! You're the same as you always were. You're nothing but a little tourist who never gave two shits about the band or Rose or the 'scene' as you call it, not that you'd know what that scene entailed or what it meant or how we can keep it going—we have to keep it going, spud. Don't you understand? We have to get back into that Panache parking lot and *show them the way*. These stupid fucks are in there pulling shows onto hard disc recorders—I scream at them, what happens? What happens when a goddamn EMP event occurs and all the hard drives are wiped? I'll have my masters, is what. My DATs. I've started running cassette backups at shows, too, on my old Sony D-5, on this stash of Maxell metal blanks I discovered on ebay. They all look at me like I'm nuts. But fuck them, and fuck you, too, Z. Gutless nitwits. Your bodies should be ground up and fed to the ducks in that goddamn pond at Drake Park."

I ground my teeth at being called a tourist—I'd barely heard another word. "Anything you have to show those Panache kids will be the wrong thing, pal. If you want to know what I really think."

And then he'd slammed the phone down.

I didn't talk to him for months afterward, not until he'd called about the rumors regarding some kind of Jack reunion that never materialized, rumors that make the rounds like they have every summer since Rose died.

And so, I'm ashamed to admit that this was the nature of our final conversation. Once he'd moved back home to Virginia the previous year, we only lived an hour apart—but not only did I decline to visit him, I didn't bother picking up the phone all year. Not even last summer on the 9th of August.

It bears repeating: Not even on the 9th of August, that awful anniversary. I didn't check on my friend. And then, less than a week later, I finally thought of him and called, only to be told by his mother that he was dead—my friend, stone dead. How about that little addendum for my report to her? That at the moment I'll bet he most needed me, I didn't give a shit whether I spoke to him ever again? Should I say that to Mrs. Godbold? Don't answer that—a coward like me already knows what he will do, which is nothing.

–4–

The Westin is a round glass tower, once the glimmering, modern centerpiece of the Atlanta skyline, but now surrounded by structures of equivalent height and varying, debatable aesthetic interest. It's a hotel a teenage me first knew from a trip to see a Braves game, and as a key visual motif in an old Burt Reynolds movie, but that I'd later most associate with seeing Jack shows at the Omni, the structure looming in the background as we stood around fending off grifters and homeless dudes and cops in riot gear in an urban parking lot while trying to get our freak on before the shows.

All afternoon we've caught glimpses of ourselves—*in flagrante delicto*—in the reflection from the blank gray TV screen, and we remain lolling about in states of mutual satisfaction and repose. After a brief discussion, we decide to have a light room service dinner. No need to go anywhere, not until time to head to the show. I ring the kitchen to rustle us up some grub.

Aimee rolls over on one elbow. "So what about these rumors?"

"What rumors?"

"I saw Chance down in the Market this morning before we left, and he said he'd heard that Linus Pullen is going to be at these shows with Jake."

"Get the eff outta here." In the post-Rose era reunion rumors have never turned out to be true.

"Those guys are worlds apart now."

"How so?"

I explain that I think Jack O'Roses is—or was—like the pieces of a shattered asteroid rolling through the black void, staying mostly together, occasionally bumping into one another, all rolling forward it the same direction, but no longer connected, and for one enormous reason: Rose. Rose was the gravitational center. Without her, I think the various fragments have drifted off into space.

"Hell, there's only the three of them now anyway. LeMoy, Pullen and Sobel do not a Jack O'Roses make, even with Lenn Circosta, if they feel motivated to pull him out of mothballs—I hear he's a recluse up in the Emerald Triangle somewhere, living with Family."

"I hope it's true. That he's here. That'd be cool—right?"

"I bet you do. But don't get your hopes up."

"I'm really excited about this," she says, dreamy.

"Me, too," I say, nuzzling her neck and pawing at one breast. "Look down there—there's even physical evidence of excitement."

She shoves me away, playful. "You cad. I'm talking about the show, sir."

I lean back, put my arms behind my head, and ponder the evening ahead. "Listen—Jake'll do some cool stuff, some Rose tunes, and all that. But dollars to doughnuts says no Pullen."

"Want to wager?"

"Sure—what's at stake?"

"I have some ideas." She disappears beneath rustling sheets. "Here's a preview of what you win."

And yet, I tell her, breathless, it is as though I've already won.

This activity, and many variations, go on for a while; at this rate, we might not even make the show. Wouldn't be the end of the world. Not like we'd be missing Rose, after all.

The second we get out of the cab outside the venerable Fox Theatre and I see the scene happening in the parking lot next to the theatre—the Jack O'Roses lot experience, in miniature—I get nervous as hell, sweating and rubbing my hands together.

I know what it is—I keep seeing guys out of the corner of my eye, big fellas in overalls and T-shirts and bajas, but none of them is Brian. And yet all of them are, and all the little blonde girlies are Halsey, and the skinny, shorthaired beerdrunk college fucks, as members of the Family would sometimes call me, are yours truly. Ghosts, yet quite corporeal.

We stroll through the crowded, tiny lot, which doesn't take long. We find the requisite veggie burritos and T-shirts and glass bowls and whispered offers of doses, shrooms, and pharmies.

"Should we eat some 'shrooms?" I ask.

"Ah . . . I don't think so. This is no Hogstomper Hootenanny on the peaceful hillside under the harvest moon."

"No—this here is downtown Atlanta."

"Not conducive."

We stand looking at one another. I rationalize that it's the New Year's run, it's a party, it's that time of year. But she's right—I don't want to have to spill out onto the sidewalk later, tripping and trying to get a cab back to the hotel. “I don’t need it. I can get to where I need to be just fine . . .”

Imagery of Rose continues to dominate the T-shirts and other artwork the gypsy vendors have for sale: Heavenly Rose, her face in a cloud floating above an endless and eternal field of vibrant floral fecundity; Earthmother Rose, her beatific visage drawn within the misty blue globe of the planet itself; Woodcut Rose; Young, Skinny Rose; Guitar God Rose; Piano Virtuoso Rose; Fat Angel Rose.

My favorite, though, has always been the famous Peace Sign Rose, a c.1968 shot of her sitting on the steps of the house on Ashbury Street and flashing the good old two-fingered salute, a stars and stripes bandana tied around her thick, black hair, an era-defining image recognized even by people that don’t know who the woman in the photo actually is. Even in death there is no denying her power, this icon of icons—her very image conveys waves of comfort and positive energy, much as the real person did while she still stomped the daisies here on the great spinning rock.

We stop to talk to a vendor, a very familiar guy who’s probably an Atlanta local, someone I might have seen one of the numerous times we came here for shows.

His shirts are lovely, hand-drawn Jake images, many of which are familiar like the Rose shirts, but with extra loving flourishes and artistic details, as though the gentleman wished to imbue Jake Sobel’s image with more *gravitas* than his role in the band has often been afforded. A variety of song-quotes adorn the back of the shirts, some from Jake’s originals, some from his big cover tune rave-ups like ‘Roadhouse Blues.’ Nice work.

I compliment the vendor on his wares.

"Right on, brother, thanks—fifteen banana-skins each, or a twofer for twenty-five."

"How's the tour been?"

"Aw, these are my only shows. I have some kids that did the whole Pallet Jack run down from New Hampshire, sold a shitload for me."

"Sweet—outsourcing."

"I got my own brick and mortar now," he says, handing me a business card with a fractal background bursting with rich, swirling, psychedelic color:

JACK-O's SCREEN PRINTING
AND MORE INC
'We Print Your Logo or Artwork
on ANYTHING, Man!'

"You started this after Rosie passed on, didn't you?"

"Sorta. Got my start on the lot back in '82, with heat-transfer of a Rose shot from Europe '74, the one with the Jake and Linus in the background leaning into the amps during the feedback segment, and Rose with her head all thrown back and pointin' the neck of that durn old white Strat up in the air . . ."

To F-Kids, the photo in question is a familiar one. "Pointing that thing up at heaven like she's showing God exactly what this band is made of."

"Right on, right *on*." We share a smile, and a fist-bump.

He takes a moment to give his twofer pricing spiel to another curiosity seeker, and by his movements I can see he's got some stiff, bad knees going. He comes back and I ask, "Miss the road?"

"Nah, not since Rose. You?"

"Yeah." A near flood of wet-eyed sincerity. "Of course I do."

"When was your last show?"

I come this close to lying—the answer is sure to leave a taint on any such discussion, but in the end I decide that to be honest will let this gentleman know I'm the real deal. "Drake Park."

"Oh, *shit*," he says. "Ouch."

"Yeah." I glance over to see that Aimee's giving me a look, nudging with her shoulder toward the old theatre—*Let's go inside!*

After buying a shirt for my girl, we get in line. She's already taken off her jacket and slipped on her souvenir.

"Want to look the part, eh?"

"Of course," she says. "So look—I heard what y'all were talking about."

"Did you now."

"So when are you going to tell me about Drake Park?"

I snort, derisive. "Well—certainly not tonight. Tonight's for dancing."

And then I hear a teenage kid walk by, one who looks like Chance but with short, dark dreads. He's talking to another kid about Linus Pullen, and how this guy heard them soundchecking 'Nebula' and it'll be the first 'Nebula' since Rose died and how he's been waiting for this night since the spring Atlanta '97 shows, the final night of which featured, well, what turned out to be the final 'Nebula Rising Suite.'

I call out after him: "Keep dreaming, kid."

But he doesn't hear me—as the line begins to move, a cheer from the impatient faithful drowns out my skepticism.

–5–

Pallet Jack: The feel and sound onstage is almost completely different from Jack O'Roses—two drummers, a sax, keys, and bass, with our boy as lead guitarist instead of rhythm as in the good old days. It's good, a chunky-funky, fat sound, but the interplay among the players is a pale imitation of the old front line of Jake, Rose, and Linus, though interesting enough on its own terms. I've had a couple glasses of wine, feel the love in the grand old theater. Like most of the crowd, Aimee's dancing and smiling and having a good time. I have to admit, the feel's like almost being home. But not quite. Jake looks good—hale and hearty and grayer than ever, but seeing him center-stage, in his old spot, with one of his familiar custom axes, I feel more than comforted.

Jake's bass player, a short African-American woman who I'm told is his current spouse—hadn't one onstage, offstage marriage been enough?—lays down a thick, solid supporting line, and as with the old 'drums' features at Jack shows, a segment is devoted strictly to her and the percussionist-drummer, at his disposal an array of midi-effects and outlandish, exotic drums. The bassist's playing is quite different from that of Linus, who eschewed traditional bottom-end lines for an unusually melodic interpretation of the instrument's role in the sound of a rock band.

But no matter—the groove is solid, the songs upbeat. I'm put off only by a first-set ending 'Save the Country' sung by the current Mrs. Sobel, a version that never quite gels into that barn-burning, door-bursting, over-the-falls jam to which Rose could take the song in those last years—when she felt up to it, that is. And frankly, I have to say that it feels *fucked up* to hear some other chick singing 'Save the Country.' But whatever. At least someone's covering the tune—both Laura Nyro and Rose Partland, after all, now sing not for us, but for the angels among whom they dwell. The lights come up, and Aimee departs to make the dreadful halftime bathroom trudge.

I lean back and watch the slow march of the cloudscape across the theater's elegant ceiling. At the top of the stage area on either side are two castle-turrets just below the stars and the clouds; it is a magical place to see music, and I ache at having missed the Jack shows that took place here back in the 70s.

I pan my red peepers around the theatre, at the faces and bodies. The trappings of the shows—the real shows—are evident in the tie-dyed couture, the blue smoke hanging in the air, the forest of microphone stands under the first balcony, but it can never quite be the same.

Then Aimee's back with a couple of fresh red wines. We chat about the first set, smooch a little, speak in whispers of private matters. Finally the lights again go down and I allow a nibble of hope that maybe the rumors are true—that Linus Pullen is wandering around backstage—but, alas, my skepticism appears to have been borne out: No Linus; just another Pallet Jack show.

The next morning we go out for breakfast, at a cheap diner that has atmosphere and character in every nook and cranny. We sit noshing and discussing the show, which unfortunately featured no special guests of any type, and grew somewhat tedious as the second set meandered its way to a conclusion that lacked *oomph,* as Aimee so astutely puts it.

"Maybe they're saving it up for tonight," she offers.

I grunt and shrug, sopping a homemade biscuit in thick, genuine maple syrup. I start picking apart the performance in truly old school, cynical F-Kid style, from song selection to sound mix to the oppressive presence of the security goons, for all the world sounding like a hungover, kvetching Nibbs Niffy.

I change the subject: In the hotel, I noticed her in the bathroom tossing back what appeared to be medication—from the mysterious doctor visit? "What'd you take earlier? Headache from the wine?"

"Oh—allergy pills. That's all. Keeps me from being sneezy." A little shadow crosses her face. "Why? A woman can't take a pill?"

"Just curious. I'd never seen you take so much as a baby aspirin before."

"It's nothing."

And so, I forget about the pills.

—6—

True to form, the New Year's show opens up with Pallet Jack's signature original tune 'Heavy Lifting,' a typically obvious Jake song title—get it?—which on most nights is the way the group starts, last night being no exception—the old rules about not repeating tunes from show to show went out the window with Rose, apparently.

The Greg Allman Band opened the evening, so already the talk is that there'll be a big jam like the Peachfest back in '73, with God knows who else showing up—perhaps Derek Trucks or Warren Haynes. Again, the Linus rumors are rampant, but I continue to dismiss them.

Pallet Jack charges through a first set spiced with many covers, one of which—'Tears of a Clown,' a big rave up that Jake ended many a Jack O'Roses show with—gets the crowd in a screaming frenzy. The band jams and jams, louder, more frenetic, until finally Jake climaxes the tune with an ascending run of triplets, higher and higher on the fret board. The lights are spinning like crazy, and if you look hard enough, you can almost see Rose looming back there in the shadows watching over her old buddy, egging him on, reminding him how to keep it all alive. How to cheat death.

The dreaded house lights, up again after this

incendiary first set, and the buzz in the room is palpable. Unlike last night, when the venue was sort-of full but not bursting at the seams, tonight the Fox is packed to the rafters. Owing to some bad ticket luck, our seats are all the way up in the second balcony, but the angle's like looking straight down on the stage, and it's cool to be so close to the faux night sky painted on the ceiling. The heavy curtains seem to be moving, but of course they're not—after some deliberation, Aimee agreed to split a chocolate, a mild, buzzy trip that has us both in blissful, giggly states of relative grace.

But then I glance over and see that Aimee's got that expression she gets when she's a little too high. I take her hand, find the palm clammy.

"My stomach feels bloated," she says. "Ack."

"It'll pass. Feel okay otherwise?"

"Yeah—something in the air, though. Like ozone. Like . . . when lightning's about to give birth."

She laughs self-consciously, but I can only nod, her insight as valuable and spot-on as anything Nibbs ever said to describe that feeling of magic in the air. I get that certain shudder up and down my neck, a remembrance of times past, or perhaps what's happening right now.

A tall, skinny guy with a graying, curly mop of hair pulled back walks by, a VIP laminate dangling around his neck. I suffer a shock of recognition—it's Doober Dougie, an oldschool Atlanta DJ to whom Nibbs used to send tapes for use on the Doober's Sunday night, Jack O'Roses-themed show, a guy who'd always hang around the section during Atlanta shows, get smoked down by the tapers.

"Dougie," I call out. "Over here, bro."

At first Dougie shakes my hand with cool standoffish politeness, until I remind him who I am: a colleague of the esteemed Nibbs Niffy.

"Well, fuck me silly," Dougie says good-naturedly, his radio voice softened by the fact that he isn't currently on the job. "Haven't heard from that boy in a coon's age. He must be down in the section."

"No. He's—not here."

"Boy's gonna be pissed—you do know what's going down, don't you?"

"No."

He starts to tell me something, then a sly smile crosses his features and he pulls back, nods, and starts bopping his way down the steep steps. "You'll see."

"Huh," I say, sitting back down.

"What?" she asks, smiling like a mischievous little scamp who's up to no good. "Tell me tell me tell me."

"Dunno. Nothing. Or, maybe something."

"*What*?"

My mind reels. "I haven't seen a look in someone's eyes like that in a long time—not since the time Nibbs scored front row tickets for Charlotte back in '91, which he didn't inform me about until we were on our way into the Coliseum. It was the greatest surprise of my life."

"So, unless I am mistaken, Mr. Holmes," Aimee says in a terrible British accent, "I'd say this Doober Dougie has told us that we ourselves have a surprise in store."

After what feels like an interminable break, the house lights are killed, and the crowd roars its collective approval, ready to ring in 2005.

Even though I can't see it, I know the taper section is alive with little flashlights and the blinking red indicators, the gearheads making a mad scramble to roll the decks and get everyone settled down amidst all the cables and stands and mixers and A>D converters. People in the general audience are already bobbing up and down despite having no music yet to which we may dance. Colorful balloons fill the smoky air. Lighters flicker and flash; the consternation of the overwhelmed ushers in this nonsmoking venue is palpable, at least in our section.

I check the time and see that it's after eleven—in the old days at a New Year's show, Jack O'Roses would come out just before the midnight hour. I suppose Jake will go into 'Auld Lang Syne' in the middle of a jam to acknowledge the milestone that is the turning of a page. Calendar pages, fluttering in the breeze.

A voice wonders if I'm getting too old for this. It's what I told my Nibbs, wasn't it?

At last, a white hot spotlight not so much bursts into life as gradually emerges into being, and what we see at the center of the stage is a bit of surprise, one that I suspect was what Dougie had hinted with such portent: Jake is alone on a stool, an acoustic guitar on his lap.

The crowd, already a tumultuous throng, goes absolutely apeshit, as do I—I'm overwhelmed in that Jack way, when some statistical anomaly presents itself in the form of a song rarely played, or an unusual combination of tunes, and you realize *this is one of the moments for which I waded through all those mediocre shows.*

I grab Aimee, yell in her ear: "There hasn't been an acoustic performance by that man in public in twenty years!"

Her understanding of such matters now approaching the level of a true F-Kid, Aimee lets loose with a yelp of excitement. We jump up and down. Other people start shushing us, tell us to sit down.

"It's an acoustic set!" an ecstatic voice yells, loud enough to be heard all through the theatre. "Fuck yeah!" The audience laughs, a veritable gale.

"Jesus, y'all," Jake says, amused. "Settle down. Ain't no thang."

A weird vibe overtakes me as Jake continues to speak rather than play, an unusual occurrence in any sort of Jack O'Roses context. The crowd finally quiets for real.

"Truth be told, folks, we did want to do something special this year, shake it up. Been a long one, ain't it?" Everybody cheers, but in a subdued, nine-eleveny kind of way: reverent, muted, a little cowed and self conscious.

He coughs and goes on in his raspy near-drawl, a voice broken and weathered by a million nights on the road, a million joints, a million moments reaching for the notes that sometimes wouldn't come. "Been a tough one, yes it has."

"Word to that!" I yell, amidst a smattering of applause that feels confused—wait, should we applaud the fact that it's been a lousy year? Not I, says he, but of course I'm talking about Nibbs and my other personal problems.

"So anyway, been a while since you cats have heard certain tunes—and some of these you ain't never heard outta me, and all, but anyway . . ." He trails off, plucks a few random notes on his guitar. "Let's have some fun."

Aimee nudges me with an elbow. "What's he up to?"

And then, as he plucks out an oh-so-familiar melody, one to which I'd referred only moments before—another Jack O'Roses, how-do-they-do-that instance—she has her answer: It's a song intro F-Kids have heard many times, but now plucked out on an Alvarez acoustic guitar instead of Rose's grand piano: A Neil Young cover, 'Borrowed Tune,' not heard since the next to last tour. Used to be that Rose would come out on the grand piano by herself for this tune, usually an encore. They said she did a mellow, quiet song like that on nights when the show had been so intense that the crowd needed to be cooled down before streaming back out into Jacktown, into the semi-real world where the gray men awaited with their craven admonitions, their attempts to corral and control us and impose their jackbooted, rulebound vision of order upon our glorious colorswept psychedelic chaos. Our shot at the spiritual brass ring. Our special brand of reality.

Jake warbles the delicate lyric, "*I'm singin' this borrowed tune, too wasted to write my own,*" his voice gruff and raw compared to Rose, or for that matter Neil himself. Everyone cheers, as though being too inebriated to create represents an accomplishment worthy of praise.

Fuck that talk, Nibbs calls out from beyond the cloudscape ceiling. *'Borrowed Tune' is a get, tater tot*!

Hot tears threaten to spill over. I think of my buddy, how he decried so many of the cover tunes—how his ideal Jack experience had to have a certain purity of artistry, with only songs penned by their collective hands; how he never ever got such an experience, only close maybe a few times. Cover tunes were a huge part of the Jack book, though. Nibbs would get overcome by some weird ideas.

I glance at Aimee, swaying, her eyes closed.

"You know this one, right?"

"Yes." She punches me in the arm, grins. "You said this was one of your top picks. Hey—you called the tune."

I choke back a sob. "Yes, I did, didn't I."

I made the call. But I didn't call the tune.

A chunk of ice settles into my gut. I think of the drive to Drake Park that last time. Nibbs ranting, fervid and febrile, about the cover tunes. The cover tunes. How no better time than the holiday weekend for Rose to pull out an all-Jack show. How this had meaning for him. How he felt that he had to have this. Compulsive, jabbering, for two hundred miles. How this idea was, inexplicably, a seeming matter of life and death. I chalked it up to the bad drugs. I had no idea what all he was into by then. Maybe even the dust, already.

A flash: At a pit stop, the mysterious call he made, on an old pay phone at a gas station. How I watched him gesticulate, stabbing the air with his fat finger. Slamming the receiver down. Marching back, self satisfied and puffed up like a cartoon rooster.

I made the call, he'd said. *That ought to do it. That will let them know we're fucking serious.*

Who, Nibbs? Who did you call?

You'll see, Z. Once you start writing down the setlist tomorrow night. You'll see.

When we got to Drake Park, and saw all the cops, how his face had drained of color. How his hands shook. How quiet he became at the impending sense of mayhem that would later come to fruition. The vibe of evil in the air; a devil in the crowd.

Who did you call, you son of a bitch? *Who?*

Aimee sees on my face that I'm troubled. "Honey—*what's wrong*?"

"Just thinking about some heavy crap."

"Well—stop it."

I wrench my attention back to the show. Next, another Rose ballad: 'Watermelon Sugar' from *Bluejean Baby*, the B-side of 'Calm Before the Storm,' and a real rarity, another get if there'd ever been one. I first caught the song at Landover, when it was a big bust-out on the spring 1990 tour, but they'd put it back into the trunk by the summer—a tease, not a return to the repertoire. I thought the Cap Centre would levitate that indelible night. Jake transports me there all over again.

Then, that rascal pulls out another gem—another cover of a cover, conjuring up the angry specter of my dead friend: the Little Feat classic 'Willin',' another Jack O'Roses encore staple. It was one of those sneaky tunes that started quiet and small, then built into a high energy, explosive concert-closer that sent everyone out on a billowing cloud of joy.

At this extreme remove from the old days, the song feels more confessional, more revelatory—a bittersweet road tune that seems to be about a hell of a lot more than driving a truck, or about weed, whites, and wine. Among the many talents Jack O'Roses possessed was an ability to imbue the most unlikely of tunes with a depth that would go far beyond what even the original songwriters could have intended, and here Jake nails the melancholy sense of loss and nostalgia the song conjures in the mind of this listener.

The covers had meaning, Nibbs. So much relevance. Now who was the nitwit?

I banish you, sir. Go away, with your calls and your covers and your ghostly bitching and moaning.

Determined to prove in that moment that I'm turning a New Year's page type-deal, I blurt out to Aimee, "I'm going to get moving on some stuff, soon as we get back. Aimee: I'm finished with all this—dilly-dallying."

Aimee, bursting into laughter and shoving me like Elaine on *Seinfeld*. "Dilly-dallying? Get-out!" She keeps laughing, 'shroomy and stoney and amused to death. It's infectious. I start laughing with her. People shush us again.

"You know what I mean—a plan. Direction."

"Oh—sure. Believe it when I see it."

"Seriously."

She can barely speak. “I’ve got . . . I’ve got a dilly you can dally.” Guffawing, honking like a goose, slapping me on the arm. Overcome with the sillies. She’s at her most beautiful, my girl. I decide she’s right—I need to let these thoughts go. These are for January 2. Or maybe the third.

Her chuckles subside, along with the song. The crowd roars. Jake stands, offers a bow. A guitar tech takes his acoustic. I kiss Aimee, which only makes her laugh harder. I don’t mind. Her spirit is childlike, joyous, infectious.

From the stage. “Y’all help me welcome another old codger up here tonight.”

The crowd hushes . . . then explodes: I fear the venerable Fox Theatre might collapse as another spotlight—a red one—comes up ever so softly, and a tall, hunched-over figure is now standing to Jake’s left, in front of the bass amps where previously Jake’s new squeeze had played, the hip lady who brings the funk, as he’d introduced her. I can’t let myself believe it, not for a second . . . but then the reality descends upon me, and Linus Pullen steps into the soft, almost-amber spotlight, that Cheshire grin of his beaming outward at a grateful audience, leaping and hugging and high-fiving from one side of the Fox Theatre to the other. Spinners begin twirling. Dozens of F-Kids prostrate themselves in the aisles, hectored by confused, flashlight wielding ushers.

The tall bass player, ever the perfectionist, ignores the tumult and turns to his stack, begins twisting knobs and stepping on pedals and playing quiet little runs of low-octave notes. Aimee and I exchange shr[g] and smiles, both of us speechless: *Can you believ*

But wait—there’s more. We ain’t seen[d a] yet.

A hulking figure climbs behind drumbeat begins—*thok thok, thok*

thok, thok thok thok—that, in its familiarity, causes me to suck my breath in and turn to Aimee with wide eyes and a slack jaw: "Oh-my-god."

A deep turquoise light comes up now behind Jake, and where Pallet Jack's drummer ought to be sitting is a bald guy, stout of gut and broad of chest, older now, but no less recognizable, a cat I'd watched at times with a fascination to match that of Rose or Linus or any of the band members: Paul LeMoy himself is perched on the drum riser, grinning and pounding out the opening beat to the 'Bayou Stomp,' a staple of Jack O'Roses concerts for over twenty years. Paul, Linus, and Jake—together.

"It's *them*," I shout in disbelief.

I fall back into my seat, overcome, my hands over my face. The crowd goes even wilder as the full stage lights come up and Greg Allman plops down behind the Hammond B-3 on stage left, and Derek Trucks emerges from the shadows; Jake straps on his Strat, and his lovely wife stands behind a solitary microphone stand to his right—Rose's old spot.

And then? This ad-hoc band launches into the wildest, most exuberant 'Bayou Stomp' that anyone in this crowd has heard in a long time, and I'm back on my feet, boogieing the likes of which you ain't never seen.

I keep on dancing, but there's some sneaky little asshole tears leaking out, and if it'd been Brian for whom I wept at the Hootenanny, I now realize I'm finally squirting a few for Nibbs Niffy, who, whatever his foibles and flaws and addictions—whatever his sins—should have had the damn sense to know that this moment, about which he'd so dreamt, would one [illegible] arrive.

–7–

Out on the sidewalk after the show, the rumors are flapping their wings and taking flight—Jack O'Roses is back, there's a spring tour in the offing, a big summer stadium tour to be announced any day, they're going to change the name, they're going out as Pallet Jack, they're going out as the F-Kid Symphonic Ensemble—a bit of a stretch—they're going out as Jake Sobel and Friends, they're back, they're back, *they're back!*

"Y'all are nuts," I insist to a couple of kind sisters hugging each other and screaming 'Summer tour twenty-oh-five! Summer tour twenty-oh-five!' over and over like a pair of F-Kid cheerleaders. "This was special."

The air outside is freezing, but no one wants to leave. Everyone, and I mean everyone—well, except for some tapers I heard running down the sound reinforcement, and how thin Linus sounded, et cetera—is beyond stoked, beyond psyched. Whatever we saw just now—and it wasn't Pallet Jack—has to be considered the closest thing to Jack O'Roses we've had in over seven long years. Came a day.

As Aimee and I wait for a cab back to the hotel, we go through the setlist, which along with the heavy rockers included a more introspective section, one in which the band—clearly under-rehearsed—did attempt a 'Nebula Suite' jam, a jam that they wisely allowed to wander off into the ether without turning into the full-fledged piece of complicated music. Once the second encore—indeed, 'Came a Day'—wrapped the evening in a psychedelic ribbon of rapturous glee, this angel band had gigged until nearly two in the morning.

"Well, that was supercool—long time coming."

"Yes, but you got hung up for a little while. Thinking about departed friends."

I hold up a hand—*don't go there.*

We buy a cold microbrew from a vendor to share, talk to people, share hugs. The cops start moving everyone out. Aimee falls down across some exposed roots in a tree well; we both convulse in a fresh rash of joyous, silly giggles.

I admonish a concerned Samaritan, a lanky baja-clad hippie guy who leans down to assist her. "Do *not* help this woman—this woman must not be *helped!*"

"Excuse me?"

"No! She's got to learn to stand on her own two feet!"

Aimee, sucking wind and overcome with laughter, kicks at me. "Unhand me, sir! Help, help, I'm being repressed!"

The kid, perplexed, walks on, and only then do I help her up. Embrace there on the dirty old Atlanta sidewalk, in the dead of winter, in the middle of the night. Kiss. Laugh some more; sigh and see our cab, pulling up as if sent from on high, the right moment, the right time.

In the cab the lights of Peachtree Street play across my face, Aimee's snuggled up next to me, and I'm thinking not about Jack O'Roses reunions or how much I'm falling in love with this woman, but about Brian, and his redacted, ruinous secrets, and the calls he did and didn't make on our trip to Drake Park.

-8-

In January, wintertime at last descends upon South Carolina for real: A modest snow and ice storm shuts everything down, and they're saying the temperatures will stay so cold that the snow will stick around for over a week, an eternity in the humid, subtropical midlands of the state that only received snow once or twice a decade, and then only for a day and a night, usually.

The evening of this winter storm, we sit in Aimee's apartment sipping cocoa and watching a DVD of an early 90s stadium show, one of the recent Jack vault releases that have started trickling out. Rose looks terrible, with a gray-faced pallor and a sheen of dust-sweat, but she's still ripping off deft solos, pounding her ivories into submission, even smiles a few times when she hands off a solo to Circosta.

A huge 'Save the Country' builds for over ten minutes, and as she gets up from the piano and straps on her axe, shredding and shredding until the tune erupts like a volcano, Rose grins and raises a fist and the stadium of 60,000 F-Kids, euphoric, roar and stomp their approval to the point that the video cameras all start bouncing.

All I can see onscreen, however, is a sick woman—Rose's hair is plastered against her forehead.

Her eyes are small, mostly downcast, skin sallow and waxy. She's pulling off her little Rose Partland act, yes, but I know when she's hurting.

"I'm surprised they released it with her color looking so bad."

"Well, listen to her—seems like a hot show. That's the principal criterion, yes?"

"Suppose so—I know one video they won't put out. For-sure."

"Too bad Drake Park had to be so awful," Aimee says, hinting. "I can't imagine."

"Twas that. And more."

"Not that I'd know—not really," leaning over, putting her head in my lap and looking up, eyebrows raised in expectancy. "You could tell me about it tonight. If you wanted."

If I didn't get squirrelly before, at the mention of Drake Park now I go numb inside, a void into which my stomach drops. This call-making business of Nibbs Niffy. If my gut is right, it's not a conclusion I could possibly say aloud.

From the Journal of Nibbs Niffy,
November 1997

Going through the '97 tapes show by show:
A short year since we only had the two national tours, and one of them cut short by one show—the lost show, my last show, which will now only ever exist as a

figment of my imagination. They're coming to take me away, haha. They're coming to take me away.

The spring tapes reveal (on most nights, anyway) a withering, lusty performance from Jake, an explosive, high-energy rock-god vibe. Linus is no slouch either. Over the winter break LeMoy's introduced yet another generation of MIDI equipment, and on many nights, the drums and electronic weirdness that he leads is probably the most spirited and intellectually engaging part of the show.

It's clear, though, that the rest of the band is on their game for one sad reason: because most of the time Rosie isn't.

The Atlanta run from April is, without a doubt, the highlight of the year. These hometown shows for Rose and Jake are usually real corkers, and the run this time was no exception, including what would turn out to be the final 'Nebula Rising Suite' attempt—final, like, ever, man. Only a short, noodling version, it appeared enigmatically in the Rose-ballad second set slot, and never reached the heights of even the most middling of versions—it was just a jam, and not even a developed one.

When the lyrics didn't come, and Rose turned back to her stack, Jake rather cruelly cut out of the jam and straight into 'Barfly.' Give the girl a chance, Jake, you impatient prick. That might have been the last real 'Nebula,' if only you'd let the fucking thing happen.

I wonder if she even cared that Jake cut her off? She turned around and played 'Barfly,' nodding and jamming along with her ex-husband. She couldn't have known there'd never be another 'Nebula,' I guess, so no big deal. Life's like that. You don't ever know what's around the next corner. Like when the person you love the most is going to die. Or you, for that matter. She once said that she tried to play every show like it could be the last one. A good approach to life in general, I think.

Now that my hackles and suspicions are simmering, I'm again digging through the post-Drake Park journals, clicking and opening file after file in the MORGUE folder, notebook after notebook of scribbled madness, suffering through the bitter rants, the wild mood swings, which range from the mild praise in the preceding passage, to bitter, vituperative excoriation of everything from ticket prices, to heavy handed security, to Rose herself—incredibly—upon whom he places much of the blame for everything that went wrong.

But later I find an interesting document—the smoking gun—in which he is like a child begging her forgiveness from on high, Rose having at last ascended to the plane of actual divinity to which many believed she already dwelled, even when her feet had still trod the fallow earth.

A passage that confirms for me the horrible suspicion about Drake Park. About what Nibbs Niffy, in his ultimate derangement, did to Rose that day:

From the Journal of Nibbs Niffy,
January 2, 2000
[typographical errors
are those of Brian Godbold]

It's a new century. Or, the bitter end of the old one. Depending on how you count.

Whether a beginning or ending, I tried not drinking today Rosie, or doing anything else like you used to, and that CONTRIBUTED but did not CAUSE YOUR DEATH three long ugly years back. It was hard. Your death.

I triedd to be open and friendly and receptive and not in hiding. In hiding. That's what you are now, you beautiful beam of light. You' wll be back in all good and due time, in fact anytime now I am sure. B u t I am in hiding, and forever. In jail, like our brothers from the road who got tagged by the iron bootheel of justice.

Rose. I'm sorry for some of the things I said about you—did you hear them? I pray that you didn't. Don't be mad at me. Please. PLEASE. I just need to have some anwser form you, in some way about what I ought to be doing with myself. Gave everything over to you, and now I got to get something back. But what? Help me Rosie, I love you I do, and I've done done the pennance I think I ought to for the mistakes I made. Come back to me and I'll show you. I'll make everything up to you, what I did to you on the third of July, under the starry sad roof of the night that fell on us. I didn't mean what I said when I called. You know that. I only wantted to make sure you knew how much the songs you wrote all meant to me. That I only wanted your words and voice, nobody elses. I udnerstand now that it was wrong. But like I said, I didn't mean it.

I didn't mean to kill you, sweet Rosie. Please forgive me.

-9-

The punditocracy, led by Fox News commentators, have turned on the President: the talking heads scream and bleat about how the government's word on Usama Bin Laden's condition, location, and purported statements admitting guilt for nine-eleven is either disinformation, absolute bunk, or at best, simply wrongheaded. The American people, the Wills and Krauthammers and Olbermanns and Stewarts insist, need to see the case made in our culture's prudent and meticulous manner, not paraded, and not a circus like OJ, but a televised cathartic trial that's just and fair and from which the country can then move on, after, of course, we've put the sodding bastard to death—maybe have that on TV, too, as Letterman jokes, bitter and unfunny. Dave hasn't been the same since that day. He can't get past too-soon.

As for the charismatic boogeyman, they've tucked our nemesis away well out of sight, in what many are calling the new American gulag at the Guantanamo Bay naval base that we control on the island of Cuba. Some people say Bin Laden's not even real, that they made him up so we'd have a face to put on the enemy. Whispers and outright exposés in alternate media suggest that during Reagan's days of supporting the mujahideen against the Soviets in Afghanistan, Bin Laden had been a CIA asset.

Whomever they have in custody, the bigger news coming this week involves a series of mail-bomb anthrax attacks on members of Congress—the letters mailed to various GOP Senators and Cabinet officers contained highly refined material, however, that some say could only have come from one of our own military labs. Curiouser and curiouser is the way of our country, and of the world. Conspiracies within conspiracies; what is truth?

Of course, there's also the dirty bomb threat, and loose backpack nukes from the former Soviet states, and who knows what else. But when hasn't there been the specter of doom hanging over our heads? How does it possibly compare to the threat of complete nuclear Armageddon, or at the very least the winter of our existence that would follow even a modest atomic war? The Beats and the Hippies and Rose Partland were the prior generation's response to this constant state of terror; what, pray tell, is that of my own, storied Gen X multitudes, and the Millennials, coming of age behind us, other than becoming followers of one side or the other?

In first few years after Rose's death, Brian and I would talk on the phone and discuss such questions, heavy and ponderous, which made us want to talk about anything else, and which of course always came back to music: Who was making the new music worth hearing? Would anyone in popular music, ever again, rise to such an artistic and commercial level of achievement and longevity as Jack?

"Could Panache get there?" I pondered aloud. "They've got the chops, their own mythos, and the years are starting to add up for them."

"Please," he said. "I'm being serious. Keep a lid on the facile and profane comparisons with our Rosie."

But I could never keep the post-Rose Nibbs on the right track to simply discuss good music—inevitably he'd start in about Rose, or the loss of the band, or the loss of the scene, and then I would have to tune him out, would have to ignore his slurring language, the errant and undisciplined thought patterns, the circular digressions leading from here to nowhere, fast. What was there left to say about Jack O'Roses? We loved the band and gave ourselves to them, were repaid in kind, and now that it's over, I believed, as I told him, that "We should count our blessings, get on with life."

"What fucking life, Z? Now that the storyteller's gone," he asked in such wondrous and sublime poetry, "to whom will I turn for the song?"

I hesitated, plunged ahead. "I had the biggest times of my life with Jack, but now they're over, it ran its course, and everyone better get on with their shit best they can. Choose *life*, for fuck's sake," I said in my best Ewan McGregor brogue. "Life is what you make of it."

"Screw life. And screw you," he'd said as a harsh goodbye. "You little college fuck." *Click*.

Adrift and enervated by the notion that I'm hunting fly poop in the pepper shaker, I go to log off Brian's HP Pavilion, a machine with the letters typed off the keys and a mouse-toe that's getting a bit dodgy. I click and clack, but instead of closing the word processor, I somehow hit ctrl+n instead.

Tabula rasa: I sit before the glowing, blank document, the cursor beckoning me with an idea—no, more than an idea: A starting place. The question in my mind now is not the meaning of *I made the call*; it is the meaning of the above-asked query:

What is truth?

In search of said concept, I begin, slowly at first, but then in a clattering torrent of words, to type. And type. And type.

-10-

A couple of days later, I drive over and trudge up the stairs to Aimee's pad, into which we've discussed my moving on a more semi-permanent cohabitation type-deal, which sounds okay to me. For the moment, however, it's not the bed, but a narrative that I wish to share with her:

I've been through the pages a few times, fixed a thousand typos, rewrote some stuff; I strove not for literary flair, but for honesty. A writer, now, of a kind. As a kid, I'd wanted to write stories and novels, but I never followed through. I didn't follow my bliss. I wonder if Nibbs Niffy would be proud of this nascent effort at being a memoirist, though not, I suspect, about the substance of what I've written.

"Take a look at this," presenting her with a sheaf of pages shiny and fresh from the inkjet.

"Oh, no way, Z, not tonight—no offense, but I'm too tired to hear what Nibbs thinks about anything. Thought you were done with that stuff."

"It's not Brian's work, it's something I wrote. A story."

I hand her the pages. She sees the title. "Well, glory be. What prompted this?"

"Hey—you kept asking, right?"

"Let me put on my PJs. Cold out there, still—they say the snow might not melt for days and days. Make me some tea, okay?"

I put the kettle on, peer out the window at a flock of cormorants following the track of the river above the snowy trees, the weeping willows drooping more than usual under their weight of snow and ice. She comes back in, settles on the couch. I bring her the tea—blueberry, with honey. I have some of my own blueberry, the spicy smoke wafting in from the kitchen.

She pages through. "You wrote all this?"

"Once it started coming, it wouldn't stop. Like I had—help."

I put on a down coat and go out on the balcony with the Sunday paper. The air, freezing, feels so good on my scarlet cheeks.

Through the vertical blinds I watch out of the corner of my eye as she begins to read: smiling at first, laughing, shaking her head, then troubled, taciturn, and utterly silent. Aimee is going to Drake Park with us, finally. She asked for it; she got it.

Drake Park: How it Went Down
By
Ashton Tobias Zemp

"Tommy always talks about the day the dee-sciples all went wild; Sally still carries a scar on her cheek to remind her of his smile."

— The Who

Fellow Traveler

This is the story of my last Jack O'Roses show, one that I attended with Brian Godbold, whose name in such a context was not Brian at all but was in actuality Nibbs Niffy. It was the last concert the band would ever give. Did I even want to go to what turned out to be not simply the worst Jack show I ever saw, but one in which everything we understood about the scene was turned on its head? No. I had to be talked into it, begged and cajoled until finally I caved.

"Like old times," he pleaded with me, and I knew that he wasn't just calling for me alone to come along. He made it clear that for the three of us, me, him, and Sally, to be together at Drake Park one more time would be a glorious thing indeed. I think Brian began to believe that if we all went back there, somehow he could change history, like Superman turning the world backwards to save Lois Lane. In this case, I thought it was to win Halsey's heart, to spin the wheel of fate in the opposite direction, to get her to love him and not me, which by that point in our lives seemed beyond delusional.

From the moment he pulled onto our property there on the Chesapeake shore, I wondered what sort of trip I had gotten myself in for. Even then I worried that Brian was turning into Rose—both physically and spiritually. His color was strange, and he was more manic than I'd seen him. He yelled at me when I demanded to know what kind of stash he had, when I asked how nervous I should be about driving seven hundred miles with a madman like Nibbs Niffy, in a Jetta with its back windshield covered in Jack stickers and god-knows-what hidden in his travel bag.

"Everything's cool," he insisted. "The cops don't have the stones to bust me. They piss in their standard-issues when they see me coming."

As we made our way out of the urban corridor and into the mountains, Nibbs commented derisively on every tune that came over the airwaves. He was already pissed—we were listening to the radio because I'd told him I didn't want to listen to Jack tapes the whole time, didn't want to get burned out so soon in the long holiday weekend. He was quite unhappy about my request for variety—for the first sixty or seventy miles, when he wasn't complaining, he was sullen and silent.

After a while I relented and went through the selection of cassettes that Nibbs had brought along, a well thought-out mix of eras, tours, and sounds, nothing less than I would have expected from a Jack scholar like him. Picking out the right combination of tapes was not so much a talent for him as an avocation. I've always been easy, though, and so I chose an '83 acoustic set from their well-received stand at Radio City, one I'm sure we'd both heard a thousand times.

The sound quality of the recording was excellent, very clean and warm. "You get this from Country Gravy or Chico? Those boys on tour this year?"

"Chico, maybe. He's one guy I definitely want to see." At the mention of Chico he got an odd look, scratched at his leg, and rubbed his eyes.

A thought occurred to me: "How many shows will this make, bud? I dare not guess."

Nibbs smiled, looking like the old F-Kid from years before, bright-eyed and fresh and open. He'd been to a run of shows the previous weekend—a twofer at Knickerbocker Arena, a one-nighter at Giant's Stadium—and now he scrunched up his face and punched the keys of an imaginary adding machine on the cracked, dusty dash of the car. "Wellsir, let me see, let me think: Saturday night will be—"

". . . insert drumroll please . . ."

"Number one-a ninety-nine . . ."

"Oh, no shit, man." Now I was seriously blown away. "Really?"

"Yeah—that's right. July 4, 1997: two fucking hundred." He let out a pent-up breath, shaking his head. "I made it."

A rush of the old excitement overwhelmed me. Two hundred shows? This was truly a monumental milestone for latter day F-Kids like us, who'd gotten started so late. No one would ever call Nibbs Niffy a tourist, or a daytripper. I congratulated him.

"Now you understand why this was so goddamn important," was all he said in reply.

We rode together on that wave of excitement for quite a few miles. The number I insisted we burn at a deserted rest stop to celebrate the news didn't hurt. Now it did feel like old times.

Once back on the road and stoned, Nibbs began ranting and raving about all the cover tunes the band had been doing. It wasn't hard to tell that something was uncool with my old friend. When he got going on some tangent, his right hand would dance up next to his face, the fingers fluttering back and forth like a big pink butterfly. In times past when he got lathered up about this or that, you might get sprayed with flecks of outraged spittle but you didn't get some freaky hand-dance.

"Covers of covers of covers of covers. What we want, no, what we DEMAND is much much much more. We insist," he said, stabbing the vinyl of the Jetta's dashboard, "on authenticity."

"I can't say I care what they play—I just want to groove, and forget my troubles." Nibbs had never

really grooved and danced like everyone else, even before he started taping the shows. He'd stand there, stock-still, leaning forward into Rose's guitar solos like they were a stiff wind coming off the stage. Everybody has their own trip, their own way of getting off. "I want to go to That Place."

His outrage was like a fog in the car. His eyes were two red pinpricks. "That's depraved. How can you not care what they play?"

"Because it's not what they play—it's HOW they play what they play. Remember?"

This aphorism only seemed to make Nibbs more agitated. He roared his disapproval, pounded the dash, thrust his thick finger in my face, cursed God and man and even Rose herself, who he accused of being disengaged to the point of uselessness.

"You need a wake-up. A wake-up call," he said, snapping his fingers. "About this whole setlist issue. You, and little miss high and mighty up there on that stage."

"Meaning what?"

"That we're fucking goddamn fucking serious about this cover song shit," he said.

Nonsense, I thought. "You are ridiculous, dude. Covers have always been part of the repertoire."

He rolled his eyes. "Maybe so, maybe not. We'll see about that."

He pulled off the freeway and into a service plaza, loped his bulk across the asphalt to a phone booth. I watched him make a call. He waited, nodding his head.

When someone answered, he yelled and screamed and stomped his huge feet. He slammed the phone down.

He strode back, goose-stepping, grinning; he

looked like he'd done a good deed. "Let's hit it," he said, thumping the door shut so hard the car frame rocked. "Full tank of gas, half a pack of smokes, it's summer, and we're on Jack tour."

"What the hell was that?"

"I called Rose. To let her know."

"Let her know what?"

"I told you," cranking the car and cracking open a high-caffeine Jolt cola, gurgling and gulping it down. "That we're serious, Z."

I hadn't a clue what he could be talking about, and chalked it up to druggy theatrics. That he'd called one of his connections—Chico, probably—to make sure he had whatever substances he needed waiting on the other end. Putz.

When we finally got to Indiana, in the middle of the night—Nibbs drove the entire way in one lengthy shot, with stops only for pizza and piss breaks—we pulled into the large campground a few miles from the venue, on acres of farmland surrounded by equally endless cornfields, which made me think of Walt Whitman's line about the 'quintillions' green', the vast and verdant fecundity of the American heartland.

The proprietors at the gate were ensconced under a white pop-up hut lit by a couple of lanterns, drinking beer and taking in money hand over fist. They took my flat-fee of forty dollars for the weekend and threw the money into a pile of similar bills spilling out of a strongbox.

"There's hoses set up and Johnny-on-the-Spots back in the north corner," the middle-aged woman said. "Y'all play nice, now."

"Yes, ma'am," Nibbs said, completely serious. "We're not like a lot of these little nitwits. We're tapers."

"Oh," she said. "Right."

We got tucked away into a decent enough spot near a copse of skinny trees separating the camping area from the farmer's back yard, met some kind neighbors, got into it with some young kids who showed up and tried to back their daddy's SUV into our turf, set up our tent. I remember feeling misty and nostalgic, and then I wished indeed that Miss Sally Simpson of the Road had accompanied us—it really felt like I'd stepped back in time. Pleasant evening weather. Cool buzz. The sound of Rose's guitar floating on the breeze from a dozen tape decks spinning. It was three in the morning. It didn't matter. Time had stopped—we were on tour.

I felt empty, though. Halsey didn't seem like the same person as when I first met her. I wasn't doing anything with my life but essentially being a househusband, and Nibbs, he was in a darker place with the dope than I myself had ever wanted to be. Those substances that we'd once used as holy sacraments had now transformed into garden-variety abuse. Acid and even weed didn't interest him that much, at least not that I could tell. I could only imagine what it was he wanted from Chico. Fucking white powders, man. Ruined the scene, almost killed Rose. Fuck that shit.

Nibbs made friends with some frat guys next door who were passing around a handle of cheap bourbon, which I declined. I watched as my friend took it and bubbled the liquor two, three, four times before passing the bottle on to the next dude. "That hits the spot," he said. In the old days, I'd never known him to drink like that.

We finally decided to crash and crawled into our bright yellow dome-tent, approximately seventy percent of which was taken up with Nibbs' considerable, ever-expanding bulk. It seemed to take him forever to fall asleep, and when he did, the snoring inside that shell of fabric was like cinder blocks being dragged across asphalt. Needless to say, I slept poorly.

"I need to find Chico!"

Those were Nibbs's first words to me in the light of morning, which came all too soon—nothing like being in a tent when the summer sun crests the tree line. The demonstrative, tripping asshole who greeted the sunrise by singing the 'Star Spangled Banner' at the top of his lungs hadn't helped.

"Why—does he have our tickets?"

"Something like that."

"Am I down in pavilion seating?" I wanted to be close, to get a good look at Rose's condition. "Please tell me I am."

Nibbs turned on me, vicious. "Fuck no you're not fucking under the goddamn fucking shed. I have an extra taper ticket—you're on the lawn with me."

The news sunk in that I'd be stuck inside the show with the tapers, a surly, type-A lot who didn't care for non-taping hangers-on like me.

"That bites."

"So you don't want to be with me? The regretful dipwad who invited you? Who's sporting these tickets," that he produced out of his hip pack and brandished in my face, a pair of mail order tickets straight from the band, threaded with glitter and psychedelic artwork, "out of the goodness of his heart, versus the cold and brutal logic of his head?"

Seeing the tickets gave me a visceral gut-punch of anticipation. There'd been nothing like the day the tickets came in the mail, and you knew you were inside. "Hey—I'm just glad to be here."

"That's more like it, you little twerp."

He wandered off. I got in the tent and put on

baby powder and changed my clothes. I brushed my teeth with water from a spigot. A party got cranked up next door—never too early for some to start getting down. Me, I stretched back out on a lounge chair and tried to nap before the sun got any higher in the sky. I twisted up a number and puffed, drank water, meditated, felt at home in this stranger's campground, surrounded by people I didn't know. Home, like I never felt anywhere else.

What seemed like only minutes later, Nibbs came running back at top speed, his big feet thumping across the hardpacked dirt covered by hay. Breathless, he exclaimed that we had to get the fuck out of Dodge—like, immediately.

"Traffic's backing up already—we have to get to the lot!"

The venue lots didn't open until two; at the time, it was only ten. I was superpissed. "The hell we do—I want to eat, chill out for a bit, get a decent head on."

But Nibbs was insistent, and all but shoved me into the car. "There's no time to eat. Now c'mon."

-11-

My boy's traffic intelligence turned out to be all too accurate—the northbound lanes of the interstate feeding into the rural music facility sat idle and jammed beneath the baking Indiana summer sun. People walked up and down the interstate with fingers in the air; some had even started abandoning their vehicles on the shoulder and hoofing it toward the venue.

Worse, there was a police checkpoint, with every fourth or fifth car getting yanked aside. We didn't get snagged by that obstacle, thankfully, which for many appeared to result in detentions and arrests. Never saw such a sight before—the cops were getting greedy, taking their game to a new level. Thanks for nothing, Slick Willie. Some lefty you turned out to be.

By the time we finally exited the freeway and started the crawl toward the south gates, which led to one of the closest parking lots—fun to be in all day, but hard to get out of after the show—Nibbs Niffy was a nervous, moist wreck of an agitated F-Kid.

Not me. I was glad to be out of the car. Now, I thought, we can relax, but we'd be depending on lot vendors for sustenance—he'd refused to stop and get food and beer.

I bought a bottled water from a guy next to us pulling the cooler out of his van. Somebody had sage burning already; the sound of a live show came from someone's speakers, and pop-up tents were appearing on every row. Security in golf carts were riding around, eyeing everyone; the cops had their own golf carts, making the lot feel more like an armed camp than Jacktown.

I asked Nibbs, "What the fuck is going on this summer?"

He shrugged, futzing with cables and batteries and blank tapes in what he called his gig-bag, a brown canvas gym bag reinforced with duct tape. "What did you expect? It's the 4th of July, on a weekend no less. That little chippy Sally Simpson doesn't know what she's missing."

I thought about how she'd said she couldn't take the crowds anymore, how nothing Rose could play would make her want to put up with the hassle and the foolishness and the fratboys getting sloppy drunk, that East Coast vibe. "Oh, I think she does. If anyone does, it's her."

"BULLSHIT!" he thundered, then wandered off, as he informed me, to get 'squared away.'

I managed to get a veggie burrito and stood around in the relentless sun, sweating and eating and feeling tired and grumpy. Hippies wandered by, seeking miracle tickets, selling dope or trinkets or artwork or T-shirts. Then more. And more. And more. Nibbs came rushing back, again in supreme crisis mode. "There's a mob scene up by the gates already—for chrissakes, we've got to go get in line!"

"What?"

"It's the only way for me to get a good taping spot! Now, come on—I need a runner for these shows."

"Oh, joy—my lucky day."

I was exhausted by all this, but I'd been through it before—the taper section at Drake Park was on the lawn, and that meant seating was first-come, first-serve. If you wanted a prime spot, once the gates opened either the taper or someone else had to run inside like a bat out of hell to throw a blanket down and reserve space. Another person, again, either the taper himself, or what was called a mule, would then carry the heavy backpack of gear, the mic stand, and whatever else. Runners and mules. Nibbs had already told me which one I'd be, which with his physique meant that I'd be doing the fleet-foot routine. I was starting to wonder if my trim build was the reason that Nibbs wanted me to come there with him in the first place.

We weaseled our way into the growing throng by the taper's entrance. Then Nibbs stretched, yawned, and started to walk off. "Be back to check on you later."

"Hey asshole," I called out after him, "get me a beer, and some more water!" My veggie burrito was decomposing and sending gas bubbles every which way.

"Dollah bills, y'all. Dollah. Dollah bills. Dollah. Dollah bills, y'all," this one kid kept saying over and over and over, waving a C-note around. I'd never seen such fervor for tickets, such begging for miracles.

I told him to cool it with his dollah-bills schtick, but that only made him chant it louder, sticking his tongue out at me and dancing around like a crazed hippie jester. He held his arms out—see? I can do what I want.

I waved my hands, a plea for calm. "Why's everybody so crazed to get inside?"

"They always bring it at Drake Park, brah,"

the sunburned, crispy tour kid, drenched in sweat and out of breath from his crazy dance, explained. "I got to be inside and see what old Rosie's got to say to us, broheem. She got a sto-ray to tell us all."

I became less annoyed with it all than swept up in the fervor—what if it WAS the big night when everything came back together? What if they were finally going to break out 'Saints at the River,' one of the psychedelic epics from the first golden age, a tune not played by the band in over twenty-five years, much requested, much beloved, and apparently much derided by Rose, who supposedly declared, "It's just too fucking hard to sing." They said 'Saints' had some juju about it; they said if the band ever played it again, you'd know that you were seeing the last Jack O'Roses show.

"Maybe they'll finally bring back 'Return of the Grievous Angel'," a young shirtless guy said, already turning pink in the bright sunlight. He couldn't have been more than sixteen or seventeen. "That's what I want to hear."

Rose's voice had been shot for a long time. "You think Rose can still sing that high Emmylou part? Forget it."

"Rose can do anything she wants, dude."

"Keep thinking that, kid."

Nibbs finally came back. I'd been left in the hot summer sun with his taping gear and nary a drop to drink, but at least I had friends aplenty thanks to the tapers and their mules. As a runner, I was treated with no more or less respect than the tapers themselves; at the Drake Parks of the world, the runner was important.

Still, I was pissed as hell. "You find what was so damn important?"

Nibbs was fit to be tied—he hadn't found Chico, who we would later find out had been busted holding an eight ball of uncut cocaine at a drug checkpoint. "Scored some good doses at least," Nibbs said, dejected at possessing the drug that'd made all this possible. LSD—not a drug like an addict needs. The addict is trying to shut some part of his mind down, not open up his consciousness to the infinite and infinitesimal connectedness of the cosmos. His attitude saddened me, filled me with empty futility. He was like Rose on a bad night—going through the motions.

"That's awesome, man," I said.

"If you say so."

In a way, I was with him—I didn't want to dose, not really. The idea scared me. With all the cops and the heat and the desperation, wrong set and setting for a fat trip—and at a Jack O'Roses outdoor summertime show. Who'd have imagined such heresy?

To wit: just inside the gates, at the first check-through, I could see men in suits operating metal detectors. Jesus Christ, as I said to Nibbs, what has it all come to? The fucking DEA set up right there at the front gates, waiting to shake us down?

"Never seen this before," is all Nibbs could say.

He fought his way out of the mass of people and went, he said, to get a couple of beers. He looked pale and sick. I figured he was starting to have withdrawal issues. Wonderful. Maybe he'd have a seizure in the middle of the drums segment.

Finally another taper we knew, Martin, came running up. Breathless and burdened by two enormous gray Pelican cases full of recording gear, his eyes were bugged out, and a vein beat in his damp forehead. "What the fuck is going on? I had to park two miles away." He leaned over, red-faced, whispering.

"Can I slip in here with you?"

"I guess."

Martin was a mental-health counselor at a northeastern inner city hospital, with Jack tour every summer being his vacation, his big release. He had a full, black beard flecked with gray, and wore a Cleveland Indians ball cap on backwards, his trademark: road name, 'Injun Joe'. I always had good conversations with him, and even though there was much grumbling from others around us, I let him slide into my limited personal space with all his crap. I'd first met him at Ventura. He was Family.

Injun Joe brought with him heap bad news, though, word which sent an ugly hubbub through the crowd: He'd heard from a parking attendant that the increased police presence was due to a death threat on Rose.

"Shades of '86," I said, disturbed.

"I'd like to get my hands on the asshat who pulled this shit."

"Probably some kid making a joke—a sick one."

Cursing and worry and dismissal and angst rippled through the crowd. A girl started crying through eyes already as red as a Carolina sunset. I shuffled my feet, folded my arms. I said to myself, self, you came all this way for this shit? Lord have mercy.

Nibbs came back with a pair of ice-cold Sierra Nevada Pale Ales, dripping and fresh from someone's cooler.

"Thank god," I said, gulping a carbonated swallow that nearly choked me. "You're trying to finish me off out here."

When told of the news of the death threat, Brian Godbold turned white as a sheet. "What a crock of shit."

Injun Joe hooked a thumb in the direction of the suits milling around behind the venue gates. "Somebody's taking it seriously."

"What the fuck have you gotten us into," I whispered to Nibbs.

He shrieked: "What do you mean?"

I gestured at the throng, growing surlier with each passing quarter-hour. "Look at this clusterfuck."

Nibbs's eyes danced. His mouth worked up and down. He laughed, shook his head. "No no no," he said. "No fucking way."

I didn't know what he meant.

Nibbs began marching back and forth, launching into a lung-busting diatribe about Ronnie Wayne Bundrick's prison sentence for attempted murder. Cartoon exclamation points appeared over his head. He bellowed and snorted like an aggrieved bull moose. He became a tie-dyed version of the Hulk, stomping his massive feet and making us all jump.

"These idiots barely protected her the first time," he shouted at the venue security team massed on the other side of the chain link fence, milling around pokerfaced in their canary-yellow Event Staff T-shirts—some of them looked like Indiana high schoolers and college kids. "You cheese-eating hayseeds had better have your goddamn shit wired tight tonight, motherfuckers!"

"Dial it back, pal," a buzzcut, thick-limbed security captain said, Popeye forearms folded across a broad chest. He seemed more bemused than angry. "Take yourself a chill-pill, big old hippie man."

Nibbs scoffed and downed his beer in two enormous gulps. He flung the bottle into a trash barrel beside the gate, which shattered, bits of brown glass exploding upwards. He let loose with a stream of invective to make blush a crusty, drunken seaman on shore leave.

"I'm not kidding," the goon said, pointing a meaty cornfed digit at the wild-eyed, gesticulating F-Kid I called my best friend. "You put a lid on the cursing, or I'm going make sure you get searched real good, pardner."

Heat and dust and sweat. Drum circles pounded; miracle kids swirled and circulated and pled for succor. The mass of bodies waiting to get in continued to swell, the crowd thicker and more boisterous and pushy than I'd ever experienced, the ticket begging now beyond the point of absurdity. Tapers yelled at all the ticket-seekers to back up, back off.

Police helicopters and a news chopper thrummed overhead, circling. The sun hit a brutal angle, no relief. I felt as though I were tripping, that I'd been dosed, that the miracle seekers were chanting and moaning and flagellating themselves bloody, and so I sat down on one of Injun Joe's pelican cases, but that didn't last because the crowd surged forward and knocked me off balance. I got back to my feet, but I felt as though I might pass out. A kind brother let me quaff a few swallows from his wineskin of tepid water, which perked me up.

Five-thirty, five forty-five. Shoving, a fight breaking out over a dropped ticket. I felt ill from the heat, but that was my fault for not being prepared. Intrepid vendors moved their coolers near the crowd at the gate, though, and I bought a couple of waters and a beer, which fortified me.

As the hour came and went, the chant started low and insistent, then built in intensity. "Let us in, let us in, let us in."

At ten after six, finally, the gates began to open, and a roar of relief rolled over our heads.

"You're ready for this," Nibbs asked, "aren't you?"

"If I have to be."

"Get me a good spot, please."

"Relax—this ain't my first rodeo."

Since all I had was a rolled-up, striped Mexican falsa blanket, a relic that Nibbs bought all the way back in '89, I made it through the pat-down and the metal detectors without delay. As his gig-bag had to be thoroughly inspected, more so than usual, I wouldn't see Nibbs again for a while.

A stab of adrenaline as I cleared the last hurdle, the tearing of my ticket, which in the old days I would have supervised carefully so that only the smallest piece of it were taken; I hauled ass, darting in and out of regular concert goers who didn't feel the crushing need to bolt for the sloping lawn.

I ran like the wind, around the walkway and through the beer and food vendors and the curve toward the lawn. I raced alongside a lithe woman in shorts and a tank and Birkenstock Arizonas she must've had taped on.

"No way," I said breathlessly. "No way, little sistah."

"Eat my dust, old timer!" We laughed and ran.

But then, my own Birks got twisted up, and I went down hard. It's a miracle I wasn't trampled.

I staggered to my feet and continued on, both knees skinned painfully like a grade-schooler in the yard at recess who's fallen off the swing set. As a result, I was in no way able to get that blanket into the sweet spot. By the time I made it up there, the taper section was almost completely covered in sheets and tie-dye tapestries and blankets like my own, so I was forced to take a shitty spot way up in the corner, halfway up the lawn.

I expressed disappointment with my luck, but a guy lying spread-eagle on his blanket—to preserve as much space as possible—told me, "Just point your mics at the repeater speakers up yonder at the back of the pavilion." The guy, who had a West Virginia hillbilly accent and said his name was Clyde, gestured at the delay speakers hanging between the square video screens on which we'd get closeups of Rose and Jake and Linus and the rest, or their fingers touching the strings and the keys, their faces contorted in concentration, remembering words, changes, tempos . . . and maybe the band would tip over the cliff into pure improvisation, searching for the sound: an all-too-rare occurrence in these, what would turn out to be the final years of the band.

"Don't know if my buddy'll go for that. He's particular."

"Sounds right good coming outta them little speakers. Did last year, anyways."

I peered upward at Clyde's speakers hanging off the back of the shed, but my eyes were drawn instead to the incongruity that was the figure I noticed on the catwalk underneath the overhang. He was scanning, scanning, scanning the increasingly crowded lawn with large binoculars. An FBI spotter, I surmised, looking for potential shooters or other threats. At a Jack show. Unreal. And yet staring me in the face.

Keep her safe, boys.

At last, Nibbs appeared down at the wall in front of the lawn, a head taller than anyone else in the area. He searched and searched, his eyes darting this way and that into the mass of people now claiming their turf and putting up mic stands. When he finally saw me standing way at the back, waving my hands, I could tell even from that far back that his face had turned the color of a brick.

He dropped his gig bag and mic stand onto the blanket. "What the fuck kind of pussy-assed cunting spot do you call this?"

"I fell."

His eyes teared up as though I'd insulted him. In a high, strange voice, he yelled, "You fell? You fell?"

"I'm sorry."

"Get out of the goddamn way."

I stood off to the side. Nibbs set up his mic stand, attached the clips, and then produced the microphones out of the padded case in which they were stored. He slipped two foam windscreens on the ends of the long tubes, attached the cables, and secured them to the stand with Velcro strips. He stood behind the rig for ten minutes trying to decide about the angle, until finally he seemed satisfied. He elevated the mics toward the sky and started futzing around with the other gear. He refused to look at me or speak.

"Point 'em at them little repeater speakers," Clyde said, stoned as a bat on a spliff of what tasted like Sour Diesel he'd been passing around to us, a sharp pungent smoke that had me into the right frame of mind. "Up yonder."

Nibbs did a slow burn, craning his enormous head at our neighbor. "Go kiss a duck. I mean, seriously. These guns need to pointed at the stacks, pal."

"Suit yourself," Clyde said, guileless and happily stoned. "I'm here to play it as it lays, brother."

A couple of young, clean-cut guys came up with

a cassette deck and asked for a patch out of Nibbs's expensive DAT machine, but with much bluster he refused. "I don't need that dusty piece of junk sucking down my juice, newbie." Annoyed and perplexed, the patchers moved on and were accommodated by the good-natured taper in front of us.

I called Brian Godbold out on his refusal to help the kids. "Remember when? Remember when you used to do the same thing, those cats like Country Gravy who gave you patches out of their decks? Or did you forget the little people already?"

He cut his eyes over at Clyde's simple, inexpensive rig. "I am one of the little people," he grumbled. "Now let's dose and get this show on the road."

All so mechanical, I thought. This is too much like work.

We both took the paper—only mine was a fake. I'd cut a little square out of a gas receipt and tabbed that on my tongue instead of the LSD, which I'd palmed and then let fall to the ground.

Tension in the air, a strange, ugly vibe. We both sat cross-legged while he flipped through his setlist notebook or otherwise fiddled with his gear, squinting downward at the stage. He held a cigarette clamped in the corner of his mouth, the smoke curling upwards into his eyes. The helicopters continued to circle out over the vast parking areas, more heard than seen.

I stood up and stretched. The venue was now packed to the gills. Seven o'clock, then seven-thirty, the audience fully charged up, growing restless, the reserved seats jammed, the tapers like sardines in the marked off square in the middle of the growing horde on the lawn, now draped in shadow thanks to the sun dropping behind the pavilion. The walkways were jammed, the lawn more full than it usually was until after they'd finally started playing. F-Kids tended to stay in Jacktown until the last possible second and beyond, either partying, shopping with the gypsy vendors—like Sally Simpson once was, with her hemp necklaces—or otherwise communing with one another. Sometimes what was happening out there was more important than the first couple of songs, in which the band, creaky, would slowly warm up and get it into gear.

There was a flurry of activity; the house music disappeared. I peered down at the stage and yelped, "Here they come—it's them."

–12–

A roar of recognition broke against the bandstand like a wave. Nibbs made a strangled sound and punched spastically at the buttons on the tiny digital tape deck, a device not much bigger than a packet of cigarettes. A red light came on, and he visibly relaxed—he was rolling tape.

Rose came billowing out in one of her flowing black dresses, the diaphanous floor-length garment blown about by the fans set up to cool down the musicians. Her feet invisible, she moved about the stage seeming almost to float.

I bent over and yelled in his ear. "Some death threat—old girl's the first one out."

His eyes bulged. "Don't say that. Don't you fucking say those words," he said, all but choking. He shook his head, fluttered the fat pink hand. "Death threat my ass."

There they were—Jack O'Roses. I never stopped getting that feeling when they walked out—I'll be damned, that's Rose Partland standing there, bigger than life. Rose. Jake. Linus. LeMoy. And here I am, sharing the space with these living legends. I became flushed with excitement. Almost three years had passed since my last show—it had been too long. I felt the old tug of anticipation.

What would they play?

HOW would they play what they played?

As Linus ambled out on stage to his own wave of approval, he peered upwards at the assembling masses, grinning. Thump-thump-thump, thok-thok-thok as LeMoy tested out the skins. Lenn Circosta twinkled on the synth, then Jake charged out in shorts and a tie-dyed wifebeater, pointing and gesturing to the lucky folks in the lower level. The band was all but ready.

A fresh roar of exultation: Rose had strapped on her axe instead of plopping down behind the baby grand. If she had the axe on already, you knew it was going to be a Rose-rocker to open.

We were not disappointed—the heavy filter effects she teased indicated that the power chord opening of 'Alphabet Avenue' would soon be upon us. A serious funk and vocal workout set in the milieu of a rough urban neighborhood, the tune had been largely derided by fans back in '77 as overt pandering to the disco market, but by the time Jack O'Roses had shown that it could master yet another musical genre, audiences became eager to hear the song. Into the modern era, 'Alphabet Avenue' remained in the rotation, but only once a tour—a treat.

I leaned over to Nibbs. "Awesome! Have they played 'AA' yet this summer?"

Nibbs shook his head. "Course not. And I called it, anyway."

I offered my upturned palm for a high five; he declined, waving me away.

His attitude couldn't despoil my pleasure—after all the BS and hardship and heat and hunger, here was the reward: The rainbow makers, onstage and doing a favorite tune. I felt extremely high, one of those contact acid-buzzes, the kind you get when you're not doing anything, but everyone around you is, and the energy somehow rubs off.

BAM went the opening power chord. As the music kicked in I started getting down. I grooved and shook my booty, as did most of the crowd.

I looked at Nibbs, his eyes cast downward at the LED readout on the DAT recorder. He had dosed but I had not, yet I was the one dancing and joyous. That was his schtick, though. This was nothing unusual.

Trouble in paradise: Rose fumbled around and dropped lyrics. The clams she laid down during the big jam were embarrassing. Like everyone, I kept dancing—I pushed open the door in my mind that had been first unlocked at Ventura. I went to That Place, and, ignoring the spotty performance from our Earthmother, felt for a time as high as I'd ever been on any drug.

The jam to close out 'AA' was lengthy and semi-interesting; in the song's roundabout vocal conclusion, Lenn Circosta blended well, providing the high harmonies in place of Rose. Circosta was a big fan of The Who, and had introduced 'Behind Blue Eyes' and 'We're Not Gonna Take It' into the repertoire of classic rock covers that Jack sprinkled throughout its setlist. The Who—I dug them a long time before I even knew about Jack O'Roses, and loved that they'd begun referencing them.

As the band played on, I felt my real life troubles melt away—all of Halsey's business stuff, the stores, the farmhouse that needed so much renovation and updating, the numbers and invoices and balance sheets, dealing with importing containers full of clothing for the boutiques, and all that bullshit—and found myself fully present and in the now.

And yet, also awash in sense-memories:

The salt air of Ventura in my lungs, the marine layer burning away, the light flashing on my sunglasses, and a pinpoint of starlight. This place—Drake Park—six years ago when I saw them lay on the world one of the best shows of the modern era, and I'd made love to Halsey back at the campground. Any of a dozen similar KOA campgrounds, in which F-Kids like Sally and Nibbs and I chilled out and talked for hours, about matters philosophical, as well as sophomoric. Driving across the Golden Gate then looking up in Muir Woods, awed, at the biggest, oldest trees I'd ever seen. The Las Vegas strip, all of us tripping, giggling, and bouncing off one another like little kids as we strolled the boulevard of bigger than life buildings and the amusements within, at least until a cop threatened us and we ducked into the Aladdin, where to Nibbs' consternation I dropped a quarter in a slot machine, and on the first spin won a sweet twenty bucks. Driving through a desert tableau out of John Ford at a moment of orange, fading dusk, a glorious open feeling of timelessness far, very far, from a rock concert held in a city, the three of us quiet, dirty, and tired from the shows and the heat, smoking, silent, chasing the sunset. At a Waffle House on the perimeter in Atlanta after a Halloween show, laughing at a guy in amazing, Hollywood-style werewolf makeup who sat calmly eating a Denver omelet and reading a thick paperback romance novel. Driving home from Cleveland after the first shows since Matt Alvin Christopher died, all night through the Appalachian mountains, listening to a scratchy, hissy cassette of Rose noodling through one of those 1974 'Nebulas' that take the listener from birth to death to glorious rebirth, resurrecting the tune as a delicately plucked restatement of the theme—and then, the whole band creeps back in for the full reprise before melting into the next song, a transition that, in its deft sublimity, catches the listener by surprise. Sally's face, her pupils blown, our bodies damp and tense and pounding away at one another until finally exploding in release, spent, high on youth and sex and music and the clear, sweet Midwestern air. That rush of anticipation in the hotel or the campground when you realize you've got another show ahead of you that night—and, oh, my, what will they play? How will they play what they play? The exquisite moment in the arena when the lights go down, and the roar goes up. The ache as the last notes at the last show of a tour fade away into the ether and the lights come up and Rose is gone, backstage, whisked away by the limousine or the white van—and when will I see Jack O'Roses again? On the next tour. Surely, this would come to pass. Like the sun rising in the East.

By the third or fourth song, the initial spurt of energy from both me as well as the musicians flagged, my nostalgia turned to fatigue, and I began to hope that this would be one of those ridiculously short sets that the band sometimes played.

But then there was a Dylan cover, followed by 'Whiskey in the Jar,' a recent sort-of bust out as an electric tune, then a new song by Linus that was not too cool to my ears, very unformed, slow, awkward in melody, and embryonic in execution. He received a perfunctory cheer, shook his head, shrugged.

Sweat rolled down my body—even though the sun was now completely behind the stage, the heat felt oppressive, the air thick and wet and with nowhere for water to evaporate to.

Circosta counted off the next tune. A hush came over the crowd, and then Jack O'Roses went into 'We're Not Gonna Take It.' Drake Park erupted. I didn't give a shit about the tapers and their precious microphones—I cheered right along with everyone else.

"Welcome to the camp, I guess you all know why we're here ..."

The harmonies were outstanding, my skin covered in gooseflesh. LeMoy pounded away at his kit as though he'd been waiting all his life to channel Keith Moon. Here was true rock and roll power. A sense of history—and perhaps a message: I remembered Peter Finch in Network. *We're as mad as hell; we're not gonna take it. A message to the cops, to the depraved idiot who'd called in the death threat, to all the little tourists and townies and daytrippers outside who'd come without a ticket. Or maybe no message at all. You could never tell with Jack.*

Nibbs, who had been thoroughly disengaged up to this point, leaned over and said, "First time closing the first set."

"Let go of all that. Be here now."

He didn't seem to hear me. He actually looked downcast, which was puzzling until I remembered his desire for a no-cover show of all Jack tunes. That had already been blown by 'Ballad of a Thin Man'. Nibbs Niffy would have to get over his foolish expectations.

I borrowed Clyde's opera glasses and peered down at the stage. From my angle Rose and her guitar were backlit and silhouetted beside Circosta, who was at the time singing the high 'see me, feel me' bit, a part Rose would have sung twenty years ago. She was ghostly, a presence hovering beside the keyboardist in her black dress, the fans making her hair dance. I felt a chill pass through me, what my grandmother would have suggested was an occurrence of someone walking over my future grave. But I know now it was Rose's grave.

You ain't gonna follow me any of those ways—although you think you must.

Epic. The end of the Who song pumped up the entire place like no time I could remember, at least not at the last dozen or so shows I'd seen before this one. The band climaxed the song beyond anything Pete Townsend could have imagined, except perhaps in volume. Rose even did a couple of modest little windmills, the tumultuous jubilance at even her smallest movements here a stupendous roar of approval.

As the band exited stage left, Rose paused and gave a big sweeping wave, which meant she was on, she was okay, she was feeling IT like we were.

"Well, damn," I said as Nibbs and the other tapers stopped their decks and the floodlights came on, illuminating the lawn under harsh light. "That rocked!"

Nibbs had a look like he'd sucked a lemon. "Eh," he said.

"Oh, come on—"

"A fucking cover. Two of them. I didn't want any covers tonight." He shook his head. I thought he was on the verge of tears. "I don't see what this stupid song from 'Tommy' has to do with any of this."

I did, but had no gut for arguing the matter with my friend.

I watched as Nibbs sat down and flipped through his book of setlists, muttering, cursing, turning down a hit from another of Clyde's fat numbers, which'd kept coming throughout the set. I tried to make conversation, to discuss what they might play, but he ignored me. I threw up my hands and went to get beer.

I spoke in passing to Injun Joe, down at the front of the taper section in a prime spot, this despite having had no runner of his own.

"Jesus—did you hear that shit?"

The exacting standards of the Nibbs's and Injun Joe's of the world were threatening to dispel my enthusiasm over the performance. "I thought it was pretty good—okay, I guess."

"I schlepped this crap two miles for this?"

"Second set's gonna rock."

"Whatever." He fumbled in his pockets and handed me a ten-spot. "Hey, get me a beer, would you? Two, if possible."

"I'll try."

The plaza, thronged with set break activity—the beer lines endless, as were the rowdy, massive queues for the restrooms. There was a commotion from around the bend at the entrance gates, but I couldn't see what was going on, only that security goons and cops were now running through the crowd in that direction.

A scared custodian, a pale, mousy teenage girl with bad skin and stringy hair, had eyes like saucers, and not from being dosed.

"It'll be all right, honey," I said to her in my sweetest Charleston twang. "These hippies ain't gonna hurt you none."

"They said there's a riot going on outside!" She sounded terrified.

"A—what? A riot?"

She whispered, "Like—oh my god," and scuttled off with her broom and dustpan.

I made my way back to the lawn. Inside the amphitheater, everything seemed fairly normal but for the crush of people. It was full dark now, but the blazing floodlights pointed at the lawn provided uncomfortably full illumination. I skirted Injun Joe; I'd give him his money back later.

No getting around Nibbs, however. "Where's the fucking beer?"

I thought of a way to assuage his ire. "Dude—I'm tripping too hard. I couldn't deal."

"Oh." He nodded, satisfied with my excuse. "No worries, bro."

I sat down beside him. He offered me a wineskin produced out of the gig bag. I drank. I smoked with Clyde and became anxious—it felt like the band had been offstage for an hour, but I looked at my watch and saw that only fifteen minutes had elapsed.

"Excuse me."

A voice came from my right—a woman in her late twenties, lovely, a natural beauty. She had on a simple T-shirt and shorts, her sandy hair pulled back from around a make-up free face, an outdoorsy look about her. A tourist, I figured.

"Hey now, sister," I said.

"Hey now," she replied, pulling from behind her a tiny blonde girl in a flower-print dress, barefoot, gorgeous, fine hair so fair as to be white. "This is my niece, Summer. She has a question for you."

"Shoot."

"Go ahead and ask him, honey."

Summer, shy, maybe eight or nine, turned to hide against her aunt's stomach.

"It's okay," I tried to reassure. "Ask away."

Summer was luminous and glowing on the floodlit lawn, a perfect, beautiful little girl if I'd ever seen one.

Finally, she spoke to me. "Will you make me a tape of my first show?" she asked in a rush, the way kids do when they're trying to remember lines they've rehearsed. "Please mister, so I can hear Rose again when I get home?"

My eyes watered, and I shared a sweet smile with the young woman.

"Sure we will," I said. "Nibbs, give me your notebook. We're going to send Miss Summer a tape."

Nibbs turned a baleful eye upon the three of us and grunted. "Negatory." He went back to flipping through his setlists, opaque and uncaring. "Already got too many assholes waiting back home."

I felt humiliated. The woman's face hardened in disappointment. "Oh, come on!"

"He'll do it, honey," I said to the little girl. I looked into her aunt's eyes. "I'll hold his big butt down and make him do it."

"Thank you," the woman said, handing me a business card. She scowled at Nibbs, or rather, the back of his head.

"He's messed up," I whispered. "He's not like that usually."

She was placated, but not much. "Okay, sorry."

"Don't be."

They walked off. I looked at the card—

Susan Becker
Interpretive Park Ranger
Indiana Dunes National Lakeshore
National Park Service
beckersusank@idnl.nps.gov

I slipped it in my pocket and slapped Nibbs on the back of his fat head. "That was shitty."

His eyes glazed, he turned to look at me, unmindful of the girl or my disappointment in him—he'd made his call. "'Barfly' to open second set."

"Wonderful. I hope you're right. Oh, by the way—they say there's a riot going on outside."

Nibbs rolled his eyes and snorted. "Rumors, rumors, rumors—if it weren't for the fucking rumors, this whole ridiculous circus would collapse in on itself."

"Cops were running every which way."

"Jackbooted fascists probably got a report that someone's smoking rabbit tobacco in the ladies room—fuck those assholes!"

"I'm just telling you what I heard."

A cheer went up. Nibbs sprang to his feet. "Holy crap."

The house lights remained on, but musicians had reappeared onstage. "They're back? Already?"

"Short break. Good."

The second set started, house lights and all, not with 'Barfly' but another drinking song: 'Gin & Vermouth.' Nibbs barely got the deck started. He was pissed about being wrong in calling the tune, his face a mask of annoyance. I was happy with the choice—good old Jake rocking the house, Rose playing her boogie-woogie barrelhouse piano routine, everybody getting down.

The video screens now on, I could see that Rose looked pretty bad, her skin waxy, the streaked gray hair plastered onto her wet forehead. Her eyes danced and seemed unfocused, but she remembered all the words. The kids were grooving; the kids were all right.

-13-

Halfway through the second song, the Rose ballad 'Take Your Coat,' a tale of betrayal and love gone wrong—a real Jack classic, a treat—a curious roar began from behind us.

I turned:

People were scaling the back fence!

From outside!

At first only a few climbed over, but then more, and more, and more. A skinny, shirtless hippie kid stood astride one of the concession stands at the back of the lawn, waving the people on in an exuberant dance of triumph. Earlier, security guards had been stationed atop the two vending stands, keeping watch; now, apparently, they'd disappeared.

"What the fuck is this?" Nibbs hissed. He turned around and stared gape-mouthed at the unfolding madness, fists clenched. "You little bastards! No trip without a ticket!"

The influx of gatecrashers trickled, but one of the copters roared over the venue in an arc, a terrifying sight. The band kept playing.

A guy came barreling straight through the taper section, breathless, his stringy hair framing his face like the wild man of Borneo. Tapers scrambled and tried get ahold of him, but in a domino effect he managed to take out three stands, and in an instant thousands of dollars in microphones went down onto people's heads and other rigs. Now even the tapers were yelling. Finally, the interloper was thrown head over heels out of the section.

I stood on the fringes, pushing against the crowd, helping keep others from spilling over into the section, but it was hard. Nibbs was furious—in all the excitement, his deck had somehow gotten turned off.

He resumed recording.

Jack ended the tune, and the band seemed to have a quick conference. Before the camera cut away, a glimpse of Rose's face, now angry instead of blissfully singing her songs. She charged over to her piano and began banging out through the opening chords of their most famous tune, the biggest hit next to 'Came a Day.' She sounded as furious as she looked. "Now is this it, or just the calm before the storm? Abstract thoughts, refuse to take form . . . a lonely bee, just trying to lead the swarm, just trying to conform . . ."

Finally, a reaction from the stage—they never did this song anymore except as a show closer, and here it was early in the second set.

Nibbs looked panicked. "They're going to call the show off!"

They didn't have to.

About halfway through the bridge, at about the time the rest of the band, caught off guard, had finally gotten in sync with her, Rose's piano playing seemed to falter, losing her sense of timing and rhythm. Two shirtless sunburned fratboys right next me started shouting and shoving each other, one of several fights I saw breaking out.

Then, Rose's piano sounded as though she'd pounded it with both fists, and a horrible cry went up through the crowd: I caught a glimpse of her pitching over and falling from her piano bench. The music stopped, the stage went dark.

Nibbs shrieked.

The crowd convulsed.

Pandemonium.

I stared down into the pavilion and saw that people were trying to jump up on the stage, the yellow shirts throwing them back into what looked to be the devil's own mosh pit. Soon they became outnumbered, and the stage was overwhelmed, a horrible sight.

People screamed and cried. A paroxysm of violence seemed to ripple upwards from the stage. In the taper section, stands and microphones and cables went everywhere. Nibbs, babbling and shaking, began shoving gear into his gig bag. He yanked the mics off by the cables, unmindful of their handling, and collapsed his stand, fumbling and fending off people trying to push through the tapers.

I grabbed him by the shirt, a size 3X black pocket T with stains and rips and the inevitable pinhole burns all down the front. "Let's get out!"

Clutching his bag like a baby, Nibbs shoved his way into the crowd, up the lawn.

"Where the fuck are you going?"

"Out the way those little bastards came in!"

A voice finally boomed out over the PA: "Everybody stop! Everybody cool out! Everything's fine! The show's over—proceed calmly toward the nearest exit and return DIRECTLY to your vehicles . . ." The voice went on, robotic, but with an edge that betrayed the speaker's fear. "Everybody cuh-cool it!"

With Nibbs leading the way, we pushed through

the surging crowd, most of whom had the same idea, all of us charging upwards toward the broken fences at the top of the hill; Nibbs, swinging his mike stand and knocking people out of his way. We spilled over the top, everyone panicking and running down toward the lots.

We wove our way through the back parking lot, past the duck pond and up on a small rise dotted with trees. Other people were hiding there, crying, puking, praying. The riot in the lots, no mere rumor, raged on. Screaming. Helicopters. The nightmare sky, glowing from the fires and the police car rollers. Tear gas wafted over the rows of cars like a thin fog rolling in, one eerily backlit by the burning cop cars and VW vans scattered throughout the endless acreage of gravel and dry grass. Haunted, angry voices echoed among the vehicles. Police in riot gear swept up and down the rows, fending off rocks and bottles. The pop-pop-pop of guns firing rubber bullets and bean bags went off every few seconds. An amplified voice boomed out—GO BACK, GO BACK TO YOUR VEHICLES. Somewhere nearby, a young girl wailed in anguish, but I couldn't get a fix on the sound. Dogs howled. I thought I heard a baby crying.

I squatted down on my haunches, trying to catch my breath, my nostrils and eyes stinging.

A girl sat cross-legged, wringing her hands back and forth. "Rose fell over, Rose fell over!"

"Don't worry—she's all right," I said. Not believing it. Not believing any of it.

She vomited into her own lap, wept.

Nibbs Niffy collapsed beside me onto the grassy knoll. He put his head in his hands. I think he was crying, but I couldn't look at his face.

A helicopter flew over our heads. I nudged

Nibbs, and together we watched the medivac land behind the gates of the venue. Barely a minute went by before it took off again.

"Oh please, god," he said, "don't let her die. Not like this."

We were so far from the car, the Jetta on the other side of the venue. "Let's walk out of here," I said.

"Excuse me?"

I stood up, craning my neck around, trying to get my bearings. "Let's just walk back to the campground. If they tow the car, they tow it—one way or another, we'll recover it."

Nibbs panicked at the thought. "But but but we can't leave the car!"

"Yes," I said, looking over my shoulder at a full-scale riot in progress. "We can."

A local kid wearing a tie-dye that looked fresh, as though he'd just bought it that day, said, "I know the way—I can show you a shortcut, along the frontage road."

A group of us banded together, began walking. The miles passed in silence but for our shuffling feet.

We found the campground subdued, and it would stay that way as stragglers like us—refugees from a war zone—made their way home either on foot, or by car.

Nibbs made a fire in a metal drum and stood there most of the night, his trip dragging on, staring as the flames licked at the blackened interior of the barrel. There was anger and sorrow on the faces of everyone I saw. I didn't sleep a wink.

Nibbs screamed out, finally: "I want the gatecrashers! I WANT THEIR GODDAMN HEADS ON A PIKE!"

An old hippie sitting on a picnic table over in

the shadows of the adjoining campsite said in a gentle voice, "No, you don't, brother. They already know what they wrought tonight."

"Get a load of the Ghost of Christmas Past over here, clanking his chains," Nibbs called out to me, keeping his eyes locked on the guy. Nibbs's words came hard-edged, like a taunt designed to start a brawl. "You were probably the first one up the hill, weren't you, you crusty old lot lizard."

The oldtimer cackled at this, flung his beaded, smelly gray dreads around, scratched himself. He took a gurgling slug out of the bottle of E&J brandy he'd been cradling like a street drunk. He got up and wandered off into the gloom.

I got in the tent and lay there, staring at the fabric and listening to the campground never truly wind down, not until nearly dawn.

The next morning the classic rock radio DJ recapped the horror—three were dead, a dozen cops injured, and mucho property damage, in the hundreds of thousands of dollars. The word was that Rose was okay, though, being treated for exhaustion and dehydration. For obvious reasons, the announcer went on to say that tonight's show was cancelled, the news of which nonetheless seemed to hit Nibbs like he hadn't expected to hear it—his 200th show would not go on, a personal tragedy, but what did he expect that morning? It wasn't as though Rose, the authorities, and the F-Kids could erase what had happened and start over the next day, at the next show, same as it ever was.

Would she ever play again? Surely. The sun had arisen, had it not?

The DJ also gave instructions about how to retrieve vehicles from the parking lot—if you left without your car, you had to present a ticket stub to get back in.

We hitched a ride back toward the venue. Cops were everywhere, and you had to be thoroughly vetted before being allowed to retrieve a vehicle. The irony of having to show a stub instead of a whole ticket was not lost on us, but we were a long way from being able to joke about what had happened.

By whatever miracle, the Jetta was intact. We putt-putted out of the lot escorted by two cops in a golf cart. Nibbs sprayed sputtering windshield fluid, trying to wiper away a layer of grime from the dusty parking lot—did tear gas leave residue? I hadn't a clue.

Once we reached the exit, I raised a hand to the cops. "Thanks," I called out with a self-effacing, high-cheeked smile. "Sorry."

"Get your fucking hippie asses out of Indiana," one said with a snarl. "You're lucky we're not conducting exit searches on these vehicles."

"Oh, fuck you," Nibbs said, but the cop didn't hear.

About twenty miles into the drive home we stopped at a gas station, one of those off-ramp places with a fast food counter attached. Nibbs called his mother from a pay phone—his second momentous call of this ill-fated trip. When he came back, he said she'd been hysterical at what was being shown on CNN.

I phoned Halsey, who was equally worried. "For god's sake," she said, " just fly back. Put it on the corporate AMEX."

"No—I'll stay with Nibbs. He's pretty upset."

"Are you?"

"I wish I knew. I don't know what to think."

I went in to get a couple of Cokes and refrigerated

sandwiches—egg salad, a turkey melt. When I got back to the car, my tour partner sat listening to radio news reports about the disastrous show.

I could see the moisture on his face.

My stomach fell into my New Balances—I don't know why, but I assumed he'd heard on the radio that Rose was dead. "Is she gone?"

Nibbs squinted at me through red eyes. "Who?"

From his reaction, I knew that Rose lived. "No one, dude. No one."

He sat gripping the steering wheel. His voice was small, like that of a child. "Oh, please don't let this be my last Jack O'Roses show," he asked the empty air. "Please don't let it end like this."

But it did. And that, fellow babies, is what really happened at Drake Park. We drove home, and it lasted twice as long as any trip I ever took.

THE END.

Aimee, exasperated and exhausted by my narrative, tosses the pages onto the coffee table and flops back onto the sofa. She's still processing it all—like I am. "He didn't do what you think he did, Z. No F-Kid in his right mind would have made such a call . . . and certainly not Brian."

"Tell me why it isn't so."

She chews her lip. Nodding. Accepting. "Jesus."

"Yes: I believe that he phoned Jack O'Roses—their business office—to say that, if they did lame cover songs . . . that he'd kill them. That he'd kill Rose

Partland. Or whatever stupid bullshit metaphor he employed."

"This is monstrous."

My voice shakes. "He didn't want to hurt anyone. He just—he wanted to call the tune. In his own wrongheaded way."

"That's ridiculous, Z."

"I know." I laugh, barking and sardonic. "But I think it did happen."

The nighttime outside is inky black—a new moon. Now it's Aimee's turn to go out onto the cold balcony. She shuts the door behind her, sits down in the patio chair. Hangs her head, rubs her temples.

I pick up my pages and dump them into the kitchen wastebasket. Whatever the truth, I think, we will now close the book—for good this time—on Drake Park. To remain sane, I must. Somewhere, I feel Nibbs watching me, nodding his head in agreement, and feel one of his huge hands resting on my shoulder, letting me know that what I have done is enough. Satisfied, I hope, that a semblance of truth—and of blame—has seen the light of day.

–14–

So one day while having lunch at a Mexican joint around the corner from the apartment, we get into this fight over what seems like nothing. The spat starts out small, but then turns into a doozy, one of our first knock-down-drag-outs, a bitter dialogue between me and the woman whom I now love. I think.

We'd come to celebrate—I put in for a position and got hired at Southeastern, in the controller's office. A number slave. At least before I could say it was in service of the family business. Now, just a bureaucrat.

"Ash—I feel strange right now." She's been calling me that instead of Z. I think it's because of the Drake Park memoir. "I'm discombobulated."

"I can tell—I've known you long enough to realize that this isn't normal."

"I've always been moody. I told you that." A shadow passes across her face; she nibbles at the side of her thumb. "The problem is that I feel like we have conversations, we talk about the future here and there—no pressure, like always—but we don't talk about ourselves much, do we?"

"Do you *want* to talk about yourself?"

"Yes." She clasps her hands, emphatic. "Don't you?"

I ponder the distasteful idea. "Not especially."

"So I noticed." She rocks her leg back and forth like she does when she's agitated. "Well, I need to talk about myself, about us, and do it in a way that I can feel is like I'm saying it to someone who's not just . . . it's like you're a confidant, just a good *friend*, or whatever . . . and a lover, okay? So it's not that. Not really." She's wringing her hands; she sounds slightly manic, her mountain accent becoming more pronounced, and I wonder what's really going on here. She folds her fingers together and shakes her clenched fists at me. "I need to put it all together."

"Are you kidding? How much more can I open up to you?"

"I know we have a good connection in so many cool ways, but you're just so *inside*, and I need more and I don't know how to get it, and this is all happening so fast . . ."

True enough.

I explain myself to Aimee as best I can—the uncertainty, the lingering ennui, the questions without answers—but apparently not very well. I blame my introversion on seasonal disorder—wintertime lingers like an unwelcome guest. She doesn't buy it.

I get frustrated, we trade insults for a while. I order a giant, quart-sized dark Mexican beer and kill it while she pouts over a *chalupa* and a side of rice. The beer is so cold it makes my head hurt.

On the freezing walk back over to the apartment complex, I try to hold her hand and apologize, but she's closed off, having none of my entreaties.

"I don't mind you staying tonight," she says. "But I'm not sure about the idea of you being here so much. Or moving in, obviously," which I figured had been settled.

"But I got this fucking job at the university because I thought—"

"You needing a job doesn't have anything to do with me. No sir. But you do need one. Wherever you end up living." Jittery, she nearly knocks her water glass over. "You, you, you have to do something. Something, anything. Everybody does."

"Maybe I should just go on back home to the folks' house tonight."

"Not after drinking all that beer. No sir."

I decide to sleep on the couch, over which she doesn't put up a fuss. I lie there looking up at the ceiling fan, thinking about Aimee, and the stupid job, and how troubled the world is—between terrorism and climate change and the coming disease pandemics and the specter of economic collapse, one might as well sign up with Phyllis and her flock, because this crap sounds straight out of Revelations.

Worse: What of this lowly microscopic existence of mine apart from all that struggle and strife? Everyone seeks an answer that makes sense, follows a path of sometimes grace, sometimes least resistance, but all in service of a ravenous and aching desire for validation—as a social animal, a sexual one, a creative one, a person who matters. Perhaps what bothers me is that, for all his sins, Brian's stab at an examined life, as much of a failure as it ended up being, puts my own to shame. Brian could have been okay. He didn't have to die. He could have taken a Jack tour off and gotten straight. Plenty of people went to the shows that way. Even Rose herself sometimes did, bless her heart.

I don't think he meant to kill himself. In the end, what I can tell his mother is the same thing I did back in his room that day—for his own reasons, he'd played too hard, is all. Sure, that's all it was. Playtime for grownups, for hippies, that got out of hand.

If I learned anything from forcing myself to go through all of Brian's papers, it's that he never got over Drake Park, and with good and obvious reason. But the idea behind what he couldn't get over was the loss of this ideal relationship for him: He loved Rose, I think, and felt close to her—we all did—even though she was, by her own words, primarily to be thought of as an entertainer rather than a teacher, and certainly not a leader. But for someone like Brian, raised on TV stars and record albums and The Beatles and media constructs designed to seem bigger than life, the Jack O'Roses experience was better than sex, a living history lesson to which all of us could make our own contribution. I think it was during the shows when Nibbs Niffy most felt a connection to the rest of the world, the very condition of which Aimee now accuses me of lacking.

Over a tense breakfast, I suggest that Brian is perhaps projecting out from the pages at me. I've been depressed about more than the weather. I've been on a downer since the New Year's Pallet Jack shows, that brief peak wherein the color leached back into the world again and made worse by writing up Drake Park. I'm stuck in a rut, I theorize.

"Well, get out of it," she tells me. "Seriously. And listen—I didn't mean what I said. I want you to move in. I love you. Really, I think I do. Forget all that yesterday."

I smile and squeeze her hand, wondering in silence about my seat here on the mood swing express. Aimee's sweet face makes me brush off my wariness, and chalk her bad mood up to hormones or an aberration. I want this to work.

Don't I?

-15-

A week later I've moved some more clothes into Aimee's closet, and toiletries into her bathroom, and in recovery from a soul-sucking, dull orientation at the Southeastern employment office that morning a call from Phyllis comes on my cell, and comes at about the worst time imaginable—my girlfriend and I are not only embroiled in the worst set-to we've had, but I find myself caught between two sudden crises: A bizarre Aimee meltdown unlike anything I've yet seen, accompanied by the frantic news that my father has been taken ill—perhaps critically so.

On the drive to the hospital we sit in silence. I grip the steering wheel and dart through a red light or two, making Aimee draw up like a cat. My father's been transported to the heart center at one of the big downtown hospitals, so luckily we're spared what would have been a forty-five minute drive to Edgewater County Memorial. I'm as stoned as a bat, and not in a good way.

Earlier she'd come in from her weekend shift at the library and walked in on what I would normally consider an innocuous enough scene—Chance and Sophie had come by, bearing gifts. At Aimee's behest I've decided to curtail my smoking, but the kids were back from Panache tour with some of the kindest nugs I've seen in years.

As Aimee came in, Sophie leaned forward gurgling the ornate glass bubbler I'd bought myself for Christmas from the reggae shop down in the Old Market.

"What exactly is going on here?"

My voice came out small and self conscious. "Just catching a buzz."

"Hi Aimee," Sophie said, coughing out a lungbuster of a hit. "Join us!"

But something more was wrong. Aimee's eyes were bugged out, and though she normally got along well with the kidlets, she barely made eye contact with them, instead motioning me onto the balcony. I could see them watching us from inside.

"This place is a *mess* since you moved in. What the *hale* are you doing having people over without straightening up first? Were you raised in a barn?"

"Cool down, sweet sister."

"Don't you dare tell me to cool down in my own apartment, Mr. Man."

The initial effects of the two enormous bong hits I'd done were creeping in along the ridge-line at the top of my scalp, an advance scouting party for the massed army that was the big buzz to come. My heart thudded in my chest as the THC entered my bloodstream. I smacked my lips and ran a coarse, dry tongue across them. "What's really wrong?"

She griped and cursed about a variety of topics, including how she's got to have some privacy and she can't have people dropping in and out and there's just too much with the smoking and these strangers, and assorted other half-whispered admonitions, complaints, and fears.

“Hey—they aren’t strangers, these are our friends.” I didn’t know what else to say.

“Just get them out. *Please*.”

Our cohabitation, off to an inglorious start.

I went back into the living room, pantomiming and whispering the notion that Aimee was not feeling herself, needed some space, and so on. The kids and I hugged. They offered to leave some of the pot, but in a gut-check moment of grim decision making, I declined. Aimee slipped by us all without saying a word.

I charged into the bedroom. “What is all this? Because the breakfast dishes were still in the sink? You remind me of Brian when he was all fucked up.”

She was still in her work clothes; she’d come home early because she told them she was sick. Sitting on the edge of the bed, biting her lip and chewing the side of her thumb and bouncing her knees up and down, she said, “I’m not on anything.” She started gripping the legs of her slacks, running her nails up the fabric.

“I’m not saying you are. I just said—”

“I’m not on anything. *Anything*.”

“Aimee, I know, what I meant was—”

She cried out and flung herself back on the bed. “I quit taking my fucking *pills*,” she screamed.

As I was about to ask what pills, what pills, what pills are you talking about, that’s when the phone rang. And then the two most important women in my life both were sobbing.

By the time we get to the hospital, my father is dead;

the blockages, as I suspect we'll be told, must have been so bad there was simply no time either for stents or surgery. He'd been lying out in the garden for a while, unnoticed by anyone. Phyllis had been having her bible study group inside, meeting with a young man named Cole Breedlove who was running for town council.

After a call to Lil in New York—the tears are hers, not yet mine—I'm this close to unloading all the cumulative shock and vitriol building up in my gut upon the weeping hairdo of Phyllis Zemp, but she's being comforted as best she can by a shell-shocked and apparently detoxing Aimee, who I've learned has stopped taking her heretofore unknown-to-me antidepressant meds, and as such sits on the precipice, apparently, of an all-time freak-out the likes of which epic poems and song-cycles will one day be written.

Shaking, I want to grab Phyllis and tell her that twas the bible study group killed my father. That if she hadn't been distracted, all might've been well. But for her wretched beliefs, my father would still live.

But I'm not a monster, and that's likely not the case. I count to ten. I breathe. I am present.

"Phyllis, I'm going to go discuss the arrangements. Aimee, would you mind staying here for a few minutes?"

Of course, Aimee mouths, frowning, looking mortified that I'd even asked. Formality is my way of dealing with crises such as this. I've probably never been more polite in my life than that drive back from Drake Park, for instance. If only I'd known then what I do now.

I come back into the waiting room. I motion for Aimee to slide over. I sit down and put my arms around Phyllis, and she clings to me, and I to her. It is then, and only then, that the tears for my father finally come.

The funeral goes by dreamlike, as I suppose everyone perceives that awful and strange time after the loss of a loved one. However I may have gotten along with my Dad, the notion of him having winked out of existence is akin to being told the mountain you climbed last week has now vanished into thin air, blown into insignificant particulate matter by a sudden gust of wind like God's own exhalation—Alston Lancaster Zemp has returned to the great pool, the eternal well.

"Gather ye rosebuds, son."

That's what one of my uncles tells me at the service in Charleston. Uncle Roland seems extremely upset, and later I'm told that he has cancer, probably won't live out the year. I feel a chill in my bones, a tapping on the shoulder: With both my parents now dead, there's no one left between my own end and me. A sobering thought that we all must face, but since owning to my youth I was never required to truly grieve for my mother, this is all new to me.

The matter of the interment has been the only dustup—when I told Phyllis that in no way would my father be buried in her family's place behind the old Baptist church out in the sticks, she wept and cursed me in her mild way, but I held steadfast. In the end I went ahead and made the arrangements right there in front of her. Who the hell was she to meddle in these matters? Unfair—she was his spouse of many years. But I know that my father would want to go home to his people. I don't know much, but about this I am certain. He had a home, and it was Charleston. As it had been for me, the only place I've ever thought of as mine.

-16-

The Ballad of Jack O'Roses, Verse Ten [last, incomplete chapter]

This story, even after all this preamble, is only the beginning of what we will need to explore together, you and I, to understand the implications of Jack O'Roses and their followers, how this phenomenon fits in our unfolding story of human history, what it says about the culture, what it says about being human and alive. We have only begun to understand what we experienced. Time will fill in the blanks, with a little help from us, the survivors, and those who go on to study what we did with ourselves.

That the Jack scene eats alive some of its best and brightest is a tricky subject, one that I will begin in the next section to explore with as much fortitude and honesty as I can. This seems a hallmark of our country's existence, and indicative of most any garden-variety empire, I think. The difference with Jack O'Roses is that Rose's empire, the grand anarchy that it was, ended up requiring the sacrifice of not mere foot soldiers, but of the leader herself.

I suppose she had to die in order for us to see the light. For me to see the light, at least. You know she had to die. Sounds familiar, and not in a good way.

That was as far as he got.

These final words of Nibbs Niffy's manuscript were written, as far as I can tell, in December of 2003, and I wonder what he did with himself up in his room for those next eight months. Maybe he wrote more and erased it. We'll never know. Died a bit more day-by-day—like all of us, when you really think about it. Dying since the moment we're born, we are. Hell of a way to think about life, I know, but there it is.

I reported to Mrs. Godbold that Brian had had heartbreaks here and there, but in the end, it was really the loss of Rose Partland that killed him, and furthermore, I could never find a suicide note of any kind, that my original supposition held true—an accident. She thanked me, hung up. Case closed. For her. And for Brian.

For me? An open question.

We're going for a walk the next evening. It's beautiful outside—over the past twenty-four hours a blush of early spring has crept in. I have on khaki shorts and a polo shirt, an avocado one with the Green Man logo embroidered above the breast, a gift that Aimee had gotten me for Christmas from the Jack O'Roses merchandise web site. Once we're close to the river, the wind picks up, and as we're making our way down the walkway, I clutch myself and whine about not having grabbed a jacket. I'm also nervous—I have some heavy shit to lay on the GF, here.

Before I can begin, however: "I never explained myself very well before," she says.

"About what?"

"Why I quit taking the meds."

"I wondered."

She bites her lip—a bad sign, I think—but as she continues, my worries fade away. "I began to wonder if all these drugs people are on these days? All the TV ads? You know?"

"I do." She sure as shit isn't talking about someone burning a number at a Jack O'Roses show. Ask your doctor, I think, if you should be taking advice from television commercials exhorting legal drug dealing. "At the risk of a bad pun, I think it's crazy."

"Me, too."

"And yet . . . the meds help you." Since going to her doctor and resuming the regimen, she's returned to what I perceive as her old self.

"Yes. I have to admit they do. But—I felt so good for weeks after the Hootenanny and the New Year's shows and those chocolate thingies we ate, that I said, heck, I don't need these pills. I thought I could just quit, but now I know I can't. Not without going back to the old me. And that doesn't work, either."

The panic attacks and depression that she started having as a teenager had at one point nearly caused her to drop out of high school. Only through force of will did she hide her troubles, not unlike the way she hid from me that she was using medication to treat her problems. As if I would have cared. As if it would have changed anything. I was thankful that in college she'd at last received an astute diagnosis, had gotten help.

I qualify my support somewhat. "But you can't just stop taking that stuff, that's the scary part to me. But I don't know that you should let the potential downside keep you from seeking relief." I clear my throat. "So why'd you try to quit?"

A troubled shadow crosses her lovely face. "Doing those mushrooms on New Year's Eve with you, at that show . . . as good as I felt during and afterwards, that residual vibe that hung on for a while, it all tripped me out maybe more than I wanted. I didn't let on. But I started feeling like . . . drugs drugs drugs, everybody doing something, all whacked out on one thing or another. Everybody trapped, in a way, whether it's coffee or cigarettes or pills or that skunk weed you sit there huffing like it's oxygen. I guess I just wanted to get clean."

"Oh, honey," I say, laughing at her hyperbole, "nobody's clean. Nobody. I have met the chemicals and we is they."

I remember her worries about me being too inside, a problem I've been working on. So, I launch into a self-reflective spiel that is my lead in to the blow I have to deal. "I've been thinking about identity. That's the question. Brian suffered with the nature of who he was, who Rose was, and I have my own unanswered questions as well . . ."

"We all do in one way or another."

"Here's the thing," and I gulp, trying to find

the words. I do love Aimee, enjoy being with her, but this isn't right, somehow. I can't simply get a job at Southeastern—running around on the same old ground, so to speak—and live in the apartment here on the river and go on with life as though nothing has happened to me, mainly because nothing *has* happened to me. I don't know where I'm going or what I will do, but like a college graduate putting off the advent of real life by going backpacking in Europe or on the Appalachian trial, I should go while I have the chance. The road, beckoning. A man, untethered.

As I huddle against a crisp wind coming off the water, I try to explain all this, tell Aimee I'm glad I met her, but that it's all happened too fast. That it's not over, but that for now I have to say goodbye.

She draws in her breath and pulls away, her voice breaking. "It's okay. Somehow I knew you were going to say that. I don't know how I did. But I did."

"It's not because you think I shouldn't be getting high all the time."

"I know. You have some living to do, don't you."

"Yeah. And learning, and growing."

The river is moving right along, the constellation of muddy, sun-baked brown rocks normally visible are submerged, subsumed, out of sight. A flock of swallows dives this way and that, greedily consuming the first cluster flies of spring.

"The mighty Congaree's running hard—they must have the gates up at the dam wide open."

"Running as hard as you are." Now she breaks down, heaving and holding onto herself. I try to hug her, but she pushes me away.

Calming down, sniffling, she points. "Look at that magnificent thing."

A Great Blue Heron soars by us, its spindly legs

and long neck imbuing the bird with grace and beauty, the sort that's found in creatures and objects that aren't made by the hands of men. To understand this beauty is to look upon it with the right eyes: eyes upon a world that is a fragile flower, a realm fraught with pain but also ecstasy, horror but also delight, and death—but only after life, ever so fleeting. In the end, Rose Partland showed us both sides, but the light behind her will live on far longer than the darkness that ultimately consumed her.

Which makes me think of Brian Godbold. "Despite what I told his mother, he did it on purpose, you know."

Her words are gentle, like a parent explaining to a child the ways of the bitter world. "Was that ever in question, sweetie?"

"To me it was. There had to be a better reason somewhere in all those pages. But there wasn't. He couldn't hang without Rose."

"Or you, Z."

My cheeks burn. "I guess he missed everyone, yes."

"Like I'm going to miss you."

Her words make me sad, but at the same time I feel open and free in the cold wind, warmth spreading outward from the persistent, thudding organ at the center of my being.

Besides departing South Carolina for a destination unknown, I decide to lay my other plan on her. "There's an idea coalescing in my mind."

"Did you get yourself an *idear*, sugar? It had to happen eventually," she ribs through a froggy, teary throat.

"Hardy-har."

As we head back through a thicket of old-growth

floodplain forest, the ornamental lamps popping on to greet the dusk, I describe in detail the plans I have about finishing Nibbs's work, my idea for revising and completing *The Ballad of Jack O'Roses*. "It's the least I can do for him. And for Rose."

Aimee applauds my little scheme, offers to assist me down the road with editing and proofing. "Maybe your sister can help get it published."

"Maybe. But that's not the point—for now, it's only for me. My father, in his own way, told me to ask the universe what I should do, and it said to do this. To write. And to hit the road."

I break out in gooseflesh—but it's only the wind. It's not the universe, or Nibbs. And it sure isn't Rose Partland. It's only an easy wind, rolling down the river. To which I say yes. Yes.

At the stairs to the apartment she gives me a hug, warming me up. We both cry, now, and hold onto one another.

"Nothing's for keeps," I say. "Nobody knows what the future holds."

Sniffling, we pull apart and go inside. "At the risk of making this seem like some silly Scooby Doo episode," she says, putting on the tea kettle, "there's one thing that still bothers me."

"*Ruh*-roh, Daphne," I say in my best talking dog, which isn't too hot. "What is it?"

"What did Brian's road name mean? I thought it might have something to do with *Peter Pan*—Nibs is one of the lost boys, the 'gay and debonair' one," she says. "He dies."

An old shudder creeps in; darkness falls, too, across a gravesite a few hundred miles away in Virginia. "However apropos that might be . . . no, don't think so."

"So what, then?"

"He told me it was something he misheard one night in a bar down in the Old Market, before he'd fully gotten the F-Kid bug, when he was a freshman. The bartender was playing some Jack song—a B-side, something rare? Anyway, he said he was talking to this old hippie burnout sitting there at the bar, guzzling beer and smoking. Anyway, Brian asked the guy a question—'This is Jack O'Roses, right?'"

"And the guy said . . .?"

"Brian said he mumbled something that sounded like 'Nibbs Niffy,' and then high-fived him in that drunk way people do, nearly missing. He asked him what he'd said, but the guy waved him off—he wanted to listen to the music, got all teary eyed, made a speech about how Jack O'Roses was the only good thing that'd ever come out of this country, the only thing that wasn't tainted and corrupt and rotten inside. The bartender ended up tossing the guy, who became completely unhinged and jabbering about the government and conspiracies and JFK and all sorts of things."

"Oh, my."

"Brian said he couldn't get the words out of his head. *Nibbs Niffy, Nibbs Niffy*. Said they just rattled around in there for days, like an earbug. Finally, while tripping and listening to a bootleg Jack tape some kid down the hall made for him, he wrote in his journal, 'Who is Nibbs Niffy? Perhaps he is me, and I am him.' After that, he said he felt free."

"Free?"

"Outside of himself—the loss of ego, a hallmark of any decent psychedelic experience. I'm not sure Brian was ever satisfied being Brian, or whatever his earthly name might otherwise have been. Being Nibbs liberated him, until it trapped him."

Aimee seems dissatisfied. "What did the old

hippie say to him, though, really?"

"He might as well have said, 'The job of the artist is to deepen the mystery'."

"Pardon?"

"What I'm trying to say is that Brian said he never knew for sure."

"Think it mattered?"

After so many months of analyzing Brian from beyond the grave, I know that conclusions are rare creatures. "I think Nibbs Niffy meant what it meant because of what he brought to the words, not what they brought to him—if that makes any sense."

Aimee is no dummy. "It does."

"And there you have the true story of Nibbs Niffy, the death of the hero and the origin issue flashback, all in one big volume."

"If this were a comic book or a movie series, though, they'd have to think of some way of bringing Nibbs back to life."

The tea kettle begins screaming from the kitchen. "Indeed."

And it is thus that, while I pack up my effects and prepare to leave, Aimee's words resonate. What I seek to do is not just honor my friend's spirit, and his vast, wounded heart, but also to shine a light back into the eternal well into which both he and Rose have now returned. I don't know if I can accomplish it, but there's no other choice but to try: It is my way, I suppose, of showing gratitude to the dead.

–17–

A season of death has fallen shadowlike upon Shady Lane in Edgewater County—first my father, and then a few weeks later Will Wrightson's wife Loretta, her cancer finally gaining the upper hand and metastasizing faster than the chemo could keep up.

When I go down the way to check on him, and to give him a check, he seems sanguine about the ordeal, but also in great pain: "She'd been dying for so long, I'd gotten used to that being the way of things, so when she passed —"

"I know, Will. It's okay."

I shook his hand, firm and strong the way a man of his generation would want it. Like my father, no hugs. This isn't Jacktown, with two hippies trading drugs and good vibes, this is a real-world transaction out here in Babylon. This is me getting the pink slip to my new ride.

He waves as I drive Bertha out of her shed and onto the highway, on the way to an RV mechanic who's going to make her roadworthy for a long trip across the fruited plain, stopping where she may, her pilot and Brian's laptop writing the story of Jack, the story of the F-Kids, and maybe the story of the writer himself, as Nibbs had attempted to do.

I don't get far on Highway 79, however, before I

see the blue rollers popping on in the huge side mirrors, covered in spring pollen and cobwebs from the long sit since I drove Bertha to the Hootenanny.

"You need a class E license for this tub," the deputy sheriff says as I hand over my bona fides. "Which you don't seem to have, Mr. Zemp."

"I just bought the vehicle—I'll get all that squared away, sir."

"You were all over the road back yonder—I don't need to ask if you've been drinking anything today, do I?"

"Nothing as dangerous as all that. Just getting my sea legs with this old girl."

"All right then, sir," handing back my papers. "Keep it between the lines, now."

I tell him I will, that I have a long drive ahead.

"Where you headed?"

I nod and gesture with two fingers. "West. Thought I'd chase the sunset."

"Sounds like a good vacation," he says, ruminating and faraway. "Out on the road."

"It's not really a getaway," taking my papers back and smiling. "More like going home."

ENCORE

Shadows Fall
(Partland, ©1989 JOR EL Publishing)

When I hear Shadows fall
In the doorway, or out in the hall
We race to find a way
To chase the night in-to the day

The ebb and flow of days
Only helps to erode our many layered code
The rowboat lifts and sways
The river passes us by bearing its hea-vy load

And I never see nothing but you
Your disguise ain't that hard to see through
The surprise in your eyes only seems to make them more blue
No, no, I never see nothing but you

When constellations rise
Above the trees into the sky
Our eyes will move our toes
Down the driveway, and across the road

The pine boughs intertwine
The silver moon illuminates your flight
I'll hold you one more time
Tomorrow's wish is coming true tonight

Banners and colorful flags snap in the breeze of a Midwestern August. The wind is warm but fresh. The air smells of dry grass, dirt, white sage, patchouli. A drum circle pounds out a tribal rhythm, a call to all those whose hearts beat along with the hands of the drummers, the circle seeking out participants until gestalt is achieved, a fellowship of spirit, of souls. A delicate guitar tone can be heard from a hundred different sources, a fragile voice lilting on the breeze, a dead angel's songbook brought to vivid life.

There is magic in the air. Can you feel it?

I pull my long hair back and cinch tight my cotton drawstring pants, walk away from the RV until I crest the hill from the lower parking lot to survey the scene outside the Fiddler's Green Music Theatre, a beautiful, lush venue in the middle of nowhere, an hour outside of one the country's great cities. I ought to be jubilant on this day, but I'm not, not yet. The sadness has fought to return ever since the day I mail ordered for tickets. But I've made a conscious decision to dwell not on the past, but instead on pushing forward.

I persuaded Lil—or 'Monty,' as my sister's assistant calls her—to help me find an editor to take a look at the book manuscript, which after three years I finally feel might be in a finished form, as much as I'm able to finish a dead man's work, that is. She tells me not to get my hopes up—it's a weird business, and considering how much people read these days, one that may be in precipitous decline.

From what she's read she says it's not-bad, but that I have a long way to go as a writer, that if this's what I want to do, I should get myself into the woodshed, as a musician would put it. So that's what I've done.

Another problem with *The Ballad of Jack O'Roses* is not merely that Nibbs Niffy and I are far from being the first out of the gate with our little biographical project, but something's happened that alters the pitch—that now, there may be something of merit left to say:

This glorious spring, when the band announced that they were coming back, like, for real, man, it felt as though the last piece of the puzzle had fallen neatly into place, as if from on high. A lovely sentiment, perhaps—but one that requires, if not another rewrite, then a final chapter—the mischievous storyteller has yet to finish the telling of the tale. The first official Jack O'Roses concert since July 3, 1997. Ten years after. A reboot, a rebirth.

I'll admit I didn't know what to expect when the announcement was posted on the Jack O'Roses website, with such breathtaking and unexpected abruptness on what was otherwise an ordinary American afternoon a few months ago. I'm a little ways off the grid, so didn't hear at first. I'm living outside Albuquerque, on a corner of a property far off the beaten track, a ranch owned by an F-Kid I met while skirting the edges of last summer's Panache tour, on which I went to get my mind back into the groove of the parking lot scene, and to hang out with Family.

And as though the news weren't astounding enough on its own terms, like all F-Kids I nearly shit myself when we found out that singer-songwriter

P. S. Jones is in actuality Jake and Rose's daughter Adelaide—unbelievable, a joke, surely, yes?—and would be taking her mother's place onstage.

Mind, officially blown.

At the news conference announcing the reunion tour, Jake compared the idea behind the group to something like the Count Basie or Glenn Miller orchestras: When the rest of us die off, he said, "Addie can get Derek Trucks or Warren Haynes or whomever to step in and keep the merry-go-round turning."

One reporter asked a tough question: Is this tour just one more chance to cash in, one more boomer oldies act trying to shake loose the last few dollars from their aging, wistful fans?

"It's the music that's driving this thing, still," Jake answered. "Always was, for Rose and for the rest of us. The music isn't dead; it's a living and breathing thing of its own volition. All the rest of it—the money, the F-Kids and the whole shebang—that was somebody else's fat trip that got laid on us. We ain't been anything but guitar pickers. And that's all we'll ever be."

In any case, the prodigal daughter will now step into her mother's shoes, and when the news broke, everybody went nuts. Once the glow wore off, though, the voices began chattering that P. S. Jones is good, sure, but she's no Rose Partland.

Of course not. She's her own person, and quite a few people have wondered how it will be to have a bluesy, growling sort of Janis-type fronting the band—Rose's mellifluous voice, like her guitar tone, was unmistakable, and Adelaide, who'll continue to go by her stage name "for the sake of personal continuity—sorry, Daddy," as she joked to the press with Jake at her side, is certainly *of* her mother, but in no way a mere carbon copy. The possibilities, if one considers them with an openness and optimism, are limitless, not constrictive. The proof, as it concerns such matters, will be in the musical pudding.

The first person I thought of, besides that big nitwit Nibbs Niffy? Aimee. I started to email her, finally, to say, what do you think about all this? But I didn't. Let sleeping dogs lie, as it were. She's probably moved on with her life.

Me? All during the drive up here, with a group of New Mexican F-Kids spanning several generations all partying and sleeping in the back of Bertha, I've been thinking of myself as a vessel within the void waiting to be filled, not by relationships or money or human endeavor, but instead by the great spirit, the connection, an assurance beyond feeling. Anyone can make it to that place—that is, so long as one is willing to give themselves over to the energy and the life force, to acknowledge the playful sleight of hand of the cosmic prankster, this zen trickster, the influence of what some still call God, but which is actually that for which we have yet to find the adequate name—that may in fact be nothing more than the collective sum total of our hearts and minds, this shared consciousness, this construct called Right Now, which is all our atoms vibrating at the just the right frequency that make us have mass, that allow us to perceive one another, and to exist in moments of liquid time watching and listening to people make amplified music.

Heavy. Groovy. I don't know where the starlight ends, and the sunbeams begin type-deal.

Makes me think again of Aimee, with whom I've lost touch for all sorts of reasons—mainly because I don't have an email address. I don't go online, I am a solitary vessel traversing the crest of a quiet lonely wave, writing my dead friend's book and teaching myself to play guitar and fooling around with writing my own poems and songs and stories.

"Here you go, brother." A skinny kid with stinky dreads and a threadbare tour shirt on his slight frame—spring of '94, a lifetime ago, now—hands me a free bumper sticker from a stack he clutches in his hands:

NO WHITE POWDERS!

Discerning advice indeed, and from one so ostensibly young. I'm duly impressed.

I stop to check out a brilliant selection of hand-twisted tie-dyes, the T-shirts laid out upon bedsheets held down at the corners by thick paperback books that are also for sale. The vendor is a large hippie lady in her 50s with long naturally gray hair pulled back, and wearing a dress like Rose might have—you see these chicks all the time in the Jack scene. They look like they're becoming Rose right before your eyes.

"Here we are," I say, looking around at the other vendors. "You believe this?"

"Somebody pinch me," she says through a grin. "Seems like it's been longer than it really has, doesn't it?"

"Yeah, it does."

She smiles and squeezes her eyes, gestures at her products. "These are fifteen each, or two for twenty-five."

I buy a couple of shirts, drape them over my shoulder. Got to keep the vibe alive, keep the scene thriving, keep the commerce flowing. How else will we get to the next show? Jack is on tour all summer, all over the country. Miles to cover.

"Look at that," the woman cries out, grabbing my arm. "Oh my god—it's Rose!"

Improbable synergistic serendipity rears its head already, the storied hallmark of the Jack O'Roses experience: A rainbow has appeared in the sky directly overhead, centered almost exactly above the amphitheater that slopes down the steep, grassy hillside to the stage below. People have stopped, gaping with wonder, their faces masks of delight, disbelief, fingers outstretched.

"When we tell people about this later," I say in a small, wondrous voice, "they won't believe us."

"But it did happen," the tie-dye saleswoman says, snapping a photo with a point-and-click. "Fading, but still there."

The world outside the Jack scene isn't so dreadful, either. After a tense confrontation last year with Saddam Hussein, in the ninth year of his extended Presidency, and the third since nine-eleven, Gore finessed the diplomacy—what could Hussein do anyway, since we had him locked down tight?—until a CIA-engineered coup ended with the death of the longtime dictator and his sons. Well, that's not the official story, but you know the way things work. That desperate country is now fracturing into civil war, but we've committed no troops other than as part of a UN coalition that may or may not yet move in to restore order. The president remains optimistic that reason and order will rule the day, about this and many other issues. Don't worry, it'll all work out—we'll just install another one of our strongman puppets in there like we always do, and oil will continue to flow, to fuel the cars and big rigs that bring the gear for the band to play, that power the onstage lights and the amps and the PA speakers, stacked and curving to the heavens.

A pressing question: Is this concert a new beginning for me?

Look, I don't see myself ever going on Jack tour again—after these shows, I'm heading back to the desert to my routine of writing and gardening and living for next to nothing. Why not go on tour, you might ask, perhaps thinking, if we've established anything at this point, it's that one doesn't outgrow an experience as momentous as Jack O'Roses. And I have not in fact done so, although I do have the feeling that I accomplished what I needed to the first time around—I'm thinking that, now that the tours are starting again, I'll be letting my ticket go to someone who needs it more than I do. Someone young, who missed the chance the first time. I feel in my heart this is the right thing to do—there's nothing you can hold for very long, another singer once whispered to me, and I think these words apply now more than ever.

I get back to the RV, its solar panels doing their job. I find the crew smoking and cracking beers and tossing the Frisbee around. A woman I don't recognize at first is leaning against Bertha's front end and talking to my friend and landlord, Delia, who everyone assumes I'm boinking, but it's not that way at all.

"Here he is right now," she says, extending an arm in my direction. "Our pilot and navigator all rolled into one, our writer in residence, the inimitable Z-man."

The woman looks at me from under her straw hat. She's wearing jeans and a Jack T-shirt. She pulls off her sunglasses. "I thought I might find you here," Aimee Pressgrove says. "Oh, Z—look at that big beard. Is that really you under there?"

I feel aglow, a warm inner light, a rightness to this moment. "Why don't you come find out?"

She does so; we embrace, kiss like friends, produce quiet tears that bookend those of our sad fare-the-well by the river. "One miracle after another today."

"That's the way it feels to me, too."

Then, we kiss less like friends than ravenous fiends. Without missing a beat, we are starcrossed, we are golden.

"I never stopped thinking about you."

"Nor I you."

Holding hands, we trudge to the top of the hill to get in line and wait for the gates to open. I take in the sight of the tapers and the rest of the excited multitude, one that grows larger with each passing moment. Aimee and I get caught up, each hearing the other out on where we are in life, who we are, what we've done, what we want, how we live now. How we both dated and loved, but never forgot one another. How we both worked out some issues for ourselves. How wonderful and strange it all is. Strange to be anything at all, much less standing here together again. At a Jack show, no less. Mind officially blown, redux.

An old man comes circulating through the crowd with his head down, mostly keeping to himself, but exchanging a brief word with certain F-Kids who notice him. Stiff and stooped, his leathery sunstruck face is partially obscured by a large straw hat flopping back and forth with the bobbing of his head. He pulls himself up the hill and stops at the crowd's edge to survey the scene, the packed parking lots, the miracle seekers shuffling back and forth on their dusty penitent feet, the snakes of the twin traffic-snarls stretching far into the distance on the highway leading to the venue. The wind ripples his simple, cotton earth-toned outfit. He takes out a small notebook and carefully jots down a few thoughts, words that remain unknown to me, as they should be.

The old man turns to look at the venue, and our eyes meet.

Oglethorpe. In the flesh.

On the verge of blurting out his identity, I'm stopped by the slender, gnarled finger he brings to his lips, and the sly wink he gives me from that face, puckered and weathered by time, but still familiar from the lovingly framed portrait that used to hang in Nibbs's old apartment.

"Big night," I say to him as he passes by. "Here in rock and roll heaven."

"Biggest ever, maybe," he suggests, squeezing my shoulder. "Or just another show."

I nod and give him a small, sharp salute, which he returns with a laugh. "Good day to you, captain."

"Godspeed, my boy."

Aimee watches him shuffle away into the crowd. "Who was that?"

"An oldschool F-Kid."

"What did he say?"

I smile. "Riders of the rainbow, let it grow."

Aimee does a happy little jig of anticipation. "I can't believe we're here. That it's real. I wish they'd hurry up and open the gates so we can go *inside* —"

"Why'd you come?"

"To see the band!" She turns sheepish. "And to find you, silly man—all I see is you."

In full confession, she tells me that Delia's a friend she made from some Jack-related Facebook group, an internet confidant who told her about this charming southern gentleman from South Carolina, a writer, she'd allowed to homestead on her land, living in an RV he called 'Bertha.'

"And so, once they announced these shows . . . I

asked her to keep this a secret from you, a surprise."

"How'd you know there wasn't someone else? That it wasn't Delia?"

"Because she says you talk about me all the time. Which I felt, somehow, all the way back in Columbia. Maybe I heard you."

"Romantic, cosmic—I like this plot development." A lingering embrace, a deep kiss. Her eyes, searching; mine saying, *Yes*.

"Maybe lose the beard," she says. "Scratchy."

Perhaps Aimee's right. Time to expose the weak chin again, find out who's been hiding under there. Return to the world, maybe. Like Jack O'Roses.

Time turns elastic: I check for the ticket in my hip pack a dozen times, look at my watch every two minutes, and nod my hirsute head to an unheard, timeless melody. Moments pass—there goes another, and another—only to make room for more moments.

Then, a joyous noise erupts from inside the amphitheater, a funky shuffle of a jam: The soundcheck is underway—the rainbow makers are again on stage.

Overcome, I fall to my knees and shout over the deafening roar from the waiting F-Kids, an exultant clamor that drowns out the sound of the band. "I've heard this before—I dreamed this!"

"What? I can't hear you!"

"MUSIC," I yell, my face and arms open to the infinite azure sky—a sun salutation. "I dreamt music."

The End

Endnote

So, why did I want to write this story? Easy—as a fuck-you to the gatecrashers at Deer Creek, individuals who, on July 2, 1995, not only ruined what turned out to be my final Grateful Dead concert, but caused what *would* have been my final show to be canceled. As with Nibbs and Z, my last show, a concert forever lost to the imagination. Sigh.

Fuck you, guys. Really and truly.

On another more serious and meaningful level, I wanted to achieve what good novelists do, which is depict some version of a particular moment and a milieu from their real lives, preferably one in which profundity, or simulacrum of the same—much like my stand-in band for the Dead—might in fact have occurred. Inspiration, move me brightly, as Robert Hunter wrote to the melodious and fluid lead-lines of his partner in musical sublimity, Jerry Garcia.

Jerry—a Rose by another name.

I began writing the manuscript that would become *Fellow Traveler* on October 3, 2000, as a kick-start to my long delayed but never forgotten dream of becoming a writer, specifically a Southern novelist. The moment had arrived: if I wanted to realize a youthful ambition or two—such as becoming a novelist—the universe whispered that I'd better set to the task, and one of the first tips I picked up in taking classes and reading books about how to write 'good' was to write what you knew. To get out of the novelistic gate, it was obvious to what I would turn, which was my Grateful Dead experience, the most striking and profound thread of life I'd discovered in my middle class, modern American existence.

As time passed I wrote *FT* through many drafts, as well as the composition of other novels and stories and articles and essays, but it was to this piece I would always return, hoping against hope to get right what I'd set out to do, which was capture a snapshot of an experience I'd considered extraordinary and vital and interesting: The band's concerts, microcosms of a time and a vibe that in the late 80s seemed in the greater culture at large to be long past dead, and the traveling community of freaks and misfits and blissed-out iconoclasts who populated the ranks of Dead-dom, had given me a sense of fellowship that no church ever had, while at the same time filling me with the spirit in a way that'd been heretofore antithetical to my cynical worldview, which'd been colored by tragedy and self-doubt and an aggregate disbelief that not much good was coming my way.

I went to see them play. And to not only listen, but to dance. I'd discovered that 'better place' they said was waiting—the hazy interior of a basketball arena, the imposing concrete temple of the football stadium, a sandy fairgrounds beside a vast ocean. Just like heaven.

Like Ashton Tobias Zemp, I, too, have dreamt and loved music, and if *FT* can be enjoyed on the level of having 'loved a band so much it hurts,' as a character in a Hollywood movie says, then I will have done my job. Loving the Dead involved ecstasy and agony in thankfully unequal measures, but when the agony came, it came hard and angry and inexorable, or so it seemed then, and seems now. All that will fall away, however, and leave only the songs. The tunes. The art.

And as Jack O'Roses lives on in this fictional milieu, the Dead, too, have soldiered on in ways both direct as well as tangential, and on this summer 2012 day the survivors tour in different bands, each exploring and expanding the repertoire; the land teems with garage-style and professional cover bands, some of whom are becoming famous in their own right, and who play late into the smoky beersign-glowing night in taverns and towns all over the country and the world; and on archive.org, with the click of a mouse much of the Dead's circulating concert catalogue may be experienced after a cursory search and with a pair of good headphones. It's especially nice to enjoy the stellar audience recordings that guys like Brian Godbold, and your humble narrator of this endnote, managed to pull.

Perhaps most important of all, the band thrives, still, in the hearts of those of who loved and continue to love the Grateful Dead, whether they got to see the so-called 'real' thing, or only just got on the bus last week. We are everywhere.

Speaking of we: how many there are to thank! My wife Jenn McCallister and her bandmates Greg Bates, Mike Mahoney, and Chris Jones in Stillhouse, my songwriting stand-ins for JoR; many many many readers through the years, friends like Steve Armato, Nick Meriwether, Nicole Cranford, Phil Ugel, Matt Martin, Samantha Goodal, Dennis Ware, Michael Spawn, Katie Braddock Rabon, Kate Harding, Lorna Festa, Cindy Patterson, the members of my online family reading this Endnote via the CDead or Deadwood Society mailing list, the esteemed members of the

Loose Lucy's family and their retail stores that kept the vibe alive in the wake of Jerry's loss, and of course my own mother and father, without whom I'd never have gotten the chance to write this book, or any others. Daniel Sobel warrants a special shout-out—without his guidance, I probably wouldn't have had this great Deadhead adventure at all. And last but far from least, gratitude to the publishers who took a chance on this manuscript, Bob Jolley and Cindi Boiter—my thanks to you both is beyond measure.

The Grateful Dead experience may also be considered codified, now, in the academic world as being officially worthy of study, and in a serious and scholarly manner that should likely last much longer than any of us can fathom. Conferences are held; the Dead's papers are stored and archived at UC Santa Cruz under the supervision and care of Mr. Meriwether, a friend and world-class scholar; papers and books are being published, and I don't mean novels and stories—I'm talking about serious, inter– and multidisciplinary attempts to record for posterity our phenomenon, which to the uninitiated may at first seem inscrutable. This, a good time to be a Deadhead—we get to see that our scene will live on, unimpeded by the vagaries and vicissitudes of the normal pop cultural attention span.

In that spirit, *FT* is my offering to this growing and vital canon of Dead-lit to be carried into the future, to cast its light and attention on this interesting and uniquely American corner of the pop cultural lexicon. I'm honored to be a part of that record, and of the conversation. It goes on, you know, our discussion—here, there, and everywhere, but most of all Right Now, which is the only time, a moment that, when you recognize it for its true colors, lasts forever.

West Columbia, SC
June 15, 2012

Fellow Traveler

CPSIA information can be obtained
at www.ICGtesting.com
Printed in the USA
FFHW010244160319
51093987-56512FF

9 780983 854425